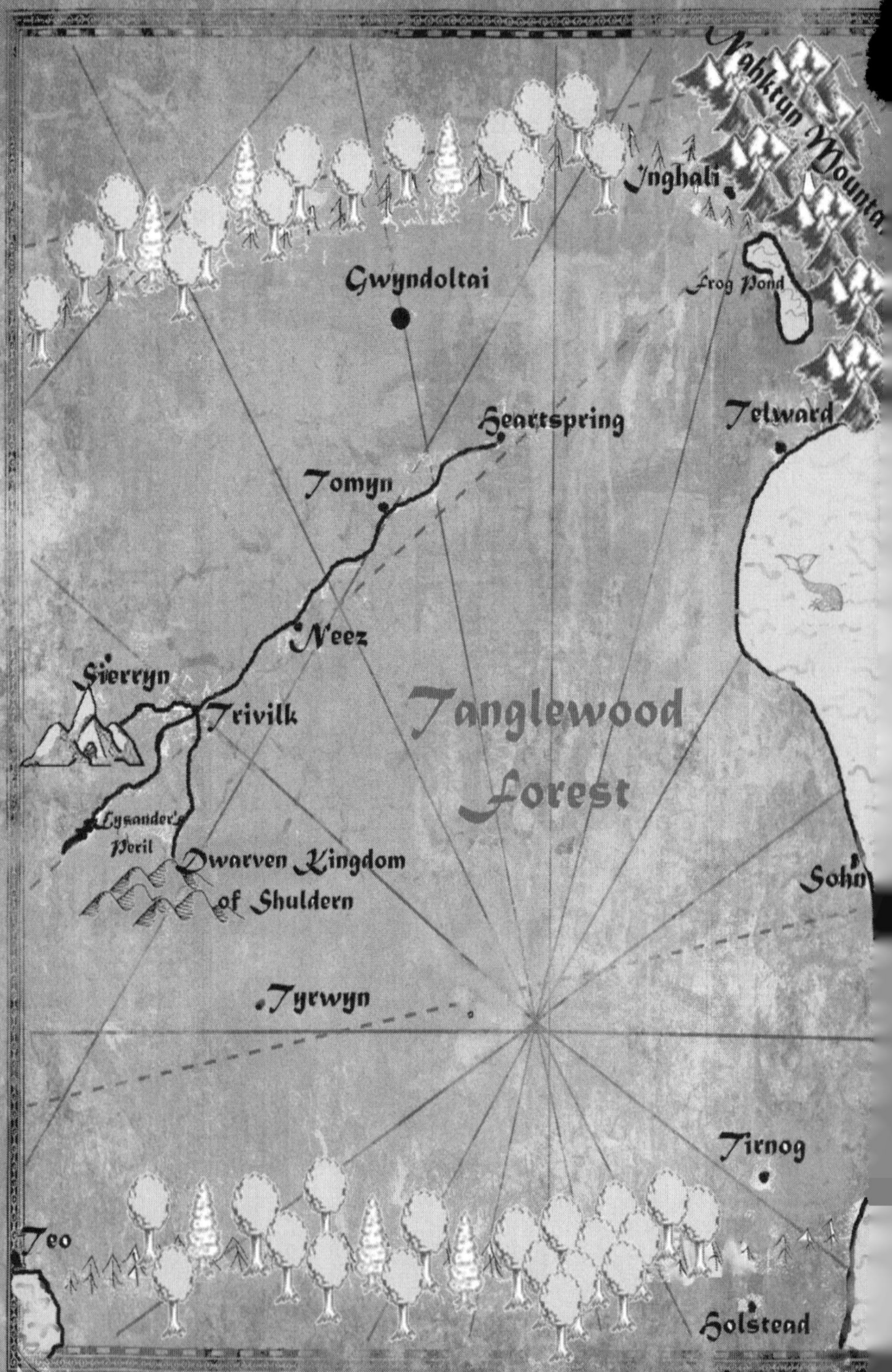
Nahktun Mountains
Inghali
Gwyndoltai
Frog Pond
Heartspring
Telward
Tomyn
Neez
Sierryn
Trivilk
Tanglewood Forest
Lysander's Peril
Dwarven Kingdom of Shuldern
Sohn
Tyrwyn
Tirnog
Teo
Holstead

# Brothers Haymaker

By

Sam Ferguson

This is a work of fiction. All of the characters, organizations, and events portrayed in this book are either products of the author's imagination or are used fictitiously.

BROTHERS HAYMAKER


Published by Dragon Scale Publishing



ISBN: 1-943183-15-5
ISBN-13: 978-1-943183-15-9

Front cover art by Bob Kehl

For J. F.

# Contents

# Other Books by Sam Ferguson

Tales from Terramyr (Short story anthology)

The Sorceress of Aspenwood Series
Dimwater's Dragon
Dimwater's Demons
Dimwater's Dagger

The Dragon's Champion Series
The Dragon's Champion
The Warlock Senator
The Dragon's Test
Erik and the Dragon
The Immortal Mystic
Return of the Dragon

The Dwarves of Roegudok Hall
The Wealth of Kings
The Dwarves of Roegudok Hall Comic Book issue 1

The Netherworld Gate Series
The Tomni'Tai Scroll
The King's Ring
Son of the Dragon

The Dragons of Kendualdern
Ascension
Dominion

The Fur Trader

# Other Books by Dragon Scale Publishing

The Protector of Esparia by Lisa M. Wilson

Kingdom of Denall Series by Eric Buffington:
The Troven
Secrets at the Keep
The Changing

Tales from the NoWhere and NeverWhen
Wisp the Wayfinder
Puck the Pathwinder
Nobb the Nightbinder

ALSO

Check you some great short fantasy stories on our website like:

Tharzule's Tome of Wishes

And

Orcs and Elves

# CHAPTER 1

Lightning crackled and popped as it soared just a few feet over Raven's head. He could smell the stale, bitter odor of the magical bolt as it ripped through the air and nearly blinded him with its blue flash. The pine tree that took the brunt of the lightning exploded ten yards away. The top end of the tree crashed through the forest while the twenty-foot-tall stub was left smoldering in place.

The wizard knew he had been lucky, but now his ward spell was consumed. He needed to find cover if he was going to live long enough to put up another defensive barrier around himself.

Raven leapt around the jagged boulder and slammed his back up against the cold, pointed surface, bits of stone digging into his flesh as he gasped for air. Another searing flash of blue light erupted around him and a pine tree splintered and cracked, showering the area in bits of light-colored wood just moments before crashing down to the ground where Raven had just been. The wizard threw up a ward, but not quickly enough to stop a mess of pine needles from scraping his right cheek.

He winced and pulled away. An arrow glanced off the left side of the boulder, ricocheting out wide, but causing the man to pause before darting out from behind the safety of the boulder.

His lungs burned and his feet ached. He scanned the area near him, knowing that to stay still would mean death. He found a sufficiently large oak and darted across for it. His left hand shot out to his side, fingers continually moving as they wove the magic that maintained his ward.

Three arrows slammed into the invisible shell around him, snapping off under the force of their collision with his magic.

The ground here was hard and dry, a far cry from the drenched, murky swamps he had been in only a little more than a year before as he hunted down the trolls in the Warrens. Yet here, in the Tanglewood Forest far to the north of the Murkle Quags, the trees and underbrush was at least as thick, if not thicker, than the swamps. Sturdy vines drooped down, threatening to catch or slow him with their lazy loops that swung slightly, right at neck level. The pines grew dense and strong, branching out and pushing their way into the forest with their sharp needles. Oaks dotted the forest, with their large trunks and their low-hanging branches that made it nearly impossible to run at a full sprint. Underfoot were patches of creeping morning glory and thick, wide-leafed ferns that slowed his legs and pulled at the hems of his robes. If that wasn't enough, there were fallen logs everywhere as well. Some were new and still hard, while others were soft and overgrown with moss and fungi. One such log nearly swallowed his right foot as he stepped up onto the fallen tree and immediately crashed through the first few layers.

Another arrow sank into a sapling nearby just as Raven managed to yank his foot free, pulling up with his boot a mess of reddish wood that smelled of dirt and dampness.

Had he the energy left, he might have thought to blast a trail before him using fire, but he knew that that would be more likely to result in a raging blaze that not even he would be able to control.

He could hear angry shouts, but he could not understand the words his enemies spoke.

As he finally ducked under a low branch that was easily thicker than his thighs, he jumped around the large, spotted oak and tried to catch his breath.

He glanced around the left side of the tree and caught the slightest hint of armor glinting gold in the little bit of sunlight that managed to permeate the heavy canopy of leaves above him. The wizard sent out a small, yet deadly ball of fire. It hurtled through the air, aiming for a point the wizard believed to be in the enemy's path. An armored archer leapt out from behind a tree and aimed his short recurve bow, but never got the chance to use it. Raven's fireball blasted through the weapon, snapping the limbs back around to smash into the archer's face. A half second later, the fireball tore through the armor and the archer squealed in pain as the magical fire burrowed through his chest. He fell to the ground, smoke issuing out from the hole in his back.

The shouting around Raven grew more frantic.

A twig snapped off to the right.

Raven turned to see someone rounding the oak, scimitar drawn and raised up in preparation to strike. Raven pulled his dagger with his left hand and lunged toward the elf with the scimitar. His blade bit into the elf's chest, which was clothed only in a forest-green tunic, and the elf fell backward. The wizard pulled the scimitar free from the dead elf's hand and held it in his right hand. He was not nearly as good with a sword as Captain

Ziegler, but his magical energy was ebbing out of him, and he knew he would need to rely on steel as well as wizardry.

He ran on through the forest, feet slamming and pounding the ground as he moved.

The shouts kept pace with him, and occasionally arrows would either slam into his ward, or hit a nearby tree. Lightning was being used less now, for which Raven was most grateful. He wasn't sure his ward could deflect another magical assault.

Lumbering footsteps pounded the ground off to the wizard's right as something large crashed and ripped through the underbrush. He glanced to the right, scanning through the dense trees to see what it was that had joined in the fight, but in doing so he failed to see the sharp decline he was approaching as it was somewhat hidden by ferns that had managed to grow tall enough to make the ground appear level.

Raven's foot failed to land on the ground as he sprinted out over the drop and began to lurch forward. He tucked and rolled as best he could, careful not to lose his grip on either the dagger or the scimitar. The thick ferns scraped and cut his cheeks, leaving stinging welts and slices across any part of bare skin that was unfortunate enough to tumble through the undergrowth. His shoulder struck a short, sharp stub of some sapling that had long ago been snapped off, and he cried out in pain as the wood tore through his skin and bit into the joint before the weight of his body tumbling yet further downhill ripped him free. The dagger in his left hand was released and he now tumbled without as much control, slamming his back and neck onto the ground more than he would have liked. He only barely managed to conjure a pillow of soft air before he flipped onto his face and would have surely dashed his forehead against a large, flat rock lying at the bottom of the hill.

Raven tried to catch his breath and moved to sit up. He started to rebuild his ward, but something was coming down the hill toward him.

He couldn't see it clearly through the large ferns, but he saw flashes of black fur and could tell by the thundering steps that it was something massive. The foliage shook and trembled around him before opening up to reveal a humungous bear lunging for him, mouth open and turned to the side, its yellow fangs on a trajectory that would surely place them around Raven's neck. Out in front of the gaping maw were the bear's paws, tipped with thick claws that could easily finish the man off.

Raven didn't think. He reflexively magicked the pillow of air up between the two of them and then hardened it, somewhat like creating a ward, and then he exploded the spell. Most of the blast was directed toward the bear, but some of the shockwave knocked back into Raven, sending the wizard flying several feet to land upon his back with a *thawump!* His left shoulder burned and he cried out in pain, unable to lift himself up. The fiery stinging in his shoulder crept up through the side of his neck and his back arched in a spasm that he could only control after calming his mind enough to focus and exhaling slowly; even then it was all he could do to sit up.

Fortunately, the bear had taken the brunt of the spell. The animal was groaning upon the ground, blood streaming out of its head and down its snout. Raven lifted his scimitar and used the last bit of energy he had to send it soaring point-first into the large, open gash he saw on the bear's forehead. It took every ounce of magic he had left, but he managed to bury nearly half of the blade in the bear's skull.

He breathed a sigh of relief, but his joy was short lived.

The ferns around him shriveled, turning black and falling like ash to the earth as they crumbled. An intense heat forced its way down from above like a ball of invisible fire. Raven put his good arm up and tried to conjure a ward, but his energy was spent. The heat enveloped his fingers, and then pressed his hand back down. Beads of sweat formed on his brow and it became hard to breath. The air grew heavy and tasted of sulfur. Then, an unseen force pushed him down to the ground. Unlike the plants, he did not burn or whither, but the sweltering force pinning him down scorched his skin, stinging and burning as it held him firm.

He looked up, barely able to squint against the heat.

A shadowy form was approaching him, making its way down the hill. Raven had to close his eyes as the heat grew more intense. Sweat was pouring over him now and he could smell burning hair coming from his arms and head. Two feet stopped beside his head, but the wizard could neither move nor look at the enemy.

"There are only two ways to deal with trespassers here," a stoic voice said. "The first option, of course, is to kill the offender."

The words hung in the air heavily as the heat bore down on Raven. The wizard found himself thinking of his daughter. She had told him not to come here alone. She had pleaded with him to take the other Ghosts of the Quags with him, but he had not listened. In the next two seconds, it was not his life that flashed through his mind, but that of his daughter. He saw her birth. He felt her toddler-sized hand reach for his and grasp his fingers. He heard her voice as she spoke her first words, and then it changed to that of a young woman filled with excitement and a zest for life. He watched Miranda grow into the young woman she now was, replaying each moment as if living it for the first time. In his heart, he knew there had been times he had been too hard on her. He had yelled too much, or been too short with her on several occasions, but mercifully none of those moments came to him now. He saw only her smiles and her achievements. His heart swelled with pride and he smiled, ready to hear his enemy's next words.

As if on cue, the enemy spoke right as the replay of Miranda's life ended.

"The second option is to use your heart, but you are a human, and therefore, your heart is useless to me," the voice said.

Raven accepted his defeat, knowing that death would be the option exercised here in Tanglewood Forest. He would have gone quietly, happily even, if the enemy had not uttered his next phrase.

"If you have loved ones, pray they do not follow you, for their death will be as inevitable as yours," the voice said.

A flash of terror ripped through Raven and his eyes opened, drying in the heat as he screamed in horror before a nightmarish wave of heat rippled through his body.

# CHAPTER 2

Jonathan shifted on the hard stump and wiggled his right foot, trying to push the encroaching needles out of his foot. As he moved, he could feel the edge of the stump pressing in along the back of his thigh. He brought the water-skin up to his lips and let the warm liquid flow into his mouth. He grimaced at his drink as he pulled it away and put the stopper back in place.

"Left it in the sun again, didn't you?" Jason called from a few yards away.

Jonathan nodded and tossed the water-skin to the ground. "Did you find her?" Jonathan asked.

Jason nodded and came over to the stump, shoving Jonathan aside just enough to make room for himself. He held up a bit of blood-streaked wool. Jason knew at once the lamb's fate.

"Pa should never have bought those dumb sheep from Nebok," Jonathan said.

Jason shrugged. "Grandfather was trying to expand the farm a bit," he said. "I can understand that."

Jonathan shook his head and stood up from his now considerably smaller seat, wiping the back of his pants free of dirt. "Nebok is a pig farmer. I mean, he is good with chickens too, but the sheep were never kept well by him. Pa should have known he wouldn't be able to control their wanderlust."

Jason set the bloody bit of wool over his knee. "It wasn't entirely Grandfather's fault. I might have talked him into it a bit."

Jonathan folded his arms across his chest. "You, the Hero of the Quags, tried to talk Pa into becoming a shepherd?" Jonathan stifled a laugh and shook his head as he looked to his older brother. "What on Terramyr would you do that for?"

"You fought in the Murkle Quags as much as I," Jason pointed out, deflecting the question.

Jonathan shrugged. "I doubt many here would agree with that, the way the townsfolk fawn over you." Jason shook his head, but Jonathan caught the hint of a grin that turned up the corner of his older brother's mouth. "Don't pretend as though you don't like it," Jonathan added. "You have always thrived on being the favored son of Holstead."

Jason laughed and waved his brother off. "If not for you, I would have been Holstead's favored *dead* son."

Jonathan smirked.

The older brother stood up. "It's been a year since the war ended. It's time we thought of what we are going to do with the rest of our lives, Jonathan. We can't go on adventures forever."

"And why not?" Jonathan teased.

"Because there are no more adventures to be had," Jason said.

Jonathan screwed up his face and pointed out at the forest around them. "There are many lands to explore. Terramyr is teeming with adventure, you just have to know where to look."

Jason shook his head. "I'm getting married, Jonathan, or have you forgotten?"

Jonathan's blue eyes lost their twinkle and his smile faded. "Yeah, I remember."

"Actually, that's why I talked with Grandfather about the sheep."

Jonathan frowned.

"I know it may not make sense, but actually I have a very logical explanation for it," Jason said. "You know that Grandfather made a deal with Mortimer. It wasn't just to arrange the marriage, but to keep me out of the war as well."

"Sure, but Mortimer didn't keep up his end of the bargain," Jonathan said quickly. "You were one of the Ghosts! That's a far cry from being kept safe behind a desk in Lehemat."

Jason nodded. "Mortimer doesn't see it that way. He paid off the appropriate people, and I should have gotten that quiet assignment Grandfather wanted, but since I was the one who put myself in danger, Mortimer believes I owe him for the money he spent."

Jonathan shook his head. "Well, then don't marry his daughter Annabell. There, problem solved."

Jason sighed. He looked down to the grassy ground and his shoulders slumped.

It was then that Jonathan realized what his brother was trying to say. "You're in love with Pig-face!?"

Jason lashed out and backhanded Jonathan in the stomach. "Don't call her that," he said as he pointed his index finger up at Jonathan's face.

Jonathan held up his hands and backed away, but he couldn't wipe the stupid grin from his face.

"Besides," Jason continued, "Annabell grew up while we were gone, and she is really quite lovely." Jason sighed again and stuffed the wool into his pocket. "Come, let's go tell Grandfather that the lamb was killed."

"So," Jonathan began, "you still haven't explained the sheep." He pointed to the pocket. "What will that prove to Mortimer?"

Jason sighed again and shrugged. "I thought if we could expand the farm, then maybe we could show Mortimer that I am just as good a businessman as he is. You're right about the town, they all love me for what I did, but Mortimer only cares about things. If it isn't tangible, then it has no value to him. I don't want to marry Annabell without something more to offer. I can't have Mortimer lording over us all the time. Imagine how suffocating that would be."

"So live with us," Jonathan said. "I'm sure Pa would help you build a cabin of your own on our lands."

Jason shook his head. "I already offered that to Annabell. She likes the idea, but Mortimer won't have it. He says that unless I can pay him back the money he wasted on me, I have to live with them and work it off."

Jonathan had never seen Jason look so defeated before. Even when Jonathan had found him in the Warrens, captured by the swamp trolls and facing near-certain death, Jason had never lost his confident grin. Now, there was a sagging frown on Jason's face and, worse than that, a dull look about his eyes.

"That's no way to start a marriage," Jason said. "If we begin our lives like that, then nothing I will ever do in the future will be good enough for Mortimer, or anyone else in the family. Even Bryce, Annabell's older brother is angry with me. He says I should have taken guard duty at Fort Sym like he did."

Jonathan nodded. "Bryce is just jealous because he now looks like a coward compared to you."

Jason nodded. "I know it, but that doesn't ease the tension."

"We should get back to Pa," Jonathan put in. "Unless you want to stop for a quick game of centers."

Jason smirked and looked around. "All right, if you think you can challenge me this time."

Jonathan watched as Jason picked out a sizeable oak tree and then fired three arrows. One bit into the tree high up on the trunk, about ten feet from the ground. The second struck it at six feet up, and the third was only two feet from the ground.

"Can't you group your shots any better than that?" Jonathan teased.

"If I group them closer, you might hit one by mistake and claim the points," Jason shot back. "Go on, hit 'em if you can."

Jonathan had been practicing nearly every day since they returned a year ago. Today was the day he was finally going to win. He pulled the first arrow back on the string. The tension was felt in his fingers, arm, and back as he drew the arrow back until it just touched the corner of his mouth. A moment before he let it fly, he called out his target. "Arrow in the middle."

The arrow flew through the air and struck the middle arrow perfectly, shattering Jason's arrow entirely.

"Bottom," Jonathan called out as he nocked another arrow and let it fly. The second missile struck its target as well. Jonathan then drew his third and final shot. He let it loose and two seconds later it exploded into the back of Jason's arrow.

Jonathan lowered his bow and looked back to Jason, wearing an obscenely large grin.

Jason's eyes went wide. He glanced from the tree back to Jonathan and then to the tree once more.

"Go on, see if you can match it," Jonathan called out.

Jason shook his head and tossed his bow to the ground. He started walking away, leaving Jonathan standing alone near the stump.

"Hey, Jason, don't be a sore loser!" Jonathan called after him. His brother didn't turn around. He walked away quietly, head down and shoulders slumped. Jonathan's mirth faded, replaced by a slight fear in his chest that he had not only failed to cheer his brother up, but he had in fact driven Jason's grief further into his heart. Jonathan slipped his bow over his shoulder, grabbed Jason's bow, and then ran off to catch up with his brother.

"Hold up," Jonathan said again as he neared Jason.

"Go on, rub it in a bit more," Jason said. This time he had recovered enough to force a grin, but Jonathan knew better than to believe it.

"Could you see what grabbed the lamb?" Jonathan asked, deciding it was best to change the subject entirely.

"The tracks were hard to decipher," Jason said. "Something big, but I can't be sure what it was. This bit of wool was the only thing left, and the ground was too compact for tracks except in the exact spot where the lamb was caught, and those were mostly claw marks in the dirt."

Jonathan could see that Jason was frustrated by this topic as well. Normally Jason was easily able to decipher tracks, even partial prints, but not this time. Jonathan decided to switch topics again. "Pa was right about Annabell though," he said with a grin.

Jason smiled, genuinely this time, and nodded his agreement. He didn't say anything, but that was all right. Jonathan could see that he had set his brother's mind on a better path now.

"When is the wedding again?" Jonathan asked.

Jason shook his head. "Two days after the fall festival. You know that already." Jason reached out and set his hand on Jonathan's shoulder. "I know what you're trying to do," he said.

Jonathan looked back at his brother curiously. "You do?"

Jason nodded. "Thanks," he offered. He stopped the two of them then and took his bow back from Jonathan. He took in a deep breath of forest air and then grinned slyly. "Bet I beat you back to the house."

"We're at least two miles away," Jonathan said. "I am not running that far back."

Jason shrugged. "Fine, but I say the last one there has to sleep outside with the sheep tonight."

"I am not…" Jonathan's words trailed off as Jason tore away, sprinting as fast as he could. "Icadion's beard," Jonathan cursed. The young man ran off after his brother, but he knew even before he started that he would never catch up to him. His feet carried him nimbly over a fallen log, around a copse of young trees and over the ground as quick as a deer, but he was falling behind his older brother with every passing second. Jonathan had slowed to a mild jog by the time he passed old Nebok's farm, and was walking before he reached the turn off that led to his cabin.

Jason was nowhere in sight, likely already inside and eating his supper.

Jonathan let his feet drift slowly over the dirt road leading up to his home. The sun had already begun to set, darkening the path and casting a long shadow over the front of the house. Not so long ago Jonathan would have seen light coming from the windows, but not now. Pa had never managed to fix the shutters correctly after the glass windows had been sold off to Mortimer. Now the windows were covered with loose fitting boards that only allowed slivers of light through. A year ago, Jonathan would have thought that Mortimer would simply give the glass panes back; after all, they had been Pa's pride and joy, a sign of his affection for Memaw, but that never happened.

A lot of things hadn't panned out the way Jonathan had expected. Oh, there had been celebrations and feasts at the end of the war, but after a couple of months things went back to normal. Jonathan wondered what it might be like if he relocated to another town that had been more intimately aware of the war and the devastation it caused. Perhaps if he had settled in Wendyn, a town pulled into the growing borders of the swamps that made up the Murkle Quags from which all of the residents had been forced to flee, then maybe he would have been received better.

Here in Holstead, he was a hero of sorts, but still a farmer. A year ago he had slain a troll king and helped kill a giant troll that would have surely destroyed any city it had attacked, but now he was just a Haymaker boy.

He still longed for adventure, though. Not even the dangers he had faced down in the Murkle Quags could beat that itch out of him that he had to travel and experience new thing. He craved adventure, and frankly felt lost without it. It was almost as if he had already hit the pinnacle of excitement that he could expect in his life, and he wasn't even twenty yet. As a farmer, that was most certainly true. What adventures would ever come to Holstead? No, he needed to find a way out. That much was confirmed when Miken, a scholar of the Order of Anorit came through Holstead about six months prior.

The man had more tales of adventure than anyone Jonathan had ever heard of, and he wasn't even a soldier! He was a traveling scholar. His whole life he visited new places and recorded important events along the way. He had even traded a book about the elven lands to the north to Jonathan in exchange for Jonathan's permission to write about his adventures. He smiled as he thought about that for a moment. A traveling scholar had come to see *him* and get *his* story.

He reached back to his pocket and pulled the small book out that Miken had given him. Jonathan must have read it a hundred times by now from cover to cover. It wasn't an overly thick book, but it detailed the main attractions in each of the major elven cities to the north. As he opened the book now, he imagined traveling north with Miranda to visit the cities. They had talked about going together before… though they had fallen out of touch as of late. Still, he liked to fantasize about going north one day, and visiting the cities he had read so much about over the last several months.

He would have left long ago if not for Pa and Memaw. No matter how much he missed the adventure beyond the village, he couldn't bring himself to abandon them again without good reason.

In their nightly prayers, Pa and Memaw still thanked the gods for the return of their grandsons.

How he could leave them?

They were the only two who really knew what it was Jonathan and Jason had done.

He stopped then and bent down to a night-bell, a purple and blue flower that bloomed only at dusk, and picked it. He put the blossom to his nose and smelled the sweet, rose-like fragrance. The color of the petals reminded him of Miranda. She had worn a dress that was similar in color to the flower, a deep blue fabric that had hugged her curves and accentuated her raven-black hair.

As he thought of her, it was almost as if he could see her standing on the porch, leaning over the front rail and watching him as he returned to the house. He smiled then, thinking how wonderful that would be. Despite their promise to remain in touch, they had lost contact with each other over the last year since his return. She was somewhere in Lehemat, and he was stuck on his family's farm. He knew then where he would go if he had the chance. He would go and find the girl who still somehow managed to maintain her spell over him.

He sniffed the flower again and then tucked it into a small, empty pouch on his belt so he could give it to Memaw. She always appreciated flowers, especially night-bells.

When he looked back up to the porch after sealing the pouch, he swore he could still see Miranda standing there, staring at him intently. He cocked his head to the side.

Someone *was* there.

*It can't be.* Jonathan started walking again, his feet pulling him along the path a little too quickly as he nearly stumbled over a rock he failed to notice.

"You lived through the Warrens to fall over a rock?" Miranda called out as she walked down the steps toward him.

It is her!

Jonathan's heart skipped once and his throat went dry. It was as if his brain forgot how to send the proper signals to his limbs. He gave a half-wave and stepped out awkwardly at the same time.

"Hi," Jonathan said.

"That's all you have to say?" Miranda quipped as she walked toward him, the soft light of dusk playing upon her long hair and beautiful face as she approached him.

He agreed that he should say something more, something poignant, something amusing… but nothing else came but a stupid grin that pulled at the left corner of his mouth.

"It's good to see you," Miranda said. She crossed the remaining distance between them, leaned in and went up on her front foot to give Jonathan a hug. Her arms wrapped around his neck and she squeezed him close for a second. He hugged her as well, his arms going around her lower back.

"It's good to see you as well," he said once his mind was able to reengage enough to form a coherent sentence. "What are you doing here?"

Miranda backed away, letting her hands slide down Jonathan's arms and then back to her sides.

"It's my father," she said. "He's missing."

"Raven is missing?" Jonathan echoed. His mind raced through the possibilities. Maybe the trolls had resurfaced. Perhaps there was a new troll king. If so, then they would likely want revenge.

Miranda clasped her hands in front of her waist and shook her head. "He left several months ago. He said he had some things he needed to look into, but he should have been back by now."

"What about the others?" Jonathan asked. "Surely Captain Ziegler wouldn't leave him behind somewhere."

"My father didn't tell the others. He went alone, and told me not to tell anyone about it."

"Where did he go?" Jonathan asked. "Jason and I can help you."

Miranda nodded. "That's why I'm here," she said matter-of-factly. "I knew you would."

Jonathan nodded and stepped in to embrace her once more. Miranda almost seemed to pull away at first, but then she leaned into his chest and stood still and silent. She didn't cry, but Jonathan knew her well enough to know that she was tougher than most, and very capable of keeping her wits about her even in the most dire of circumstances. Slowly, Jonathan slid his left hand down to retrieve the night-bell. Miranda could use the gesture now more than Memaw. His fingers spread the pouch open and then pushed inside gently, fishing for the delicate flower. He just managed to grab it and pull it out of the pouch when he heard the knob on the door turn.

The door to the cabin opened and a flood of yellow light poured out around the shadowy figure of another man. He was taller than Jason by a bit, but Jonathan didn't recognize the form and his face was hidden in shadows thanks to the light from behind.

"Miranda, can you come back in?" the man called out.

Miranda stiffened and pulled away from Jonathan. "We should go inside," she said.

"Who is that?" Jonathan asked. "Is it a new member of the Ghosts?"

Miranda shook her head. "His name is Ruben Faelwyn. He is my fiancé."

Jonathan felt as if someone had punched him in the stomach. He watched Miranda turn around quickly and make her way back up to the porch. She reached out her hand and Ruben took it as the two of them entered the house. They left the door open behind them, obviously intending for Jonathan to follow them, but his feet wouldn't move. He stood there, replaying in his mind the day that Miranda had taken *his* hand in hers. Now she was not only with someone else, but engaged to be married.

He likely would have stood outside for the remainder of the night, hoping that Miranda would disappear somehow, if not for Jason sticking his head out the door and shouting at him.

"Are you coming or not?" Jason called out.

Jonathan shook his head. Maybe he could make an excuse to go into town—no, it was already fast becoming dark. His mind thought of the sheep. After all, he had lost the race to Jason. He should go and be with the sheep. He looked down to the ground, fumbling for something to say.

"Come on," Jason said. Jonathan had been so stunned that he hadn't even noticed Jason's approach. Jason put an arm around Jonathan's shoulders and started pulling him along toward the porch. "Buck up, buttercup," Jason said. It was a saying that Memaw had often said to them while growing up, though this wound stung a bit more than the usual skinned knee or sliver that had plagued Jonathan's youth.

Jonathan tossed the night-bell a step in front of him and then let his left foot fall onto it, crushing it into the ground.

"What was that?" Jason asked.

Jonathan shrugged. "Nothing important," he said.

Jason squeezed Jonathan's shoulders once and then gave him a gentle shove up the stairs and into the doorway.

Aside from Miranda and Ruben, Jonathan saw three others in the front room with Pa and Memaw. Captain Ziegler, standing closest to the doorway, was the first to greet Jonathan. The three scars on his right cheek stretched as he smiled and held out his thick hand.

"Good to see you again," Ziegler said. Jonathan looked down and took the proffered hand in his and gave it a shake. As he did so, he noticed the many skull tattoos on Ziegler's arm. There was one for each human soldier that had fought under Ziegler's command and died in the Murkle Quags. Jonathan knew that the tattoos stretched up the arm, and down Captain Ziegler's torso as well. The wars with the trolls in the Murkle Quags had been the deadliest conflict ever to reach their realm. Jonathan glanced back to Miranda, and then wondered if there would soon be another black tattoo in memory of Raven.

Bull, a bald, heavily muscled man rushed in and wrapped his arms around Jonathan's waist, catching Jonathan's left arm and pinning it in the hug as he lifted the boy up and squeezed him. "Oh, it is good to see you again!" Bull said. He shook Jonathan to each side, grunting and laughing before setting Jonathan back down on the floor.

"Hello, Bull," Jonathan said. The young man then looked up and saw Moose, a mountain of a man standing seven feet tall, with shoulders wider than the doorway and harrier than the animal that was his namesake, holding up the back wall of the room with a sour look on his face. "Well met, Moose," Jonathan greeted.

Moose waved flippantly and then folded his meaty arms across his barrel-like chest.

Captain Ziegler leaned in and whispered to Jonathan, "Don't worry about him. He's happy to see you too, it's just that your grandmother scolded him for trying to smoke in the house not more than two minutes ago."

Jonathan's mouth fell open and he glanced to Memaw. No one, ever, had even asked Moose to stop smoking in their presence, let alone scolded him for it.

"Don't look at me like that, Jonathan," Memaw said when she caught his look. "He can turn himself into a chimney if he likes, but I won't let the smell fester in my house or clog up my body."

Captain Ziegler stifled a laugh when Moose audibly snorted and looked away at the far wall.

"I offered a roll with apple butter," Memaw said.

Jonathan closed his mouth and stepped into the room when he felt Jason pushing from behind. The door squeaked closed and everyone remained silent for a few moments. Jonathan looked at the Ghosts of the Quags, letting it sink in just how serious this was.

"Gentlemen," Pa spoke up as he sat forward in his reading chair. "You know how I feel about this, but I will leave it up to my grandson to decide for himself."

Jonathan glanced from Ziegler to Pa and then to Memaw.

Pa didn't seem nearly as upset as he had the night Jason had spoken of entering the army and going with the Ghosts of the Quags to fight the trolls, but there was an edge to his voice, and a coldness in his eyes. Something was definitely amiss. Memaw sat silently next to Pa, staring at the floor and holding Pa's hand.

Jonathan turned back to Ziegler. "Where did Raven go?"

"He went north, into Tanglewood Forest."

Jonathan frowned. What could Raven have been looking for up there?

Jason slapped Jonathan on the back and spoke up next. "You can always count on me, Captain Ziegler. I'm in."

"*We* are in," Jonathan said.

Ziegler shook his head. "No, we only came for Boar, er, I mean Jason, this time."

Jonathan bristled and stared indignantly at the large man for a moment. He glanced to Miranda, who returned his gaze with sad eyes. No, he had helped her find Raven once before, and he could help again. "I think you are forgetting that *I* am the one who slew the troll king. *I* also helped kill the giant troll afterward. Besides that, Miranda and I survived the Murkle Quags and made it all the way down to the Warrens without your help, thank you very much. If anything, it was us who helped *you*."

Ziegler nodded and patted the air. "We know that, Jonathan. No one here has forgotten what you did. However, you *are* still very young. We don't know what dangers await us in the north, but you can bet they won't be anything to take on lightly. We are leaving you here as our way of keeping *you* alive."

"No, that doesn't make any sense." Jonathan glanced to Pa and Memaw, but Memaw was silent, and Pa soon threw in his lot with Ziegler.

"Captain Ziegler is right, Jonathan," Pa said. "The gods may have smiled upon you once, but this is not a journey any of us want you to be a part of."

Jonathan shook his head. He knew that wasn't true. Miranda wanted him along. But then again, why wasn't she speaking up? He looked to her again, but she looked to the floor.

Ziegler nodded and smiled faintly. "Jason, it will be good to have you back with us."

"Where are we going first?" Jason asked.

"All we have is a cryptic letter from Raven. It talks about finding some sort of mystical creature in Tirnog, called a Wyrebin, but that doesn't make any sense because the Wyrebin has been extinct for over a thousand years. As far as we know, Tirnog doesn't even have a statue or museum exhibit of such a creature, as it was viewed as a nuisance."

"It was essentially a giant beaver the size of a mammoth," Ruben put in.

Ziegler nodded. "Exactly, and there are no places in Tirnog where they could keep such a thing alive or dead. Best we can figure is he was giving us a visual clue."

"Like maybe a painting on a sign somewhere, or perhaps a symbol in a library, that sort of thing," Bull said, trying to sound smart.

Jonathan perked up. This was his way in. He knew what the letter was speaking about. Not only did he know of a place that was home to strange creatures, the Scholar of the Order of Anorit had even told him about stopping in to see a colony of Wyrebins in Tirnog, tucked away safely and protected from harm. "No, that isn't it," he said. "There *is* a place in Tirnog where they keep mystical creatures. They have an actual Mystical Creature Preserve there, I have read about it. They have several Wyrebins there too." He was nearly jumping with joy at having something the group needed. Now he could buy his way into the group.

"Tell us where it is then, and we'll be sure to check it out," Ziegler commented.

Jonathan shook his head. No one knew about his book, not even Jason. There was no way they could force him to give the information without letting him come along. "Nope, I can take you there, but I won't tell you where it is."

"He's bluffing," Bull said.

"I never bluff," Jonathan replied curtly.

"It's true," Jason said as he slapped Jonathan on the shoulder. "My brother is a terrible liar. Can't even bluff his way out of a card game. If he says there is a preserve, then there is. It's as simple as that."

Ziegler sighed and finally nodded his head. "All right, but he's your responsibility then," he said pointing to Jason. "Keep him out of trouble. We have another lead to follow up in Tirnog. I'll let you two check out the preserve he claims is there."

Miranda perked up just then. "I want to go with them as well," she said. "To the preserve, I mean. I want to see it. If my father was there, then maybe he left another clue for us."

Ziegler nodded.

Jonathan heard Pa emit a sound that was akin to a growl shortly before rising from his chair and leaving the room.

"You have only until the Fall Festival," Pa shouted over his shoulder. "Then you get your skinny behind back here and marry Annabell!" Pa stormed into his room and slammed the door.

Jonathan and Jason shared a look.

Bull laughed and pointed at Jason. "Putting on the ball and chain a bit early, aren't you Jason?"

Memaw spoke up, clearing her throat loudly and directing her words at Bull. "A man can do worse than settle down and get married. After all, without families how would the civilized world continue?"

Bull blushed, something he rarely did, and quietly apologized. "Sorry, ma'am, didn't mean nothing by it."

"No, I am sure you didn't," Memaw said, her voice scathing and her eyes glaring at Bull.

Everyone was stunned for a bit, that is until Ruben broke the silence.

"We are to be wed as well," he announced as he pulled Miranda tighter to him. "I would agree with Mrs. Haymaker that marriage ought to be the goal of every person."

Jonathan wanted to spit on the floor to show his contempt, but he didn't for fear of his Memaw's wrath. He felt Jason pat him twice on the back, then his older brother moved away.

"I'll get packed," Jason said.

"Pack light, we need to move quickly," Ziegler instructed.

"When is the wedding, dears?" Memaw asked Miranda and Ruben as if she was oblivious to the fact that Jason was already preparing to leave.

Jonathan caught the sheepish glance Miranda shot his way. He couldn't tell if she was uncomfortable about the wedding, or if she was feeling guilty for not having told him sooner. Either way, he stuffed it down and turned to follow his brother. He would rather pack than listen to Miranda's wedding details. Truth be told, he would rather be back in the Warrens again, but with the cabin's size, he overheard more than he ever wanted to know anyway.

"We plan to be wed next spring. Miranda will be eighteen then, and we will have the ceremony in Lehemat."

"That sounds lovely," Memaw said.

Jonathan grabbed an extra shirt and stuffed it into his backpack. He must have made a face while doing so, for Jason was smirking at him and trying hard to keep his budding grin from erupting all over his face.

"Easy, little brother, maybe he'll die on the trip and the wedding will be canceled," Jason whispered as he leaned in.

Jonathan glared back at him. He didn't dignify the jest with a response. Though, truth be told, he had thought of the same thing himself already, but that only made him feel like an animal for imagining such a thing.

"It'll be alright, maybe he'll turn out to be a coward, and run away from battle. Then she'll remember who her hero really is."

Jason made a kissing face in the air.

Only a short while ago Jonathan would have given anything to cheer his brother up, but this was not the way he had imagined that going. He looked down and packed an extra pair of pants.

"And what is it you do in Lehemat, dear?" Memaw asked.

Jonathan paused, half hoping Ruben would announce he sold horse manure fertilizer, or maybe mucked out the king's stables. He was not so lucky.

"I am the head of arcane research at the Lehemat College of Mystics," Ruben replied.

"He is the youngest man to ever be appointed to the position," Captain Ziegler commented. "He was put in charge just two years ago, at the age of twenty."

Jonathan closed his eyes and sighed. His hands went down for his good pair of boots that were tucked in a chest at the foot of his bed.

Jason moved in close and bent down to Jonathan. "Sorry little brother, tough break." He patted Jonathan on the shoulder and then turned away.

Despite his anger and embarrassment, Jonathan knew that this time his brother meant his words genuinely. Jonathan continued packing. "Why are you so eager to go north?" Jonathan asked.

Jason finished stuffing his backpack and then pulled out a small piece of paper from his bedside table drawer. He sat down and began writing a note. Jonathan maneuvered around to try to get a look at it, but Jason twisted and put his shoulders in the way.

"Not polite to read other peoples' letters," Jason said.

"Then tell me why you are so quick to leave Annabell."

Jason sighed. "It's nothing," he said. "Just…"

"Just what?" Jonathan prodded.

"Well, partly it's because I owe the Ghosts. After all, I was a part of them for a while during the war. Raven is my brother-in-arms."

"Sure, I understand that," Jonathan mused.

"Also, maybe I can do something that will make Mortimer impressed. You know, come back with something, or achieve something that will ease the tension."

Jonathan shook his head. "I know I am young, and all, but if Mortimer doesn't respect what you have already done, I don't think anything else is going to help unless you come back with a lot of gold. That seems to be all he cares about."

Jason nodded and hurried to finish his letter. "Then I'll just have to do that," he commented as he signed the letter and folded the paper.

Jonathan quickly finished packing and returned to the front room with the others. Memaw rose from her chair and bid the others farewell and then embraced Jason in a grandmotherly hug.

"You be sure to watch out for yourself out there. After all, you're getting married soon."

Jason smiled garishly and patted her on the back. "I'll be back before the festival," he promised. "Give this to Annabell for me?" he asked as he held up the folded letter.

Memaw nodded and then moved toward Jonathan and stopped short of hugging him. She took his shoulders in her arms and looked into his eyes. Her blue orbs had lost a bit of their brightness over the years, and now appeared equal parts blue and gray, but they were as kind as ever. She smiled and nodded, as if convincing herself of something, then she pulled Jonathan in close. "You watch over your brother. You brought him back once, and you can make sure he returns again."

"I will, Memaw," Jonathan said.

Memaw gave him a squeeze and then turned to whisper in his ear. "Don't worry about the girl, you'll get her back," she said. She pushed away and gave Jonathan a quick wink, then she retired to her room.

Jonathan followed her with his eyes, stunned that she would say such a thing. He had never confessed to anyone but Jason how much he liked Miranda. A moment after the door closed, he could hear Pa grumbling in a muffled voice.

"We should get moving," Ziegler said. "If you're ready, that is," he added.

Jason nodded enthusiastically. "You would do the same for me," he said. "Let's go find Raven."

"And quick too," Bull said with a snort. "The little guy has to get back for his wedding!" Bull couldn't contain his laughter as they all exited the cabin.

Jonathan was the last out the door, locking it just before heading out into the night.

# CHAPTER 3

Jonathan barely took two steps before he passed through a thick fog of cigar smoke that made him gag. He looked up to Moose. The big man was making a show of blowing the smoke back toward the door. Unlike Memaw, Jonathan was not about to say anything to the mountain of a man about it. He held his breath as best he could and walked by. He passed by Miranda and Ruben quickly, careful not to let her notice his sideways glance as he hurried to catch up with Captain Ziegler.

The large warrior offered a nod to Jonathan and then held his left hand up, signaling everyone to stop.

"There is one more thing you need to know," Ziegler said. He motioned for Jason to come up closer. "Dell didn't approve this mission."

"Why not?" Jason asked as he rested an elbow on Jonathan's shoulder.

Ziegler shook his head. "Said that the elves would never forgive a foray into their territory. He made it clear that if we went in, we would be branded criminals."

"Why did you tell him?" Jason asked.

"The two of you may be done with your service, but we have contracts that last a little longer. Our absence had to be approved."

"But it wasn't approved, so how are you here?"

"Put in for holiday leave," Bull grunted. "We each have about two weeks coming to us, so we all took it at the same time."

Ziegler shot the bald man a look and Bull closed his mouth. The captain then turned back to Jonathan and Jason. "The truth is, he knows what we are doing. In two weeks' time, or earlier if our true intentions are discovered, he will come for us. We will be branded traitors."

"So we need to be very fast, then," Jason said with a nod.

"Even still, Dell will likely punish any who go with us. He can pretend to look the other way only until Commander Kilgrave finds out, then we will be in more trouble than ever."

"Bah!" Bull shouted. "We'll just find Raven and then all go north beyond Tanglewood Forest."

"We're still coming along," Jason said.

Jonathan nodded his agreement. "Raven would do it for us," he said.

"What about you two?" Jason asked Miranda and Ruben. "Won't you be in trouble as well?"

"I convinced the council that I needed some time off to prepare for the wedding, though I will likely be expelled from Lehemat once they discover my involvement," Ruben said.

Great. Not only is he in a high position, but he is risking everything for Miranda. How could I ever compete with that? Jonathan wanted to shake his head and grumble some sort of insult, but he kept calm and held the urges in.

"Let's move," Captain Ziegler said. "I hope you packed light. We are on foot, and we must make good time."

Jason looked down at Jonathan and nudged his little brother. "Ready for another run?"

Jonathan grunted. A moment later the entire group was jogging away from the cabin and into the darkness. Jonathan glanced over his shoulder once, just before turning onto the main road, and silently wished his grandparents farewell one last time.

Despite the war having ended a little more than a year before, each member of the Ghosts of the Quags maintained their pace easily. Even Moose, as large as he was, made the journey look easy as they jogged along the path before turning up north along Threadwyrm Road, which led into Tanglewood Forest. Much to Jonathan's chagrin, even Ruben the wizard appeared to have an easier time running him. The young boy developed a cramp in his left side that stung miserably and threatened to bend Jonathan at the waist. On the other hand, Ruben was lithe and not even breathing hard after several miles. Luckily, Jason dropped back to run beside Jonathan, helping the younger brother concentrate on moving forward.

They didn't stop until they reached the opening into the forest, which took nearly three hours. By that time, Jonathan had long forgotten about the single stitch in his side. His calves ached, his lungs burned, and his stomach threatened to eject anything inside of it as he doubled over and gasped for air.

"Looks like you should train more," Bull jested as he slapped Jonathan on the back.

"I'm sure he already put in a full day's work on the farm," Ruben said.

*Great. Now he is defending me.* Jonathan forced himself upright and waved at Bull. "I'm okay. Just need a short break."

"You have two minutes," Ziegler put in. The large captain stepped over to Miranda and the two began pointing at the forest and talking quietly between themselves.

Jonathan moved away from Ruben, who smiled at him as if he had no idea the distaste Jonathan was developing for him, and went to inspect the woods. The stars and half moon above gave a decent amount of silvery light, but it was nowhere near enough to penetrate the trees. Beyond the large opening of wood and leaves was a gaping darkness the likes of which Jonathan had never seen before. He had, in fact, been to this spot many times, but never at night. During the day, the forest always looked so inviting. Birds were often heard singing loudly, and deer and elk were commonly seen in this very area, nibbling upon the soft grasses that flanked the well-made dirt road. This time, however, the forest was quiet and cold. It appeared as though the woods themselves were a great beast lying low to the ground, mouth agape and waiting for foolish prey to wander inside to be consumed in the darkness.

"It will be fun to finally go inside Tanglewood," Jason said as he moved to step beside Jonathan. "I doubt there are any trolls in there."

"Trolls no, but there are other dangers to be aware of," Bull said as he came up on Jonathan's other side. "I heard there are jungle cats that roam the forest."

Jonathan shook his head. "Those are rumors. We've never seen anything like that."

Bull shrugged. "Well, you haven't ever been inside, have you? A jungle cat can sneak up on its prey without ever making a sound. Then, all at once, the beast launches and tackles its quarry, pinning it under several hundred pounds of teeth and claws!" Bull snatched out and shook Jonathan's shoulders for emphasis. Jonathan didn't jump, which obviously rankled Bull, for his mirth disappeared and he offered only a snort as he eyed Jonathan. "It's true, you know," Bull put in.

Jonathan shrugged. "I went into the heart of the Kigyo lands and found Kigabané by myself. I guess cats just aren't as scary as a nest of fifty-foot long snakes."

Moose chuckled to himself and lit another cigar, the orange and red flare of the match nearly blinding Jonathan for a moment.

"No one asked you to chime in," Bull shouted at Moose.

Now it was Jason's turn to offer a little ribbing of his own. He turned to Bull and put a mock expression of concern on his face. "Is Bull scared of cats?" Jason teased.

Bull growled and half-heartedly elbowed Jason in the side as he moved away from them.

Jason turned and winked to Jonathan, careful not to let anyone but Jonathan see him rub the spot where Bull had struck him.

"Simmer down!" Captain Ziegler snarled. "We are Ghosts, not a drunken murder of crows cackling on in the night!"

"Crows don't drink," Bull called out.

Ziegler took a step after Bull, but then stopped when the bald warrior set his pack down and turned to face a bush while undoing his trousers. The captain huffed and turned back to Miranda.

"Bull seems mouthier than I recall," Jason said quietly.

Jonathan nodded, but didn't say anything.

Before Bull had even finished watering the bush, Ziegler gave the order to move out. The group took off toward the opening in the forest, leaving Bull to grumble and hurry to catch up.

Jonathan couldn't help but feel a bit overwhelmed as they jogged into the darkness. He could see the first few trees, but then the forest pulled them in completely. He glanced back over his shoulder after his eyes adjusted a bit and the group slowed to a walk. He was surprised by how bright the field out beyond the forest looked now in comparison.

"Light," Ziegler commanded.

Jonathan turned back around just in time to be painfully blinded by an orb of white light that erupted in the air above Ruben. Jonathan winced away and had to blink for several seconds before the dozen spots disappeared from his vision and allowed him to refocus on the light in their path. Ruben set the orb floating over them effortlessly and the group continued on as if it were daytime.

"I thought we were being secret?" Jason asked.

"Only about our true intentions," Ziegler responded. "If anyone sees us, we tell them that we are all on holiday, and traveling to see the wonders of the elven cities."

"And then we pray they don't look in our packs," Bull said.

Ziegler nodded and turned to Jason. "It would look more suspicious if travelers didn't use light at night. Don't worry, we'll be alright."

Ruben nodded and said, "I have academic reasons to call upon some of the elven elders to discuss several books that I brought with me. This way we can look for clues without raising suspicions."

The thread of conversation unraveled then and Jonathan looked out to the trees with the aid of Ruben's light. Massive trunks stood with hardly any gap between them. Some of their branches grew out and around neighboring trees, while others shot up at an angle, twisting around other branches as they fought a slow war for dominance. The canopy of leaves above appeared as solid as any stone ceiling Jonathan had seen before, blocking out any view of the sky above, and greedily taking in all the light for themselves. Jonathan noted the lower branches had far fewer, if any, leaves upon them. There were, however, vines and creeping flowers that grew upon the lower branches. Moss and ivy covered many of the trunks, in some cases covering the base of the trees for only a few inches off the ground, and in others creating a full sheath of green that covered entire trees. It was a beautiful sight, and easily explained the forest's name. Jonathan doubted whether a horse could maneuver through the forest at all, with the thick webbing of branches and foliage closing off any passage wide enough to go through.

The group made excellent time, covering many miles before they stopped to make camp a few hours before dawn. Each of them slept in the open, using only their outer cloaks to keep themselves warm. Jonathan would have liked to set a fire, but Captain Ziegler insisted that fire was too dangerous in Tanglewood Forest.

"The tiniest of sparks can wreak havoc on the forest if an ember were to catch hold of some of the dead growth," he said. "Besides, Ruben can keep us warm."

Jonathan didn't even bother waiting to see what spell Ruben would cast this time. He just threw his pack down at the base of a large elm tree and dropped down onto the ground, lying back and looking up at the underside of the green canopy above.

A few moments later, a wave of warmth rolled over the young boy amidst whispers of thanks and appreciation aimed at Ruben.

"Don't let 'im get to ya," Jason said softly as he moved to position his pack next to Jonathan's. "I bet he can't fire a bow half as well as you can."

Jonathan nodded and then turned onto his side, putting his back to Jason. The older brother got the hint apparently, for he didn't say anything else as the two of them drifted off to sleep.

A sharp nudge bumped into Jonathan's back, just above his tailbone. It seemed as though it had only been a few minutes since the boy had closed his eyes, but light was now breaking through the thick mess of leaves above, and Ziegler was casting a fuzzy shadow over Jonathan.

"It's morning; time to move," Ziegler said.

Jonathan pushed up from the warm dirt, rubbing his neck when a sharp pain prevented him from looking over his left shoulder. He grabbed his pack and stood on his feet, noting that Ruben was still snoring.

Jason elbowed Jonathan in the ribs. "Well, at least he has *one* bad quality eh?"

Jonathan smiled at that one. Jason's blue eyes lit up and he scrunched his face for emphasis when Ruben let out a particularly loud snort. Jason pulled a stale roll out of his pack, broke it in half, and offered one portion to Jonathan. The two ate quickly, barely managing to finish their last bites before Ziegler had everyone, including a groggy, yawning Ruben, back on the road.

"Keep pace," Ziegler called out as he broke into a jog.

"I don't remember him running so much last time," Jonathan complained.

Jason slapped Jonathan on the back. "You'll get used to it."

Jonathan shook his head and frowned. He doubted very much that he would ever get used to running. It was the only activity he knew of that was both boring, yet mentally demanding as well. The forest droned on tree after tree, passing him by as his feet plodded the road and his mind began to drift. Unfortunately, as his mind drifted, so too did his feet. He veered to the side, slowed pace, or nearly tripped maybe a dozen times before he finally had no choice but to reengage his mind and focus on the road. That was the part he hated the most. The dirt road stretched out before him like a never-ending snake slithering its way through the forest. There were no visible goal markers or end points to focus on.

As if that wasn't enough, the stitch in his left side sprang upon him without warning, and much earlier than he would have expected. The pain was sharp, sending a vertical line of stings up the left side of his abdomen that altered his gait and slowed his pace.

"Keep up back there!" Bull called out.

Jonathan winced and came to a full stop.

"I'll get him," Jason said.

Just before Jonathan bent down to catch his breath and relieve the tension in his side, he caught sight of Miranda shooting him a disapproving glance.

"Come on, Jonathan, we've run farther than this before. Let's go," Jason called out as he circled back around Jonathan.

Jonathan shook his head. "Give me a second."

Jason threw his head back and let out a frustrated sigh.

Jonathan pushed upright again and was about to start running again when something moved off to the left. It was subtle, a shadow in the darkness of the forest really, but he had seen it. He squinted and focused in on the forest, his eyes scanning the sides of each tree and peering through the thick mess of vines and boughs.

"What is it?" Jason asked.

Jonathan shrugged. "Not sure, but there is something out there," he said.

Jason slapped his shoulder. "Come on, let's catch up with the others."

Jonathan noticed that they had all disappeared around a bend nearly one hundred yards away from them. He nodded and started jogging alongside Jason, but he stayed on the outside of the road in order to scan the forest.

"Tanglewood Forest is docile," Jason said. "It was probably just a deer, or maybe something smaller, if there was anything at all."

Jonathan shook his head. He was already breathing hard and trying to banish any recognition of the stitch in his side from his mind, so he didn't bother to respond. He just kept his eyes glued to the forest.

The two of them rounded the bend just as Bull let out a feral yell and lunged at something emerging from the trees. Jason and Jonathan broke into a sprint. A flash of yellow shot out from Ruben's hands and something screamed against the magic and slumped back against a large oak tree.

Jason and Jonathan arrived on the scene after the fighting was over. There on the ground were a pair of creatures the likes of which Jonathan had never seen before. Each had legs like those of a human, but they were made of wood. A thick torso of green, moss-covered wood coiled upward until a pair of long, spindly arms stretched out. Their heads had no mouths or noses. Only a pair of glowing eyes that dimmed with each passing second until the light left them entirely and a puff of dust erupted out from their bodies.

"These are wood sprites," Ruben said. "Usually they are mischievous, but harmless creatures. They tend to shy away from large groups like ours. However, I caught this pair rushing toward us."

"Good thing too," Miranda put in.

"I saw them, back there in the woods where I stopped," Jonathan blurted out as he pointed back behind himself.

"Then you should have sent out a warning," Bull said harshly. "At least Ruben here had the sense to tell us they were coming."

Jason cut in. "We weren't sure what we saw," he said. "They were only faint movements in the forest. I thought they were deer."

Bull snorted and shook his head, but diverted his anger toward Jason then. "You should have known better," he said.

"What's done is done," Ziegler said, ending the conversation then and there. "Let's keep moving. Everyone keep your eyes open." He turned and patted Ruben on the shoulder then. "Good job, Ruben," Ziegler said.

The group set off without so much as dragging the wood sprite corpses out of the road. As they jogged down the road, Jonathan thought of Ruben whenever the stitch in his side returned. He was not going to spend the entire journey being outdone by a wizard, much less by Miranda's fiancé. The boy's willpower pushed him through the growing aches in his feet and legs until Ziegler ordered everyone to halt and make camp a short while after sundown.

Like the first night, there was no fire, but at least they had enough time to eat and drink from their supplies before turning in for sleep. Bull took first watch, and Ziegler was to take the second, with Ruben taking the third and final shift for the night.

As Jonathan made his bed for the night, he couldn't help but wish that maybe, just maybe, something would come and disturb the camp during Ruben's shift. Then maybe he wouldn't feel so bad about the wood sprites from earlier in the day.

He was not to get his ill-conceived wish. In fact, the rest of the journey to Tirnog was completely smooth and free of any incidents whatsoever. After several more days of travel, the group stopped as the trees of the forest opened up to reveal a great city the likes of which Jonathan had never laid eyes upon. It was exactly as he had imagined it based upon the travel guide that the scholar had given him. He smiled and excitedly quickened his pace, ready to finally see in person the place he had imagined so many times in his mind.

Walls of white stone rose thirty feet into the air before them with crenelated parapets. Several guards dressed in white armor walked along the battlements, their flowing, golden cloaks waving behind them gracefully. Even from the ground Jonathan could easily see the spears the guards held, though they were not as large or foreboding as the slender halberds the guards near the gate wielded. Behind the walls rose a series of towers and spires of white stone that sparkled in the sunlight. Green ivy snaked up a few of the towers, but most were bare of any growth. Roofs of bronze tiles reflected the sunlight down and lent the city an almost heavenly appearance.

"Remember, we are here on holiday," Ziegler said. "Ruben, you will accompany Bull, and Moose and me. Miranda, you will go with Jason and Jonathan. Try and find that mystical reserve."

"Mystical Creature Preserve," Jonathan corrected.

Ziegler eyed the young boy and exhaled impatiently. "We have another lead we will follow up on. There is an elf here named Gadrien who might be able to shed some light on things. He and Raven used to exchange letters from time to time."

"As recently as last year, in fact," Ruben put in.

Ziegler nodded. "We'll go to his office. If we can't find him there, then we will meet him at his home." Ziegler turned to Jason then, obviously intending to address the ranking member of the three. "Jason, keep your eyes open. If you can't find the Wyrebin," Ziegler paused and eyed Jonathan suspiciously, "then meet us at Gadrien's house. Here is the address. Anyone should be able to tell you where it is, just be sure to play along as though you are visiting a friend on holiday."

Jason nodded dutifully. "Of course, Captain Ziegler."

Ziegler nodded and then turned to his backpack, fishing out a roll of parchment. "These are our official papers. Elves are big on lists and order."

"If no one knows about this mission, then how did you get official papers?" Jonathan blurted out.

Ruben raised a fist and coughed into it.

Ziegler smiled. "Ruben is more than a wizard. He can also make excellent copies of official documents."

Jonathan looked to Ruben.

"Don't get any ideas," Ruben said. "I only use the skill when someone is in serious trouble."

The others quietly fell into line and followed Ziegler as he walked to the front gate.

Jonathan shifted nervously when Miranda moved back in the line to walk between him and Jason. She smiled softly, her green eyes sparkling in the warm sunlight. Jonathan forced a smile and then walked half a step behind her as they approached the gates, stuffing his nerves down and deciding instead to focus on the sights around him. After all, he had never been to Tirnog before.

Ziegler gave the papers to the first guard, a tall elf the same height as Ziegler, but built much leaner. The elf turned and surveyed the group. The elf stood stoic, with angular features that showed something between disdain and indifference as his golden eyes inspected each member of the group. Jonathan tried to get a look at the elf's pointed ears, but they, along with most of the elf's hair, were covered by the helmet he wore. As Jonathan studied the helmet, he suddenly understood the difference between elves and men, at least in terms of craftsmanship.

In Fort Sym, or anywhere else groups of soldiers gathered together in Jonathan's homeland, a guard's helmet would have been little more than a large bowl of iron or steel shaped to fit around a man's head. Some would have a strip of metal hanging down as a nose-guard, while other helmets wouldn't. If the guard was lucky, there might be a coif of chainmail hanging down to protect the neck. This elf, on the other hand, wore a helmet that appeared to consist of some sort of steel alloy, for it was yellow, almost golden in appearance. The main cap of the helmet formed the base layer, but built onto that were a pair of bronze wings that fanned out behind either side of the elf's head. Each wing was formed with carefully etched feathers of bronze. The metal then extended down the elf's neck, flaring out at the bottom to allow for movement. A hinged, curved piece of metal closed the front of the elf's neck, but it was not a simple piece of metal, like one might find for a human's visor. No, it had silver inlay along the outer rim, forming a pattern of swirling ivy and leaves. Though the elf's face was uncovered, there was a visor that was resting atop the helmet, waiting to be pulled down to cover the face. Jonathan couldn't see it clearly, but the glaring shine in the sunlight was more than enough to assure him that the visor was every bit as ornate as the rest of the helmet.

The rest of the guard's armor was just as lavish. The white metal breastplate was carved to present the onlooker with a wall of pectoral and abdominal muscles flanked with a black metal inlay of ivy and leaves growing along the sides. Atop the collarbones, a cloak of gold was fastened to the breastplate with golden clasps. The legs were covered in greaves that attached via a series of leather buckles along the inner side of the legs, giving Jonathan a clear view of the golden colored trousers underneath the armor.

No human would have ever wasted the money, or the time for that matter, on creating such an elaborate set of armor for a city guard. A simple, smooth set of plate mail, or possibly even just a set of chainmail set over a leather hauberk would have been more than sufficient. Such was not the case here.

Nor was the armor the only overt difference between the two cultures either.

As they walked through the gates, Jonathan stopped and gawked at the mahogany door leading into the guard's office inside the gatehouse. The door was arced, standing roughly eight feet at the apex, and every inch was carved into a scene of grape vines, fruit, and leaves. The more Jonathan studied the door, the more intricacies he found. There were honeybees, hummingbirds, and even a small caterpillar carved into the wood. The knocker itself was made of bronze, but cast in the shape of a hand holding an apple.

"Come on," Jason said as he tugged on Jonathan's arm. "Let's go inside to the wildlife refuge."

Jonathan nodded his head. He glanced back toward the guard that had let them in. For a moment, the two locked eyes. The elf's golden eyes were no longer welcoming as they had been when Ziegler gave him the papers. They were studying Jonathan carefully, seemingly boring into his very soul. The boy felt his brother tug at his arm again and broke the guard's gaze.

Something about the guard didn't sit right with him, but he kept it to himself for now, thinking there would be a better, more private opportunity to discuss the matter after they were inside the city.

Within the walls the city was much like the larger settlements Jonathan had visited before. The streets were filled with the hustle and bustle of daily life. Elves pushed handcarts, or drove carts pulled by large elk through the streets while pedestrians walked along the outer edges in a rather orderly fashion.

Jonathan kept pace with his brother and Miranda, but his eyes were constantly moving through the crowds. He scanned the buildings, and the small, but elaborate, flower gardens that lined the grounds between the buildings and the street. He saw a pair of short elves with tan skin tending to a particularly large rose bush with fiery orange blossoms. One of them turned and looked at him with icy blue eyes that lingered upon him only for a moment before he returned to his work.

Looking back to the elves in the street, Jonathan realized that the pair of short elves he had seen were not simply shorter than most others here, they were a different race of elves altogether.

"They are Nizhni'Tai," Miranda said as she nudged him on the right side.

Jonathan almost jumped when she touched him, but managed to crack a weak smile. "That means 'little elf,' right?" He had read the term in his travel guide that the scholar had given him.

Miranda giggled and shook her head, her smile drawing her lips tight across her face. "Not exactly. Nizhni'Tai actually translates better as 'lower elf' or 'shorter elf' actually."

"Lower elf," Jonathan echoed as he thought about it. He wondered what else the scholar might have gotten wrong in the travel guide.

Miranda pointed with her chin, indicating the trio of elves walking in front of them a few yards away. "Those are Svetli'Tai," she said.

Jonathan studied the trio and then looked at a group of four walking the opposite direction. "And those?" he asked with a nod of his head.

Miranda smiled. "Those are Vishi'Tai," she said.

Jonathan stopped to study them all, but couldn't see much difference. Both groups wore similar, flowing robes of silk and fine cloth that shimmered and moved elegantly as they walked along. They all had long hair, and he was able to see that one group had both gold and white hair, while the other group had only white hair. But the two groups appeared to be similar enough in other respects. The book the scholar had given him had talked about some of the various physical differences between the elf races, but seeing the elves in person it was hard to put the knowledge to use confidently.

"Look closely," Miranda said. "The Svetli'Tai have skin that is a golden tan, almost shiny appearance if the sun hits it just right. The Vishi'Tai have skin that it much whiter. Even those who are tan appear different, for a Vishi'Tai who is tan will have a brown tint to his or her skin. A Svetli'Tai will always have the golden tint. Also, if you look closely, the Vishi'Tai are taller than the others."

Jonathan could see that as the two groups passed each other.

"Vishi'Tai males average between six and seven feet tall."

"So are all Nizhni'Tai short then?" Jonathan asked.

Miranda nodded. "Nizhni'Tai are like the pair you saw, usually averaging three to four feet tall, but they are built like an elf, with elegant proportions and nimble bodies, whereas a dwarf is much stockier."

Jonathan nodded.

"Vishi'Tai also see themselves as the rightful rulers of the elven peoples. There are some families among the nobility that believe Icadion favors them because he made the Vishi'Tai first, before all other sentient beings."

Jonathan snorted derisively and shook his head. "We all bleed the same," Jonathan quipped.

His comment had been loud enough to draw the attention of a tall Vishi'Tai passing by. The elf looked down on him, arching his left brow and drawing his lips into a thin, straight line across his face. The look was enough to make Jonathan squirm.

"Come on, let's go," he said.

The three of them broke off down a street to the right while Ziegler and the others pressed forward.

"Where do we go?" Jason asked.

Not wanting to reveal his book to them, Jonathan suggested asking one of the elves on the street for directions. Jason huffed, obviously starting to question his little brother's intentions. As Jason and Miranda turned to ask someone, Jonathan whipped out the travel guide. He shot a quick glance over his shoulder to ensure that Ziegler and the others were far enough away so they wouldn't see his book either. Then he flipped through it to find a map of Tirnog. He traced his fingers down the lines that represented the streets and quickly memorized the way to the preserve, then he stuffed the book back in his pocket just as Miranda and Jason finished talking with a tall elf.

"All right, let's go," Jason said. Jason seemed to know well enough where he was going thanks to the other elf's advice, so Jonathan let him lead for a bit while he and Miranda walked behind him a half-pace slower.

"There are other races of elves as well," Miranda put in as they walked, restarting the conversation they had been in.

Jonathan looked to her with an expectant expression.

Miranda smiled matter-of-factly and listed them off one by one. "Vishi'Tai, which means 'tall elf,' or 'high elf,' then Svetli'Tai, which means 'bright elf,' or 'golden elf,' Nizhni'Tai we covered, and then there are Korr'Tai, which are the wood elves, Pes'Tai, which means 'sand elf,' and then there are the two drow races."

"Drow races?" Jonathan had not seen that term in the travel book.

Miranda nodded. She glanced around and then leaned in and spoke in a more hushed tone. "The drow are elves in all respects, but they are very different. While occasionally you might see a dark-skinned elf among the Korr'Tai or Nizhni'Tai, all of the drow are dark-skinned."

"You mean they look like Konnons?" Jonathan asked. He had seen a Konnon once come through Holstead. The man was quite old, but he was nearly as large as Moose, with skin as black as the night and hair the color of snow. Pa had told Jonathan that Konnons were among the fiercest and best warriors to ever set foot upon Terramyr, but Jonathan remembered the old man as a friendly, gentle giant who told stories to the children that would gather around his knees. The man had passed on from Holstead only a couple of weeks after his arrival, but it was enough to leave an impression upon Jonathan.

"Not exactly like a Konnon," Miranda said. "The drow are broken into two main races, the Sierri'Tai and the Tomni'Tai. The words Tomni'Tai mean 'dark elf,' and their skin can actually be black, dark blue, or even have a purple tint to it."

"That sounds beautiful," Jonathan said as he pictured what a dark purple she-elf might look like with silver hair and green eyes.

Miranda continued. "Sierri'Tai means 'gray elf,' and their skin is usually a shade of dark gray, or sometimes black. But, their skin isn't the main difference between the drow and other elves. The Sierri'Tai often live in underground tunnels or caves, which most of the other elf races find abhorrent and unnatural. It's said that the drow used to live in Tanglewood

Forest, for it is the birthplace of all elves, but they had a falling out with the other races, and eventually were forced out for their bloodthirsty ways and abhorrent customs."

Jonathan looked at her curiously. "Where did you learn all of this about elves?"

Miranda shrugged. "My father taught me some of what he knew, but the rest I learned from Ruben."

There it was again. He had almost managed to forget about her fiancé, but now his mind was forced to remember the truth of this outing. He was not touring Tirnog with Miranda on some fanciful get away as they had once discussed. He was here on a mission to find her father, and she was with her future husband.

"If you two are done lollygagging, can we get a move on?" Jason asked as he turned around to face them. He turned back around and moved to ask another elf for more directions.

"Seems like he is lost a bit," Jonathan said with a smirk.

Miranda nodded and turned to catch up with Jason. Jonathan waited for just a second and put some distance between himself and the other two so he could glance at the map in the book one more time. He opened it, checked their progress, and then oriented himself to the sign he saw on a nearby building. As he moved to put the book back in his pocket, he felt a piece of paper that had not been there before. He replaced the book and pulled the paper out and looked at it curiously. He spun around, suspecting someone had just put it into his pocket, but he didn't see anything suspicious.

Jonathan unfolded it and read it.

You're in danger.

Jonathan looked around again, scanning the passersby for any sign of who had slipped him the note. He didn't see anyone that he could pinpoint as the culprit. Elves walked in an orderly fashion, some talking amongst themselves in small groups, others carrying books or walking alone, but none seemed to even notice him, let alone have taken interest enough in him to place a note in his pocket.

He turned and jogged to catch up with Jason and Miranda just as they were veering down a side street on the right that Jason was pointing out to Miranda.

"Wrong way," Jonathan called out. The preserve is down this street," he said as he pointed to a side street on the left side of the main road they were on.

"Are you sure?" Jason asked.

Jonathan nodded and grinned boyishly at Miranda. "I'm certain, come on then, slowpokes." When they caught up to him, Jonathan pushed the note toward Jason. "Someone put this in my pocket just now."

Jason took it and read it, then he showed it to Miranda. The two of them looked out over Jonathan's shoulders, surveying the streets, but obviously came up empty when they both shrugged.

"We'll keep our eyes open, but let's go along with the plan for now," Jason said.

The three of them walked down the side street until they came to a large building with a golden door.

Jonathan smiled and pointed to it. "Here it is," he said. He would have been excited normally. He had fantasized about coming to this very building for months, but now he was too busy worrying about the letter in his pocket.

"Wow, I guess they spared no expense for the refuge," Jason commented. "If I could get a door like this sent to Mortimer, then I bet he would finally treat me like an equal."

Then, at the other end of the street, a shadowy form moved along the side of a building.

The hairs on Jonathan's neck stood on end.

He reached forward and forced the door open, then he shoved the others inside.

# CHAPTER 4

"What in Icadion's name do you think you're doing?!" Jason shouted as he stumbled into the building.

Jonathan slammed the door shut and looked for a way to lock the door. "Someone was out there."

"There were a lot of elves out there," Jason said. Jason pushed Jonathan aside and reached for the door. Jonathan protested, but Jason pulled the door open and stuck his head out. He looked to the left, and then glanced right for half a second before ducking back into the building.

A blast of red fire struck the doorway where Jason's head had just been.

"Believe me now?" Jonathan quipped as he threw the door shut.

"We have to take cover!" Miranda said.

Jonathan turned around, expecting to see some sort of office, but instead he saw only a sign set upon a bronze marker with the words 'Mystical Creature Preserve' written across the plaque. There were no workers that he could see. There was only a large area of grassland inside the building. Jonathan looked up and saw that the ceiling was made entirely of glass.

"Is this a joke?" Jonathan asked. The building wasn't nearly large enough to house one Wyrebin, let alone a whole colony of them as the scholar had claimed to have seen.

Miranda shook her head and spun around. "There has to be more to it than this," she said.

The room they were in was maybe forty feet long and thirty feet wide. All of that space was filled with a level pad of grass, except for the three-foot-wide walkway that ran along the outer edges.

"This is hardly enough for more than a pair of exhibits, let alone an entire preserve," Miranda said putting words to Jonathan's thoughts.

"This has to be the wrong address," Jason said.

"No, this is exactly it should be," Jonathan replied. "I know it!"

Jonathan spied a door on the opposite side of the room, across the large pad of grass.

"Come on," Jonathan said as he pulled the others along and darted into the grass.

No sooner had they crossed the golden line in the floor that separated the stone floor from the grassy ground in the middle of the building than they all fell to their faces. The grass rushed up around them, stretching higher and higher until each blade of grass was the height of a fully grown pine tree. They all tumbled to the ground, huffing and puffing as they shook themselves off.

Jonathan was the first to his feet. He looked around, confused by the sights around him. Had they fallen down into tall grass? Maybe what he thought was the ground was really just the top level of some large pit filled with tall grass. No, that couldn't be it. The grass wasn't just tall, it was huge. He walked to a blade of grass and placed his right hand on the warm, rough surface. The blade hardly moved under his weight. The width of the blade was twice as wide as he was.

They hadn't simply fallen. They had shrunk!

"Welcome to the first exhibit in Tirnog's Mystical Creature Preserve," a shrill voice called out from behind them.

Jonathan turned to see a young woman with long, black hair and olive-colored skin. She had big, black eyes and a warm smile on her face. The white dress she wore seemed to float with her every move as she approached them.

"Where are we?" Jason asked.

The young woman looked puzzled. "Why, you are here, of course." She held her hand out to the side as if the simple gesture explained everything.

"You shrunk us?" Jonathan asked.

The young woman smiled and a pair of wings unfolded behind her as she floated up into the air. "I am Vindriel, and I will be your guide through my homeland."

Just then, an incredibly loud *boom* erupted around them and the ground shook. Jonathan looked up and saw a shadowy form move into the area near the grass. The form looked enormous now that the others were so small. They could hear his breathing and feel his every step. The large form turned and slammed the door shut, creating a sound so loud that each of them had to clasp hands over their ears.

"Where are you?" a raspy voice called out.

Jason turned to speak, but Vindriel fluttered in front of him and placed a hand on his mouth. She pressed her finger to her lips and then motioned for everyone to follow her through the enormous grass. The three of them ran while the fairie hovered through the air before them, leading them through the winding grass until they came to a door built into the side of a mushroom stalk. Vindriel waved her hand and the door swung open, then she ushered the three of them inside.

Jonathan found the inside of the mushroom to be much larger than he had thought. From the outside he had figured they might be able to fit easily enough and have a bit of room to spare, but once he was actually in the mushroom he found the inside to be like that of a large manor. There was an entryway with a long bench along one wall and a washbasin set upon a credenza on the other wall. Beyond the entryway there was a large foyer with a grand rug stretching to the walls of the rectangular room that had a staircase twisting upward at the end of it and a pair of doorways on the right side.

"Quick, into the first room on the right," Vindriel said.

Jonathan and the others dashed across the foyer as Vindriel locked the door behind them. They rushed into the room and then halted in the doorway, nearly tripping on each other when Miranda and Jason froze. Jonathan looked past them and saw a massive creature munching on a strange, green creature that was squeaking and gasping as the larger one ate it.

"What in Hammenfein?" Jason whispered.

Miranda was the first to spot the tell-tale red shell with black spots. "It's a ladybug," she said. "Come on, it won't hurt us."

"Ladybugs don't bite big people, but have you ever seen a ladybug that was the size of your house before?" Jason said.

Miranda shrugged off the comment and moved in toward the ladybug. She reached up and petted the beetle on the side of its face. The ladybug swallowed the rest of the aphid it was chewing and then turned to regard Miranda. The beetle had a pair of antennae that twitched and swayed as it let out a clicking noise.

"Miranda," Jason said cautiously.

Miranda shook her head and continued petting the large beetle.

Vindriel entered the room then and pushed Jason and Jonathan further inside.

It occurred to Jonathan then that perhaps the fairie was about to sacrifice them to her giant pet, but his fears were put at ease when the ladybug saw the fairie and then laid down lazily upon the floor.

"This is Alfax, he guards my home."

"He?" Jason echoed.

"Not all ladybugs are female," Miranda said impatiently.

"Who is after you?" Vindriel asked.

"We don't know," Jason replied.

Vindriel then looked to Miranda and pointed at her. "You, you look like the man who came here a while back."

"You met my father?" Miranda asked.

Vindriel nodded. "He came to speak with—"

A banging came at the door.

"He is here," Vindriel said breathlessly. "Quickly, hide!"

The fairie shoved the three of them behind Alfax and then exited the room.

Jonathan peeked around the edge of the bug to see Vindriel standing just outside the room, in the foyer. She was weaving her hands in the air and a glowing, glittering line began to appear before her.

A loud explosion erupted and the house shook.

"Where are they?" someone shouted. Heavy footsteps echoed in the hall outside the room and Jonathan understood that whoever was chasing them had just blasted his way into the mushroom house.

Vindriel stood tall in her white dress. "You are not welcome here!" She sent out a blast of energy and another force shook the house.

A male voice laughed wickedly and then Vindriel was engulfed in fire.

Jonathan moved to step around the large ladybug, but Alfax lashed out with a kick that knocked Jonathan to the floor. The beetle then scurried out of the room faster than any of them would have thought possible. With a shriek that nearly pierced their ears, the insect wheeled around to the left and its shell opened to reveal a set of thin, translucent black wings. The male voice yelled out and there was a great commotion.

Jason helped Jonathan up to his feet while Miranda sprinted for Vindriel. The three of them got to her just as a thunderous humming noise swarmed around the house. Jonathan looked to the doorway, but couldn't see the attacker, for the ladybug blocked his view. A bit of blood splattered onto the floor and then there was a puff of smoke and flame. Alfax hissed and rose up on his hind legs, and the attacker fled.

Outside, the commotion grew louder and louder. Shouts and cries could be heard coming from all directions. Then there was a loud *ka-slam!* The echoes reverberated through the air like thunder.

"Sounds like he got away," Miranda commented.

Jonathan nodded and then looked up to see a pair of fairies enter the house.

"Vindriel!" one of them called out.

"She's over here," Miranda cried.

The two fairie warriors flew over to them and began administering to Vindriel with a strange, icy blue magic that flowed out from their palms.

"Who was that?" one of the warriors asked.

"We don't know," Jason answered. "Did he get away?"

"Yes, but not before he dropped this," one of the warriors said as he handed a strange, silver charm to Jonathan. Jonathan studied the symbol on it, but didn't recognize it. He tossed it to Jason. "Do you recognize this?"

Jason shook his head and pocketed the item.

"The bees are here now," one of the fairies said.

"Who are the bees?" Jason asked.

One of the warriors looked up to Jason incredulously. "Honeybees," he said simply. "They help protect our lands from intruders."

"Are there many intruders here?" Jonathan asked. "I thought this was a sanctuary."

One of the warriors shook his head. "Not many intruders, but it happens from time to time."

They went back to their work, healing some of Vindriel's larger burns with their magic.

"I thought there was no magic that could heal burns," Miranda said breathlessly. "This is incredible."

Vindriel coughed and sat up slowly. "Fairie magic is among the most ancient and potent of powers on Terramyr," she said. "We have many skills."

"Can you teach me?" Miranda asked.

Vindriel shook her head as she waved the other two fairies off. "No, our magic only works in our realm. Even if you could master the skills, you would only be able to use it while living within our borders."

"Do you know who the intruder was?" one of the warriors asked her.

Vindriel shook her head. "These three came, and then he came in after them."

The two warriors looked to Jonathan menacingly.

"Explain," one of them said.

Jonathan let his mouth fall open and he looked to Jason for help. His brother, who was usually good with words, faltered and floundered as much as he did. It was Miranda who spoke up.

"I have come in search of my father," she said. "I believe something terrible has happened to him, and I think maybe the person who attacked us might have had something to do with my father's disappearance."

The warriors looked to each other and then took to wing, hovering in the air just below the ceiling. They offered a nod to Vindriel and then flew out the front door, which was in process of being repaired by yet another pair of fairies.

"Your father, was he an older wizard?" Vindriel asked softly.

Miranda nodded. "Tall, thin, with gray eyes and hair, and a long nose."

Vindriel nodded. "That is the man I saw before, the one I told you about. He was here," she said. "He went to ask the scholars about some sort of artifact."

"What was it?" Jason asked.

Vindriel shook her head. "I am not sure, and the scholars told me they had never seen it, or anything like it before. They couldn't help him. He left rather unsatisfied, I'm afraid."

"Well, did he speak with anyone else?" Jason asked.

"He mentioned seeing Wyrebins in a letter to us, does that mean anything to you?" Miranda pressed.

Vindriel thought for a moment, rubbing the side of her head where some smudge covered a scrape she had received when the attacker had knocked her down. Her eyes lit up and she nodded. "There was one other he spoke to, though I imagine it will be rather difficult to find him."

"Who?" Miranda asked. "Please, if you know anything that will help me find my father, you must tell me."

Vindriel nodded. "Alfax," she called out. The ladybug turned to her and approached. Jason and Jonathan backed away, giving the insect plenty of room. "Oh, my poor friend, you're hurt as well," Vindriel said. She rose to her feet and stretched her hand out to Alfax's left antenna, which had been burned down to a nub. A green and blue energy flowed out from Vindriel's hand and the antenna grew back before Jonathan's eyes in a matter of seconds.

Alfax made a soft clicking noise and then nuzzled Vindriel delicately.

"Take them to Nebenuk," she said.

Alfax clicked twice and then turned to walk outside.

"Follow him outside, then he will carry you to Nebenuk."

"Who is that?" Miranda asked.

"He is the last person your father spoke to," Vindriel replied.

The three of them shared a glance and then offered their sincere thanks to Vindriel for her help. The other fairies stood to one side as the three humans walked out of the mushroom and toward Alfax.

"How do you suppose he is going to carry all of us on his back?" Jason asked.

As they got closer to Alfax, the ladybug took to flight and then swooped down, scooping them all up with his strong feet and legs, and then he turned to fly through the tall, massive blades of grass.

Jonathan let out a holler as they flew at what seemed to be a blinding speed. His hair flattened back against his head and his eyes struggled to stay open as the wind rushed around them. Alfax tilted this way and that, swerving around blades of grass as he ascended higher and higher. They passed over rivers and valleys, or at least it seemed to them that they were rivers and valleys now that they were the same size as the fairies.

"Look there," Miranda called out as she pointed to a small clearing where the grass was thinned out.

Jonathan turned his head to see a herd of white horses galloping alongside a stream. As he watched them run, one of the animals turned its head and then Jonathan saw a horn clearly situated upon the animal's head.

"Unicorns!" Jason shouted. "I thought those were only a legend."

Alfax chirped happily and swung them back into the thick of the grasses. A few moments later, the large ladybug chirped three times and flew yet higher into the air. Jason was the first to see the mud nests built onto the side of the blades of grass.

Swallows poked their heads out from inside the nests. Strangely enough, the swallows were the right proportion to Jonathan and the others, despite the fact that Alfax was very much his normal size. It appeared that all other life in the preserve was magically scaled down to exist within the small area of the building as though it were miles and miles of vast valleys and forests.

A pair of swallows launched from their nest and flew up beside Alfax, diving and looping through the air. Their feathers were golden in color, and emitted a strange gold and purple dust as they flew.

"Those are the Golden Swallows of Tirnyn," Miranda said. "I used to read about them from a collection of bedtime stories when I was a child."

"What do they do?" Jonathan asked.

"They are supposed to grant wishes, if you can catch them," Miranda replied. "Trouble is, they can't survive captivity. The only tales I ever heard either resulted in the swallow dying or being released back into the wild. They were hunted nearly to extinction by the Talman Mages a couple centuries ago."

"I heard about them," Jason said. "Weren't they the ones who tried to overthrow the king?"

Miranda nodded. "Not just the king, but they also sought to establish rule over the elves."

"I bet that didn't go well," Jonathan commented wryly as he watched the golden swallows swoop under them, their golden trail of dust glistening in the sunlight.

Then, as they rounded a particularly wide blade of tall grass, Jonathan shouted with excitement and pointed downward. "Look there! Wyrebins!"

The others looked down to see large, beaver-like animals chewing though the tree-sized grass and making a dam in another stream to create a pond for themselves.

"You were right!" Miranda shouted.

Jonathan smiled and watched the Wyrebins work until he could no longer see them.

It was nearly an hour before the group landed on a small mound of dark green, soft moss next to a river and flanked by what looked like miniature oak trees that stood half as tall as the grasses around them. Alfax hovered in the air while he released the three, then he turned and flew away.

"Wait," Jason called out. "How will we get out of here?" he asked.

Alfax simply chirped twice and disappeared into the tall forest of grass.

"Now what do we do?" Jason huffed.

Jonathan was the first to answer. "We wait, right here."

"Sure, we'll wait here on a patch of moss in the middle of a giant forest where no one will know where we are. Probably get eaten by some sort of rat, or maybe a giant snake."

Jonathan smirked then and had to stifle a laugh. He had already dealt with giant snakes. The Kigyo had caught him trespassing in their lands, but in the end it was the Kigyo who had given Jonathan the magical bow, Kigabané, that proved so helpful in his fight against the trolls.

"A snake?" a voice called out.

Jonathan and the others turned around, looking for the source of the voice, but none of them saw anything.

"Nebenuk is most certainly not a snake," the voice said.

"Show yourself," Jason commanded.

"No," the voice said curtly. "You must show *yourselves.*"

Jason huffed and glanced to Jonathan. "We're right here in the open," he said.

"No, you must show your inner selves!" the voice said loudly. "I can see the physical you, the embodiment of what your spirit walks around in, but to judge you by what I see of your flesh is not much different than judging you by your clothes. Hardly a suitable standard."

Miranda folded her arms. "What must we do?" she asked.

"You must convince Ma'at that you are pure of intentions," the voice replied.

"And who is that?" Jason asked.

"Look up," the voice said smugly.

Jonathan and the others did as they were told and saw a most peculiar form in the air above them. Great wings stretched out, carrying the body of what appeared to be a horse as easily as though it were an eagle circling above them. A great tail of white hair flowed out gently as it came ever lower. Its gray fur was marked with black and white spots that covered the whole of the animal, except for the nose and muzzle, which was one solid patch of black. Ma'at dropped down onto the mossy ground near to them and folded its wings as it shook its head. Great, chestnut eyes scanned Jonathan and the others.

"I am Ma'at," the pegasus said.

"I am Jonathan Haymaker, this is my brother Jason, and our friend, Miranda."

Ma'at came two steps closer to Jonathan and angled his head to the side slightly. "Why have you come?"

Jonathan indicated toward Miranda with his hand. "Her father is missing, and we believe he may have come here before he disappeared. Can you help us?"

Ma'at moved three steps to his left and looked at Jason. "You are soon to be married," Ma'at said.

Jason nodded. "I am," he said.

Ma'at nickered and shook his head, flinging his silvery mane back and forth several times. "When you come to the Kingdom of Shuldern, you must impress Dignar. If you succeed in this, Dignar will open the way for you to acquire what you seek."

Jason nodded silently, apparently understanding what Ma'at was saying. Jonathan could only guess that maybe Dignar would give Jason something which he could in turn give to Mortimer.

The pegasus then moved in close to Miranda. His eyes locked with hers and he snorted softly. "Young wizardess, be not troubled, for your heart will attain what it seeks. Your father is yet alive, but he is in great peril."

"Can you tell me where he is?" Miranda asked.

Ma'at shook his head. "I can only see his shadow. His form I cannot see. You will have to search for him. You are his only hope."

Jonathan saw a tear form and then slide down Miranda's right cheek. She put a hand up to her mouth and closed her eyes, turning away from Ma'at.

The pegasus then turned to Jonathan and stepped in close enough for the young man to feel its hot breath.

"And then there is you," Ma'at said softly. Jonathan fidgeted with his fingers and shifted his weight as he tried to meet Ma'at's gaze. The pegasus stared into his eyes for what felt like an eternity. Then, Ma'at bent his head low, nodded twice, and unfurled his wings. "Nebenuk, these are worthy creatures." The pegasus then took flight and soared across the river. He landed and then began drinking peacefully without so much as another glance to the party.

"That's it?" Jonathan asked aloud. *No prophecy for me? No advice?* He never voiced his disappointment aloud, for Nebenuk appeared and commanded all of their attention with his grandiose entrance.

A teardrop of blue and silver formed in the midst of them, spreading out with tendrils of white and black smoke that sizzled and popped with sparks of gold and green. The mossy ground beneath the strange orb bent under its weight and then the light cleared to reveal a peculiar man dressed in black robes with gold trim around the hem. Fiery red hair flowed down into a single plait that laid lazily over Nebenuk's right shoulder, fastened with a gold bow near the bottom. His skin was so dark it almost appeared to have a purple tint to its blackness, which wonderfully set off the pair of silver spectacles over his purple eyes. The frames extended out and wrapped around Nebenuk's slightly pointed ears.

"You're an elf," Jonathan said quickly.

Nebenuk nodded. "I am one of the patriarchs of the Tomni'Tai," Nebenuk said. "Few know of my existence here, and so Ma'at carefully screens any who come seeking my wisdom."

"Why do you hide here?" Jason asked.

Nebenuk held up a long pointer finger and shook his head. "I am not here to answer questions about myself. As I understand it, you are searching for her father. If I can help you with that endeavor, then I will."

"Did he come to see you?" Miranda asked quickly.

"Yes, he did." Pain struck Nebenuk's eyes then and he took in a deep breath. "Your father had just spoken with Gadrien, one of my few confidants, who had sent him to me."

"You know Gadrien?" Jason asked.

Nebenuk nodded. "I have known him for a very long time." He turned back to Miranda then and continued recounting what had happened. "Your father carried an amulet with him, something he wished to know more about. It was made of a deep purple stone."

"No, it can't be," Jonathan said. "I destroyed that amulet in the Murkle Quags!" He was speaking of the amulet that the troll king had worn to control the monsoons that spread throughout the peninsula and extended the reach of the swamps. While it made sense that Raven might have been inquiring about the amulet, it was entirely impossible for the amulet to be whole. Jason had personally smashed it over a magic altar, which subsequently released such a powerful blast of magic that it collapsed the troll king's tunnels in the Warrens.

Nebenuk frowned and shook his head. "The amulet was whole when he brought it to me," he said. "He told me that you had destroyed it, but that the idea of something so powerful being used by the trolls nagged at him after you all left the Murkle Quags. He told me that he went to see if he could find any pieces of it to help him identify where it had come from, for he did not believe the trolls could fashion such an enchanted item. He was right. When he returned, he found the amulet had not only reformed and healed itself, but it had worked its way to the surface, and was lying in the open."

"No, it's impossible," Jonathan said.

Nebenuk shook his head. "The amulet is an ancient relic from the days when the first council of the elves sat in congress together. It was used to create and control weather patterns."

"Who created it?" Jason asked.

Nebenuk sighed once more. "I did," he said. "I fashioned it several millennia ago, but I was not the one who made it what it has become today."

"What do you mean?" Miranda asked.

"I fashioned the amulet to help Tanglewood Forest. You may not be aware of this, but the first several centuries of Terramyr's history were rife with conflict. There was a time when even the Gods themselves could not fully control the world. That is when I fashioned the amulet."

"If that's true, then you would be thousands of years old," Jason put in suddenly. "Elves don't live that long."

Nebenuk held up his hand again. "Most elves live for one thousand years, it is true, but I have extended my life."

"How?" Jason asked.

Nebenuk shook his head. "We are here to talk about Raven," he said, bringing the subject back to Miranda's father. "He brought the amulet and I told him the same thing I will tell you. There was a family struggle among my posterity after the amulet began to lose power. My nephew, Lidaryn, altered the amulet so that we could put our very life essence into it to fuel it. Unfortunately, the council deemed it was too dangerous an artifact to keep after that point.

"They were right. Soon, the family fought over the amulet, and eventually a small group managed to steal it, and hide it away. It was discovered after some centuries that the amulet needed more life force to operate. Soon, elves began disappearing." Nebenuk's eyes welled with tears and he looked down to his feet. "I led a few of my most valiant sons to crush the wicked sect of necromancers that had taken to sacrificing their own kin for the glory of controlling the weather. We rid Tanglewood Forest of Lidaryn and his followers' putrescence, and then we banished the amulet to the Netherworld."

"Why not destroy it?" Miranda asked.

Nebenuk shook his head. "We tried, but we were unable to do it. Like you, we used weapons and tools to shatter it, but the crystal regrew and healed itself no matter what we did. So, the sitting council at the time opened a small rift to the Netherworld, and we sent it through. I had thought our work was done, but when Raven came to me with the amulet, I knew we had failed. Someone has followed in Lidaryn's footsteps, and the realm is in dire straits so long as the amulet is out there."

"Did my father give it back to you?" Miranda asked.

Nebenuk shook his head. "I alone do not have the power to seal it away."

"So he went to seek out the council then?" Jason surmised.

Miranda shook her head. "No, the council is no longer complete."

Nebenuk smiled and nodded at her. "That is true. The council used to be comprised of three elders from each of the seven elf races. Now, however, many of the elves have moved on from Tanglewood Forest. Even if the council wished to banish this relic, I doubt they would have the strength to do so. The elves of my day, especially the patriarchs, had a power and level of skill that few elves ever achieve these days. Raven may have gone to the council for guidance, however, as they may know of a method to dispose of it, or perhaps to seal its danger."

"Where did he go then?" Jonathan asked.

Nebenuk smiled slyly at him. "After I gave him the amulet's history, he traveled northward, to Telward, via the causeway that travels through Sohn."

Miranda screwed up her face and frowned. "But the council lies in Gwyndoltai, why not travel through Heartspring directly to Gwyndoltai?"

"Because," Nebenuk said with a frown. "He told me of the trolls in the Murkle Quags. He enlightened me to the war that had been raging in your lands."

"You have been living here for thousands of years and yet you didn't know?" Jason asked.

"I suppose Gadrien had not realized the importance of informing me. He would have been my only connection to the world outside this preserve." Nebenuk gestured to the area around them, reminding them that he was in fact hiding within a magical preserve of mystical creatures. "Had he told me, I would have suspected that they had found the amulet."

"They?" Miranda pressed.

Nebenuk nodded. "You know about the rift between the drow and other elves, yes?"

Miranda nodded.

"Since that time, there have been pockets of drow who seek powerful artifacts in an attempt to restore their long lost power. Gadrien told me of one troublesome youth, a descendant of mine who, unfortunately, seeks to bring our family back to power." Nebenuk sighed and folded his arms. "His name is Larkyn, and he is a Tomni'Tai noble, the son of my eldest son's eldest son, and heir to the council seat we held. However, he, along with any drow who remained behind after the drow exodus from Tanglewood Forest, have always been rejected by the council. Therefore, the only way he can claim the seat is to take it by force."

"A war among the elves," Jason whispered breathlessly.

"And he will stop at nothing to get what he wants, or to prevent others from stopping him."

Jonathan suddenly remembered the letter shoved into his pocket and he pulled it out and offered it to Nebenuk. "I was given this on the street, just before we were attacked."

Nebenuk took the note and opened it. "This is written in Gadrien's handwriting," Nebenuk said. "He told me that he would be working to solve the mystery after Raven had traveled north. Go to him, see if he can offer clues where I cannot. Here, I will write his address and draw a map to his home from here."

"Actually, I have his address," Jason said referring to the paper Ziegler had already given him. Jason then reached into his pocket and pulled out the strange silver charm left by their attacker. "Do you recognize this?"

Nebenuk took the charm in his hand and sighed. "This is the symbol of my family. Where did you find it?"

"Someone attacked us. He got away, but he dropped that," Jonathan said.

"Oh, he wouldn't drop it," Nebenuk said decisively. "This is a charm that belongs on a bracelet. There would be seven such charms on the bracelet by now, possibly more. One for each generation of my posterity. I was the first to carry it."

"Then Larkyn is the one who attacked us?" Jason asked.

Nebenuk's eyes grew dim and watery. "I never intended to create pain for this world. I had created the amulet to use for good, to bring peace and order to Tanglewood Forest." He looked to Jonathan with sorrow in his purple eyes. "I am afraid I cannot go with you. To leave the preserve would be to die for me. However, should you ever need assistance, return to me and I will tell you what I can. Now you must go to Gadrien."

Jonathan nodded, then he pointed to Ma'at. "Can he help us get out of here quickly?"

Nebenuk smiled and nodded once. "Ma'at," he called. "Please take our friends to the edge of the preserve so they can resume their quest."

The pegasus whinnied and unfurled his great wings once more.

# CHAPTER 5

Jonathan, Jason, and Miranda stopped on the opposite side of the street from what Ziegler had marked down as Gadrien's house. The building was made of the same, sparkling white stone, and rose three stories tall with a sloped roof of tile facing the street. Two stained glass windows in the top floor depicted floral scenes with hummingbirds, while the windows on the second and first levels were made of plain glass. The door to the house was made of mahogany, and sat twenty feet back from the road, separated from the group by a small fence with a waist-high gate that marked the border of the exquisite orange and yellow rose bushes and the expertly trimmed rows of hedges flanking the coral and gray flagstone path to the door.

"Should we go up and knock?" Miranda asked.

Jonathan nodded and led the way. He pushed open the gate and approached the door with a determined gait, only to find it already open when he struck it with the bottom of his fist to knock. The door creaked eerily and the hall inside was cluttered with overturned chairs and bits of scorched wood. Jonathan looked up to see a large, charred circle in the wall nearby and his stomach tightened.

"Larkyn was here, come on!" Jonathan said.

Jason followed him in and pulled a pair of knives from his pack, handing one to Jonathan. "Eyes open, little brother."

A rustling sound was heard up the stairway to their left. The three shared a nod and then crept up the stairs. Thankfully, the thick green carpet runner muffled their steps and the stairs did not squeak. Jonathan then heard what sounded like voices, but he couldn't be sure. When they reached the top of the stairs, a door to the right was ajar just enough to see a shadow cross the doorway.

Someone was inside.

Jason snuck to the far side of the door, while Jonathan crept up to the near side on the right. Miranda moved into position and lifted her hands, preparing a spell. Jonathan nodded to Jason and then the two took a breath. Jason kicked the door the rest of the way open and the two brothers rushed in, breaking out wide to the sides.

A large hand seized Jonathan and tossed him into the wall face-first.

"Easy Moose! It's our boys!" Ziegler shouted.

Jonathan stumbled back from the wall, a bit too dazed to realize that they had just rushed in on the other Ghosts. He waved his knife around a bit as his eyes regained their focus. As his vision came back in and his head stopped ringing, Jonathan noticed Bull standing in front of him with a wide grin.

"Shouldn't try sneaking up on Ghosts of the Quags, you ought to know that by now."

"We thought you were him," Jason said.

"Him who?" Ziegler asked.

Jonathan put the knife away and turned around to see what had happened. Ziegler was kneeling next to a dead body. An elf with long, golden hair was face-down upon the wooden floor. A bookcase was overturned, covering the elf's lower half. Blood was pooling around the elf's head and right arm. Books and papers were everywhere.

"We got here too late," Jonathan said.

"Too late?" Ziegler echoed. The captain stood up and approached the brothers. "If you two know something I don't, I suggest you tell me, now."

"We were attacked on our way to the preserve," Jonathan said.

Ziegler shook his head. "Who attacked you?"

"Not sure, never got a good look at him, but we think his name is Larkyn, a drow relative of Nebenuk, the elf who made the amulet Raven has been investigating."

"Slow down," Ziegler said. "Who is Larkyn, and where did he attack you?"

"He might be the one Raven is after," Jason reported. "He attacked us with fire spells. We were saved with the help of others in the preserve," Jason said.

"Who helped you?" Ziegler pressed.

Jason opened his mouth but then hesitated. "It might sound a bit crazy, but we were saved by fairies."

"Bwahaha!" Bull shouted as he clapped his hands together. "Oh, you boys are *never* going to live that down. Saved by a bunch of pixies!"

"Bull, tuck it away, now." Ziegler silenced the bald warrior with a stern glare, then he turned back to the body. "And what makes you think this Larkyn fellow was after Gadrien too?"

With Jason still red in the face over Bull's comment, Jonathan spoke up. "The fairies sent us to see Nebenuk, an old elf living in the preserve. He gave us clues about Raven and the amulet the troll king used in the Murkle Quags. Then told us to come here and speak with Gadrien. Seems he knew him as well. We came as soon as we could, but it wasn't fast enough."

Moose pulled a mammoth cigar from a pouch on his belt and lit it, then he turned toward the window and scanned the street below, grunting as he let out a puff of smoke.

"Moose is right," Bull said respectfully. "We'll need to leave soon, before the guards catch us in here. Someone is sure to have seen or heard something."

Ziegler shook his head. "No," he said. "Whoever killed Gadrien was quiet about it."

Bull gestured around and scoffed. "How is someone quiet while doing this?"

"The intruder tore the place apart after he killed Gadrien. Either way, he killed the elf silently."

Jonathan shook his head. "But there were signs of a struggle," he said. "Downstairs there are scorch marks on the wall and floor."

Ziegler raised an eyebrow and moved back to Gadrien. Bull picked up the overturned bookcase and Ziegler flipped the corpse up to show the others the wound in Gadrien's chest. Jonathan saw a small, deep hole in the right side of Gadrien's chest. The copious amount of blood pooling around him proved that this was the fatal wound. From the small bubbles in the blood, Jonathan knew that the wound had pierced Gadrien's lung. He had seen similar wounds plenty of times before while hunting deer.

"Whoever did this knew Gadrien well enough to allow them to come in close, from the front," Ziegler said.

"Then what of the scorch marks on the first floor?" Jonathan pressed.

"Maybe two intruders," Bull pointed out. "Perhaps we have more than one person who wanted Gadrien dead, and they ran into each other."

"Or maybe Larkyn killed Gadrien quietly and then wanted to cause a ruckus to make neighbors aware of the fight," Jason said. "Maybe he was hoping we would come here and then get caught by the guards, and they could deal with us since he failed."

Ziegler nodded. "Could be. We didn't see the scorch marks, we came in from the back door. Show us where they are."

Jonathan took the others back down to the landing near the entryway, showing them the large circle on the wall and the bits of charred wood on the floor.

"Kid's right," Bull said. "Does look like a fight."

Ziegler bent down and picked up a piece of silver from the floor. "Anyone recognize this?" he asked.

Jason immediately produced the charm from his pocket and moved in close to examine the second one. "It's a match," Jason announced. "Larkyn was here."

Suddenly, Moose made a quick line for the front door and leaned to the side, peering out. He closed the door and then locked it.

"Time to go, guards are here," Moose said.

"Snake piss, this is poor timing!" Bull swore.

Ziegler gestured with his hands for Moose to lead the way and the group quickly fell into a line, running through the rubble to the back side of the house. Not two moments after they were out and had the back door closed before Jonathan heard a large explosion.

"That'll be them knocking in the door with their own magic," Bull said.

Ziegler pointed to a large well in the middle of the rear garden. The group ran toward it. Moose reached down into the water and then jerked to the side.

Jonathan was a bit confused at first, but then he heard a low, metallic clicking noise inside the well. That was soon followed by a grinding sound, like stone being slid over another bit of rock, and Jonathan understood that Moose was activating some sort of hidden passageway.

"Come on," Ziegler said.

Jonathan followed the others to a large family monument that was swiveling out and away from a large hole in the ground.

"In you go, cross your ankles and fold your arms over your chest!"

Bull jumped in feet first, locking his ankles before he disappeared in the darkness. Miranda went next, then Ruben. Jason jumped in a second before Jonathan, Captain Ziegler and Moose brought up the rear. Jonathan felt something hard and smooth slam into his back and buttocks, and then he began sliding at a steep angle downward. Darkness closed in as the statue above moved back into place, and then it was as if he was traveling through a void of sorts. The only sound was the rough slipping of cloth and occasional grunt as someone was jarred on the smooth, cold stone chute. The ride felt as though it lasted an hour, though in reality it was only a few seconds before they were dumped out into a pool of water.

Jonathan only managed to suck in half a breath before his body was enveloped by the warm water. He had no way of knowing how deep he had fallen, but he immediately threw his arms out and began clawing his way up to the surface.

FAWOMP!

A wave of water pushed Jonathan out to the side as Ziegler plummeted into the water beside him. The boy thanked the gods that Ziegler hadn't landed on top of him, and then resumed swimming to the surface. His face was greeted by cool, musty air as he broke free from the water and took in a new breath.

"Jonathan, over here!" Jason called in the darkness.

Jonathan swam toward his brother, but was dragged below the surface when something heavy fell upon his ankle. A large hand pushed him aside in the water and Jonathan realized that Moose had just landed in the pool. Once again he swam to the surface and then called out for his brother. The voices guided him to a solid surface, but it was still darker than any place Jonathan had ever been before.

"Kind of like the chute in the Warrens right?" Jason said as he slapped Jonathan's back.

Jonathan wished Jason hadn't drudged up that memory. That particular chute had led down to the troll king, and resulted in a terrifying battle. Worse than that, Jonathan hadn't known whether that particular chute would open up to anything, or drown him inside of it, as it had actually been an underground waterway.

"No," Jonathan said. "Not exactly like that one."

"Ruben, give us light," Ziegler said.

An instant later there was a soft, blue, glowing orb in the air over them. Jonathan looked around to see that the underground pool extended for another thirty yards in the opposite direction, where it then met a sheer wall of brown stone.

Jonathan then realized that something was missing. His heart skipped when he patted the pocket that had held his book. It was gone.

"Come on," Ziegler said. "The guards may still be able to track us unless we hurry."

Jonathan almost thought to go back into the water after it, but he knew it was a lost cause. Even if he could find it in the depths, which was doubtful at best, the pages were surely ruined by now. The book was lost. He took in a breath, and tried to push it out of his mind. "What is this place?" Jonathan asked, hoping conversation would take his mind off of his precious travel guide.

"Let's just say that Gadrien was a bit of an eccentric," Ziegler replied.

"Fat lot of good that did the poor fellow," Bull commented.

"Jason, Moose, scout on up ahead and make sure the way is clear. The rest of you stick with me," Ziegler commanded.

Jason and Moose broke into a light run, staying just beyond the reaches of Ruben's light as the rest of the group moved at a marginally slower pace. Jonathan kept his eyes peeled as they followed the underground walkway through a tunnel beside the water. At the end of the pool, the walkway continued on into a cavern that was barely tall enough for Ziegler to walk upright. The air here was warm and smelled of salt and musk. They followed this path for nearly twenty minutes before it came to a dead end.

"Moose?" Ziegler asked.

The large man turned around, quite a feat as he was hunched over in the tunnel, and shrugged. He pulled a cigar and lit it. The first match wouldn't take, but undeterred he lit two more until the end of the cigar was burning brightly.

Jonathan could only imagine what his Memaw would say if she saw the mountain of a man lighting his cigar at a time like this, let alone blowing the smoke into the small tunnel where everyone else was standing. Memaw would likely have chewed the large man up one side and down the other, but none of those present dared even look at Moose while he smoked.

"Ruben, there should be a latch here, or a lever, or something," Ziegler said.

Jonathan, not about to be outdone by Ruben today, started scouring the sides of the cavern. He placed his hands on the stone and felt around for anything out of the ordinary. He managed to find a hole in the rock just big enough for his hand. He dug at the thick, soggy moss growing out of it and then snaked his left hand inside, examining the inside of the hole with the pads of his fingers. He found a round shaft that felt like wood. He wrapped his fingers around it and tried to pull.

As he did so, what had felt like wood writhed in his hand and only then did Jonathan realize that it was made of sections that were hard, like large scales. He pulled his hand back reflexively, but something struck him before he could get completely out of the hole.

"Gah!" Jonathan cried out. He jumped back and held his left wrist with his right hand. Blood was beginning to ooze out from two puncture wounds on the inside of his hand between his index finger and thumb. "Something bit me!" he shouted.

Ruben came over immediately and whispered something as he waved a hand at the hole in the wall. A moment later, a very large creature was pulled out of the hole, held still inside a ball of green energy. It looked much like a centipede, except the creature had no legs. The body looked as though it might slither much the same way a snake would. The plates of its shell were black with large red and orange spots on them. The creature's head was certainly more bug-like, however. A pair of antennae protruded out from two yellow spots on the top of its head, while seven eyes sat in a row upon the front of the head, just under a pair of white spots. A pair of nasty looking pinchers opened and closed, struggling against the magic Ruben was using. Behind those pinchers were two long fangs dripping with a clear liquid.

"This is a Kabba," Ruben said in a serious tone. "Highly venomous to—"

Jonathan's heart leapt into his throat. "Is there an antidote?" he interrupted.

Ruben kept his eyes glued on the Kabba as he turned to magically send it further down the tunnel away from them. "Antidote is for poison," Ruben corrected. "What you mean to ask for is an antivenom."

"I don't care what it's called, I want to know if I am about to die!" Jonathan squeaked.

Ruben muttered something and the Kabba flew, sprawling and writhing through the air down the tunnel to disappear in the darkness, its angry screeches echoing through the tunnel. The wizard then turned to

Jonathan. "I was about to say that it is highly venomous to fish, but has no ill effects on humans or elves."

Jonathan's beating heart slowed. "Oh," he said simply.

"It will be sore for a day or two, but you'll heal up just fine."

"Are you sure we don't need to call the fairies over for help again?" Bull poked.

"That's enough," Ziegler said. "We need to find the way out."

Ruben turned around and pointed at the dead end. "I managed to find the secret just before Jonathan got his hand stuck in that hole over there."

*Great.* Jonathan thought.

Ruben walked to the door and traced his finger along the stone. As he did so, a set of orange runes began to glow in the stone. A light was born at the base of the wall and it rose slowly through the rock, sizzling and cracking as it grew up to the ceiling, and then the stone wall split in twain and opened to a small clearing in front of the forest.

"This should let us out about a mile north of Tirnog," Ziegler said. "This should help us put some distance between ourselves and the guards."

"Won't they come looking for us?" Jonathan asked. "I mean, we had to show them papers to get in."

Ziegler turned around and nodded. "I suggest we hurry then. We have a long way to go to reach our next destination."

"Where is that?" Jonathan asked.

"Telward," Ziegler responded.

Jonathan shook his head and stepped up closer to Ziegler. "Nebenuk told us that Raven went to Telward, but that he stopped in Sohn first."

Ziegler frowned. "Why would he do that?"

Jonathan shrugged. "I'm not sure. We were hoping Gadrien would tell us. Whatever it was, there must have been a lead he was following there."

Ziegler motioned for Jonathan to walk beside him. The party exited the tunnel; Ruben and Moose out in front, with Bull walking alone in the middle, and Jonathan, Jason, and Miranda walking with Ziegler. Together, they told him all Nebenuk had said about the amulet, and Larkyn.

“Well then, I suppose we are headed to Sohn as well,” Ziegler said after they finished.

# CHAPTER 6

The trio arrived in Sohn after a week of traveling over the road through the forest. Fortunately, they were not pursued from Tirnog, nor did they meet with any dangers on the road. Ziegler produced the travel papers to the guards and gained entrance for all of them rather easily. Jonathan was struck by Sohn's similarities to large human settlements. Based on the descriptions of Sohn in the travel book, he had expected something a bit different.

There were a few buildings that stood tall, but instead of the crystalline rock of Tirnog, these buildings were made of brick, wood, and stone. While most utilized either stone and wood or brick, some did in fact use all three materials, which gave a rather distinct atmosphere to the city. The roads were made of cobblestone and there didn't appear to be nearly as much regularity to their width or overall evenness as there had been in Tirnog. Alleys varied in size and most were made of compacted dirt. Roads didn't have equal gutters, nor were they bordered by finely kept rose gardens in front of the buildings that lined the streets.

It did, however, have an inn close to the main gate, and that is where the group was heading.

Jonathan looked up to see a wooden sign with painted letters of gold that read, "The Chubby Bunny."

Ziegler and Moose were first through the doors. Inside was a raucous mess of activity and noise that Jonathan would not have expected to find within an elven city. None of the passages in the travel guide had ever depicted the elves as anything but an austere, sober nation that frowned upon unruly and boisterous behaviors. Yet, here a quartet of string instruments that he didn't recognize were busy playing fancy, quick-paced jigs while a trio of she-elves danced in shirts that barely covered their chests and skirts that flared out carelessly with heavy, clicking shoes that pounded the floor so violently that the drinks on nearby tables shook and quaked. There was nearly two feet of thick, gray smoke clouding the top of the ceiling and swirling around the patrons' heads. At the tables, elves played card or dice games. It was every bit as loud and obnoxious as any human pub might have been when the day laborers had ended their shifts, except there were no humans here.

More than a few of the gamblers gave Ziegler a sidelong glance as he made his way to the bar. Several pair of eyes found their way to Miranda, surveying her hungrily as smiles stretched around pipes teeming with thick smoke.

"This looks fun," Ruben said with a doubting frown.

Miranda's lip curled back and she almost laughed. The dark-haired beauty then glanced over to Jonathan, still smirking.

Jonathan smiled back at her. After all, he had met her in a place not so different from this one. Judging from the look on her face, she remembered that fact as well.

They pushed through the throng, ignoring the stares from the elves and following Captain Ziegler. By the time they reached him, he had already procured beds for the night. The seven of them would all sleep in one room.

The party left the main floor and made their way up a slightly curved set of well-worn, stained and cracked stairs. On the top floor there was a long, narrow corridor with three doors on either side. Ziegler walked over the creaking floor to the third door on the left. He slipped the key into the lock and opened it.

"Inn keeper said that normally they would hold the key downstairs, but seeing as we paid for all of the beds in the room, I convinced 'im to let us have it."

The others filed into the room. Jonathan was caught in the shuffle and waited until all the others had gone inside and claimed their beds. He was left with a rickety cot made of green canvas set upon a wooden frame. A thin, wool blanket was folded at the foot of the cot. There was no pillow. Jonathan kept his disappointment inside, not wanting the others to see him complain. After all, it was better than the endless torrents of rain he had faced in the Murkle Quags. At least here he was dry.

He took off his pack and slid it under the cot. The others unpacked a few things and set their items on their beds. Jonathan looked around and was about to ask what the plan was when a knock came at the door.

Ziegler glanced around and gave a silent nod of his head. Moose tip-toed to stand beside the door and drew a long, slightly curved knife from under his shirt. Ziegler went to the door and pulled it open.

Jonathan was able to catch a clear view of the visitor from his position by the cot.

A tall elf with white hair and deeply black skin stood in the doorway. He wore a cloak of green trimmed with black at the hem, held on his slender shoulders with a sparkling brooch of gold with a single ruby set inside. He reached out a hand, adorned with an emerald ring and a silver bracelet, for Ziegler to take.

"I was not expecting visitors," Ziegler said as he stood motionless.

The elf let his hand linger in the air before Ziegler and arched his exceedingly white brow over his green eyes. "I have been expecting you for some time now."

"And who are you?" Ziegler prodded.

"I am Friil Bosien, descendant of Commander Horiatu Bosien, Founder of Sohn, and the scourge of the Merfolk."

Ziegler's muscles relaxed and with his left hand he issued an almost imperceptible signal to Moose. The mountainous warrior sheathed his knife and stepped out from behind the door without casting a glance back at Friil.

Friil's eyebrow arched ever higher when he noted Moose. His keen, vibrant eyes followed the warrior for a moment and then a sly grin pulled his lips apart to reveal stunningly white teeth. "So it is true then," Friil began cryptically. "You are the Ghosts of the Quags."

"Our reputation precedes us, it seems," Ziegler said. The captain finally reached his hand out to take Friil's. "I am Captain Ziegler."

Friil nodded. "Yes, I thought so." Ziegler stepped to the side and offered to let Friil in. The tall drow stepped into the room and glanced around. "The large one is Moose," he said. Friil then pointed to Bull. "The bald one is Bull. The young one with the black hair and the blue eyes is Jason Haymaker. The younger brother with the blonde hair is Jonathan. And that means this other fellow is Ruben Faelwyn, an accomplished wizard from Lehemat, and then there is his bride-to-be, Miranda, who is also Raven's daughter."

Everyone in the room glanced around nervously at each other. Jonathan wondered if perhaps a bounty had been put upon them back in Tirnog. Surely that would be the only way this drow would know their names and descriptions.

Friil, sensing the tension, put his hand in the air and smiled. "I was told to expect you."

"Who would tell you such a thing?" Ziegler asked.

"Raven, of course," Friil replied evenly. "He gave me your descriptions so that I may prove my status as a friend to the cause."

"What cause is that?" Bull put in. "We're here to get Raven, and I doubt he told you he was missing."

Friil set his hands together before his waist so that his fingertips touched and he took in a breath. "My dear, impatient Bull, Raven did in fact tell me just that. He came to see me, after meeting with Nebenuk in Tirnog. He had some questions about an amulet, and then he told me that if he went missing he would be followed by the Ghosts of the Quags."

"He predicted he would go missing?" Ziegler asked.

Friil offered a half shrug. "He said only that you would look for him should he fail to return to Lehemat. I, on the other hand, suspected that he would fail most assuredly, and thus I have been waiting for you since he left. I must say, it took you longer to arrive than I would have guessed, but then I suppose humans have never had the most acute perception of time."

Bull opened his mouth to speak, but Ziegler held up a hand and shot him a deadly serious glare.

Ziegler turned back to Friil. "What were you able to tell him about the amulet?"

Friil shook his head. "Nothing more than Nebenuk, I am afraid. My family ranks among the nobility, but never were we privy to the council in Gwyndoltai. However, I did have a piece of information for him that I believe may assist you as well." Friil's green eyes scanned the room, settling on Jonathan for a moment before returning to Ziegler. "There is a member of the higher nobility that has made quite a name for himself. Mostly he is whispered about in hushed circles among close friends, as no one has ever been able to prove his misdeeds, but I think it a worthy clue for you."

"Give me the name," Ziegler said.

"His name is Larkyn, a direct descendant of Nebenuk. There are rumors that he has formed dark alliances in a bid for power. Those of us who still remember some of the old relics believe him to be after the amulet Raven carried."

Ziegler folded his arms across his chest. "Why tell us any of this?"

Friil's eyes grew hard and his voice took on a strained tone. "Elves have gone missing in the middle of Tanglewood. The trees are no longer safe for our people."

"And you believe these disappearances to be linked to Larkyn?" Ziegler pressed.

Friil nodded, casting a nervous glance over his shoulder at the closed door. "As I said, his involvement is only spoken of in rumors, but the disappearances are real. Three elves from Sohn have gone missing in the last four years alone. There are reports of others."

"There are dangerous creatures in the forest," Ruben put in. "Why, we ourselves were set upon by a pair of wood sprites on our journey to Tirnog. Perhaps something else is responsible for the disappearances."

Friil shook his head. "The forest has been clean since its creation. Tanglewood has always been a haven for the elves. It is our birthplace. I am not ignorant of the fact that there are some abominations that have managed to creep their way into the forest, but I believe they have come at Larkyn's invitation."

"Why would you say that?" Ziegler asked.

Friil grinned wide. "I found a troll in the woods five summers past. When I approached him, he spoke. He called me 'Larkyn,' and waited for a response."

"What did you say?" Ruben asked.

"I let my scimitar speak for me." Friil pulled the left side of his cloak out to reveal an exquisitely crafted sheath of leather embroidered with velvet and stamped with silver runes. The handle protruding from the sheath appeared to be made of mithril, for the pommel shined silvery and bright, but was not like iron or steel. The handle was wrapped in leather and the guard glistened with the same silvery tone as the pommel, with runes of gold carefully placed into the guard. "I took the troll's head, and then I pierced his heart and set the corpse ablaze. It was not until the disappearances that I heard the rumors of Larkyn's evil deeds, otherwise I would have interrogated the foul creature."

"What on Terramyr was a swamp troll doing in Tanglewood Forest?" Ruben squeaked. "For that matter, how in Hammenfein did he even manage to get here in the first place?"

Friil nodded. "That is the question I have often asked myself. Now, seeing Raven come with Nebenuk's amulet, and then to have him disappear as well only deepens my suspicions."

"Why not confront Larkyn directly?" Jonathan asked.

Friil's eyes widened and his brows shot up a bit as he turned to regard the younger Haymaker. However, his expression was not one of pomp or offense, as Jonathan had experienced in Fort Sym. Friil put on a warm smile and seemed to nod almost as if he approved of the outburst. "Unfortunately, I can ill afford to be as impetuous as you might, Master Haymaker. If I were to make such an accusation without evidence, it would be a crime worthy of banishment for me. I am afraid a drow does not need to do much these days to be cast out from Tanglewood, even if his family founded an entire city and never wished to join the exodus."

"Where do we find Larkyn?" Ziegler asked.

"His home is in Telward. There you will also find a council of powerful elven wizards who may be able to shed more light on the subject. However, they do not take kindly to prying eyes. You will have to be careful, for they will not likely give you the answers you seek."

"What are you suggesting?" Ziegler pressed.

Friil frowned ever so slightly and glanced back to the closed door one more time. "If you hope to find out the true danger of Nebenuk's amulet, then you should look for a council disciplinary record." Friil stuck his right hand into his pants' pocket and came out with a small, tan square of folded parchment. "I have written down the details so you can find the correct record. If you can find it, hopefully it will put you one step ahead of Larkyn."

"We could also take a look at Larkyn's home," Bull put in. "Moose can get in and out without raising any eyebrows."

Friil looked to the large man and shook his head. "I am afraid Larkyn's home may be more challenging than the council chambers. Whatever you decide to do, please be careful. Elven law will not look upon you with any degree of mercy if you are found trespassing."

"Why help us?" Ziegler asked. "There has to be more to this than just some missing elves in order for you to risk exposing yourself like this."

Friil exhaled sadly and folded his slender arms across his chest. "My niece, Bedora, was the most recent elf to turn up missing after a short venture into Tanglewood. I have exhausted all honorable resources at my disposal to find her, but to no avail. I ask only this, if you discover Larkyn is involved, treat him with the same respect you would a den of trolls hiding in the Murkle Quags."

Ziegler smiled and put his hand out once more. "By my head, I swear if Larkyn is responsible for the disappearances, my blade will judge him."

Friil smiled and shook Ziegler's hand. "Then, there is no time to lose. I will repay you for your room, but you will not be sleeping here tonight. I have a small ship waiting for you in the bay. My men will transport you directly to Telward."

"Is there nothing else you can tell us about my father?" Miranda asked as she stepped forward.

Friil shook his head. "Your father was very determined to uncover the mystery behind the amulet. He said he was close, but he didn't remain here for very long. We spoke for a few minutes, and then he left. I offered to send him to Telward with one of my ships, as I have offered to you, but he refused. He said he wanted to remain unnoticed." Friil's frown deepened and he sighed. "I fear he failed to remain undetected, for that is the last I heard of him."

"Thank you," Ziegler offered.

"An escort will be waiting outside your door to take you to the ship. Farewell, and may Icadion watch over your travels." Friil bowed graciously and then exited the room, leaving the door open behind himself.

"Pack up," Ziegler instructed as he turned back to his bed. "Looks like we'll be resting our legs for a bit."

*****

Jonathan sat upon a crate filled with oysters, staring out across the breaking ridges of the blue and white waves coming at the small ship as it rose upward, then lurched down to crash into the water. A happy smile was firmly planted across his face as he wiped the ocean spray from his brow. The crew was busy running to and fro on the deck, working the sails and securing various crates or barrels that came loose in the choppy waters.

Jason was down below deck with the others. Ruben was across from Jonathan on the starboard side, heaving and retching with nearly every bump the ship made. Jonathan ignored the guilt creeping into the back of his mind whenever he glanced over at Ruben to take the slightest bit of pleasure from the man's misery. For all Jonathan cared, it served Ruben right for stealing Miranda.

A sudden ripple in the water nearby pulled Jonathan's attention back to the water. A strange glimmer of blue and green broke the surface and then disappeared again.

Jonathan stood from the crate and strained his eyes against the swells to get a better look. A few yards out beyond where the first ripple had appeared there was a sudden flurry of white, followed by blue and green again.

The boy wondered if it was some sort of shark perhaps, hunting fish in the rough seas.

He leaned over the rail and looked down. Something flashed beneath the ship. He turned to see if anyone else had noticed it, but a stern drow pulled him back from the rail and pulled him down to the deck.

"What are you doing?" Jonathan asked.

"Stay down, lad, there is danger near."

"Sharks?" Jonathan asked.

The drow scoffed and shook his head of red hair. His green eyes flitted out toward the rail and he said, "No, merfolk."

A bell rang out clear and frantic over the ship. Jonathan looked up and saw Ruben similarly pulled from the side of the ship by another crew member. Ruben tried to protest, but the drow shoved a bucket under his pale face and pushed him down to the deck.

"Stations!" the ship's captain called out as he stepped out from behind the wheel on the upper deck.

The ship's captain was a shorter drow with stern, icy blue eyes that seemed to burn like a cold fire against his deep, dark sin. His long silvery hair was held in a neat braid behind his head, and he wore a leather jerkin over a twilled cotton shirt. "Quickly now!"

The drow holding Jonathan pressed him down again for emphasis. "Stay down," he said.

The drow jumped up and ran along the deck. He took a short recurve bow made of steel and then turned to the port side. He fired three arrows as quick as lightning. Jonathan then saw an arrow fly up and strike the drow in the right shoulder.

The drow grunted and fell backward, dropping his bow.

Jonathan scurried toward the drow and reached out to grab the arrow, but the drow swatted his hand away.

"Poison, you fool!" the drow shouted. "Get below deck!"

Jonathan studied the arrow and only then did he notice that there were sharp barbs and ridges along the entire shaft. The arrow was also void of any fletching, leaving Jonathan to surmise that the bows used by the merfolk must be exceedingly strong to make the missile fly straight without the aid of fletching. As he looked closer still, he noticed that the arrow appeared to have a thin, yet distinct, layer of green slime along the shaft. Surely that was the poison the drow spoke of.

"I'll be fine," the drow said. "Elves are renowned for their constitution."

Another arrow sailed by overhead and dug deeply into the wooden rail near the stairs leading up to the captain. Jonathan looked up to see several drow firing into the waters.

He didn't wait any longer. He ripped the steel bow from the fallen drow and took the quiver as well.

"What do you think you are doing?"

Jonathan wasn't listening. He turned and leapt onto the oyster crate.

A flash of white rose up three yards to the right, just a foot away from the ship's hull.

Jonathan fired two arrows.

The water turned red and a merman's head snapped backward. The now lifeless body floated up and Jonathan saw that from the waist up, the merman was much like a human, with skin and large muscles resembling any man he had seen before. From the waist down, the merman had a thick tail like that of a blue fish, with scaled as large as small eggs. A strange weapon floated away from the dead merman. It was not a bow, as Jonathan had thought, but some sort of sling used to launch small javelins. It looked as though it were made of bone, and it had a groove that perfectly fit the strange "arrows" Jonathan had already seen fired at the ship.

Another ripple appeared several feet away and Jonathan caught a glimpse of the weapon in action.

A mermaid broke through the surface, a pair of large shells covering her breasts and right arm holding a weapon identical to the merman's. She pulled her arm back and then launched forward. The missile flew out from the strange sling and sailed directly for Jonathan.

The young man leapt out to the side and fired back with an arrow of his own.

The mermaid's attack missed by inches, but Jonathan's arrow struck the mermaid in the chest as she began to descend into the water. She let out a terrible screech that sounded like metal raking across glass and then she violently swam below the surface.

"Get below, boy!" the captain shouted. "If one of those so much as grazes your arm, the poison will kill you!"

Jonathan wasn't listening. He was good with a bow, and he was already set on helping defend the ship.

He continued to scan the waters and fire at merfolk warriors. He killed four more before the attacks ceased. By that time Ziegler and Bull had tried to come to the deck, but the drow captain convince them to stay down below. Even Ziegler called for Jonathan to come to safety, but he saw no reason to do that. He continued to scan the waters long after the last attack, bow in hand and several arrows itching to be loosed from the quiver.

Only when the other drow put away their bows did Jonathan begin to calm down.

He turned and smiled to the drow captain, but the elf only arched a brow and shook his head. "By Oda's bones it is a wonder humans live as long as they do," he said as he approached Jonathan. "One would think that a life span of less than a century would be enough to scare even the largest human into a peaceful life, but then here you are, barely able to put hair on your chin and ready to die by a merman's poison arrow."

"I never was good at letting others fight battles for me," Jonathan said as he offered the bow back.

The captain shook his head. "Keep it. It is yours now."

Jonathan smiled wide and looked at the bow. He hadn't noticed the design of ivy etched into the sides of the limbs before, nor had he seen the runes on the inside. "What do these mean?" Jonathan asked.

"They are charms, believed to bring luck to the archer who uses the bow," the captain said. "The top one means 'swift,' the middle one means 'accurate,' and the bottom rune means 'luck.' They are not enchanted bows, but we have a tradition whereby each bow at sea must have three symbols. It is something like naming a sword or other weapon. Take care of it, and it will take care of you."

Jonathan bowed his head in thanks.

Just then, the ship was jarred to the side, lifted from the water and creaking in protest against something striking the bottom of the hull. The captain was the only person able to remain on his feet, and even then it was only because he reached out to catch himself on the mast while the others tumbled across the deck.

"What in Khullan's unholy name was that?" Bull snorted.

Another impact rocked the ship, this time pitching it to portside. An unfortunate drow crewman tumbled over the rail and was caught by a gaping maw filled with a mess of sharp, triangular teeth. The jaws snapped closed, swallowing the drow whole.

Jonathan's eyes shot wide and a great dorsal fin as large as the main sail of the ship rose out of the water. Soon afterward a massive tail appeared, swishing right and left as the gargantuan shark swam away.

"We can't take another hit like that!" one of the crewmen shouted.

"Bellis!" the captain shouted. "Bellis we need you now!"

The doors to the sleeping cabins were thrown open and a tall, slender drow came out with a fierce look in his red eyes and fire in his palm. The flames swirled about in a ball, not burning the mage, but obviously ready to consume any target the mage wished to destroy. His gray robes flared out behind him as he walked to the side of the ship and threw his arms up into the air. The fireball grew as it rose above him and he called out over the waters in his language.

The massive shark turned in the waters and redirected itself toward the ship.

Bellis shouted louder and looked as though he was preparing to send the fireball at the shark.

A ripple appeared next to the ship and up jumped a large mermaid. She lunged out with a great, barbed spear and caught Bellis in the chest. The drow coughed and choked, then he was pulled overboard and into the water.

Two elves rushed to the side and slew the mermaid with their bows, but the damage was done.

The ship's mage was now descending the dark, cold depths of the cold sea below.

The shark was coming in, lowering in the water just slightly.

"Icadion be merciful," the ship's captain said.

"Arrows!" another drow shouted.

Everyone with a bow, including Jonathan, ran to the side of the ship and fired at the beast. The arrows stuck in its skin, but none of them pierced deep enough to draw so much as a drop of blood.

Jonathan tried to aim for the shark's eyes, but the great fish dropped just enough below the surface to make its eyes unreachable. Jonathan's arrows shot into the water, but not with nearly enough force to reach the shark's eyes.

"Move!" someone shouted in an authoritative voice.

Jonathan turned to see Ruben. The seasickness was now gone from his face, replaced by a determination and ferocity Jonathan had not before thought the wizard capable of. Ruben pushed back his sleeves and stepped up onto the oyster crate Jonathan had been using before.

The man's hands weaved curious, glowing designs in the air before his face as he chanted a strange phrase over and over.

"Guard him!" the captain shouted. All of the drow archers peered into the water, ready to strike down any merman who dared attack Ruben.

Jonathan glanced back to the massive shark. What could little Ruben do that would stop such a monster?

Ruben then clapped his hands together and shouted, "Lisei, lend to me your light and rescue us from ou09r plight!"

The glowing symbols in front of Ruben soared high into the sky and turned black amidst the roll of thunder and a great wind from the south. A cloud as black as night formed out of the symbol and then bright silver spots appeared on the cloud's belly. A strange odor filled the air and Jonathan felt the hairs on his arms and neck rise to stand on end.

A flash of lightning struck down from the cloud and pummeled the monster. The first bolt was instantly followed by seven more that slammed down, drilling the massive shark in the head and spine. The dull, gray skin on the beast turned red and then charred black under the brutal force of the lightning. A terrible thunder rolled out over the sea, nearly deafening the entire crew as everyone but Ruben clapped their hands to their ears.

The shark tried to turn away and dive down, but the lightning was relentless.

Bolt after bolt of the sizzling energy blasted into the shark's skin. As the great fish dove down, the lightning bored through the water and continued to strike the beast. Then, the shark groaned and turned its belly to the sky, rising to float upon the surface of the water. Three more bursts of lightning zapped into the shark's underbelly, and then the cloud disappeared.

The captain let out a cheer as did the rest of the crew.

"Huzzah for Ruben! Huzzah for Ruben Faelwyn!"

Even Jonathan had to admit that the feat was impressive. He looked out at the vanquished shark. Watching it bob it the waves he could easily see that one or two more strike from the gargantuan thing would have destroyed the ship. They all would have been eaten after that, assuming none of them were caught by the merfolk Jonathan was sure were waiting in the depths below.

"What you did was pretty good too," Jason said as he came up to Jonathan. "You were brave to take the bow and help the others."

Jonathan smiled. "It isn't the same," he said. "Ruben summoned lightning."

Jason nodded. "Yeah, he was better, that's for sure. I just wasn't going to rub it in." Jason tousled Jonathan's hair a bit and then walked over to congratulate Ruben.

Ruben was standing in the middle of the group, face reddening with each passing second.

"I don't normally respect followers of the demi-gods, but I think I shall make an exception in this case," the ship's captain told Ruben. "I am grateful to have a follower of Lisei on this ship. You can return anytime."

Ruben shook his head and wrapped his arm around Miranda's waist. Jonathan's smile faded then and he sighed. Had he not looked away, he would have seen an exhausted Ruben leaning on Miranda for support, instead of what he thought was an affectionate embrace. Ruben was taken down below deck, and then Jonathan watched from his oyster crate as the seas calmed and the elves stopped the ship in order to administer a farewell of sorts for Bellis and the other drow crew member who had perished in the battle. That night there was a celebration when it was announced that the drow struck by a merman's arrow would pull through and live, despite the poison.

From that point on, it was smooth sailing to Telward.

# CHAPTER 7

Several days later, Jonathan and the others were saying farewell to the crew and stepping onto the wooden docks at Telward. As Jonathan had expected from his reading of the travel guide, there were several warehouses and open walled markets just off the pier and lining the gently sloping hill that led up to the walled city.

Elven merchants moved goods back and forth, some loading their ships and others unloading. Jonathan had to keep alert, for the elves carrying the crates and bags of goods cared little if they knocked into someone, as Jason learned the hard way when a pair of longshoremen nearly pushed him into the water as they carried a hefty crate between the two of them. Had it not been for Moose's long arm, Jason would very likely have taken a salty bath.

The longshoremen continued on to a nearby ship, not even bothering to look back at Jason.

Going through the market wasn't much better either.

The pleasant aromas of spices and herbs filled the air, but Jonathan's joy in the sensation was overshadowed by the thick crowds pushing and squeezing their way around the market.

Jonathan followed Ziegler, with most of the others filing into a line of sorts behind him as they snaked through the pressing throng. Moose, however, moved from stall to stall, purchasing some fruits and other supplies for the group. Jonathan smiled as he heard a couple of elves complain loudly about a large man blowing smoke at them.

Moose never was patient when the mood to smoke struck him.

Jonathan was sure the effects of all those cigars were bound to catch up with the man someday. He had seen a few men die from the habit back in Holstead, and if that hadn't been enough to dissuade him from ever trying it, the idea of his Memaw catching him certainly did. Forget about trolls, elf warriors, or even the giant shark, Jonathan's Memaw would become the most ferocious creature upon all of Terramyr if she ever caught him doing something so foolish.

He smiled thinking about her, wondering what she and Pa were doing at the very moment he was about to explore another elven city.

Strange to think he had lived so close to something so different as the elvish culture, cities, and people, and yet had never experienced them before. He doubted whether more than a handful of people from Holstead had ever ventured into Tanglewood Forest before.

He glanced up at the gray walls and saw the open portcullis before him. This city also had a set of guards at the gate, but they were not stopping anyone as they passed through. The guards played some sort of dice game upon wooden tables off to the side of the gatehouse while Ziegler and the rest of the crew walked through to the city.

Ziegler turned around and shot Jonathan a wink that seemed to underscore the ease with which they had entered the city. A mischievous grin appeared on the large man's face and then he turned back around and sped his pace so that Jonathan had to quick-step to keep up with him.

They walked down a cobblestone street to the left that wound its way between several tall, thin buildings, each complete with brass plaques on them. Jonathan squinted to read them, but soon found that the signs were not posted in Common Tongue. They were written in the fine, elegant letters of the Taish language.

"Government buildings," Ruben said from behind.

Jonathan started, unaware that Ruben had been so close to him.

The tall, handsome wizard quickened his pace to match Jonathan's and pointed out the buildings. "The red brick building there is the office of the Dockmaster. The gray building beside it is a government warehouse. Over there," Ruben said as he pointed to the other side of the street, "I see a shipwright's guild, a lawyer's office, and the accounting guild."

Jonathan nodded appreciatively as his mind was able to connect each building with their purpose.

"Looks like a fishing guild is over here," Ruben said as he pointed to a green and tan building on the left. The brownstone building beside it is a cartography guild, they'll have exquisite maps inside there."

Jonathan nodded, but was not nearly as excited about the prospect of maps as Ruben apparently was. The young wizard rubbed his hands together and smiled wide, looking back to Jonathan excitedly.

"Come with me," he said.

"In there?" Jonathan asked, indicating the cartography guild.

Ruben nodded enthusiastically. "Come on, we can find something to help with our journey."

Jonathan couldn't decide whether to agree or protest. On the one hand, he didn't want to do anything with Ruben. On the other hand, since his precious travel guide had been lost in the waters under Gadrien's house, he was more than a little excited to see the maps of the elven nation made by actual elves. This was a once in a lifetime opportunity.

Ruben made the decision for Jonathan, wrapping an arm around the boy's shoulders and pulling him toward the cartography guild. Separated from the group now, Jonathan knew it would likely look worse to everyone if he pulled away to rejoin the others, and he didn't want Ruben to catch on to how much he disliked the fellow. In another life they might have been friends, perhaps, but with things the way they were now, Jonathan was very uncomfortable to be in Ruben's presence. In any case, he decided to make the best of it, choosing to focus on the treasures of knowledge he might find inside.

Ruben pulled the door open, ringing out a loud brass bell that bounced over the doorway, announcing their arrival. Jonathan walked in and smelled the unmistakable scent of old paper. Large, hand-drawn maps were framed upon the walls. A set of wooden counters lined each wall, some with rolled maps stacked neatly on top, and others left bare, with rectangular leather mats upon the wood surface. He smiled despite himself, eager to get his hands on a new map of Tanglewood Forest. Everything in here was so much bigger than the pages in the book he had lost that almost any map was bound to have more detailed information than what he had previously had access to.

A frail, elderly elf sat upon a stool, his left knee up nearly under his chin as he fiddled with the laces on his brown leather boots. The elf adjusted his spectacles and looked up to them with a kind smile.

"Don't get many visitors from beyond the elven lands," he said as he slid off the stool and stepped forward to place his hands upon the counter. "What is it you are looking for? Directions to the nearest inn perhaps?"

Ruben shook his head. "I am Ruben Faelwyn," Ruben said. "I am here on holiday, but thought I might peruse some of your maps, if I may."

The elf's gray eyes seemed to light up and his bushy, white brows lifted with his widening smile. "Master Faelwyn, a pleasure to meet you. I have heard of you. I am a cartographer by profession, but my first passion has always been the arcane arts. I have visited Lehemat even, and counseled with wizards there, oh but that was a few centuries before your time."

Jonathan glanced to Ruben, who was smiling modestly and nodding as if he had heard of the elf as well.

"I am Master Cartographer Eustinian Fink."

Jonathan drew his brows together at the name. It sounded familiar somehow, but he couldn't quite place it.

Ruben turned to indicate Jonathan. "This is Jonathan Haymaker, a famous hero from our wars with the trolls."

At that, Eustinian wrinkled his nose and his smile turned to a sour grimace. "Disgusting creatures, trolls. We'd all be better off if the lot of them had never been born in the muddy quags in the south, that's for sure."

Ruben pressed the matter. "Jonathan made it into the Warrens, and managed to slay the troll king."

Jonathan couldn't help but let a small, proud grin creep onto his face.

Eustinian nodded. "Yes, yes, that's a fine feat." The elf's tone was flat, entirely void of surprise or wonder. Usually, such a statement in Holstead would have a stranger gushing over Jonathan, or at least it had for the first many months after he returned. Even with the people of Holstead growing used to seeing Jonathan around again, none of them had ever given him quite the cold greeting this elf had. Eustinian drummed his bony fingers on the counter and looked back to Ruben. "What kind of maps interest you, Master Faelwyn?"

The elf turned and pointed to a bookshelf replete with rolled maps. "I have maps of the peninsula, or more detailed depictions of each region. I also have many wonderful maps of the sea. Of course, the maps that detail the migrations and settlements of the merfolk are all sold out at the moment. We seem to have an increase of attacks lately. But, I do have many other fine maps of the sea if you wish."

"What about the forest?" Ruben asked. "Have you any maps of Tanglewood?"

Eustinian's eyes lit up again and he let out a slight chuckle.

"Do I have maps of Tanglewood?" Eustinian repeated with a laugh. "My dear friend, I am an elf cartographer. I cut my teeth surveying Tanglewood Forest. I have so many maps of Tanglewood that you would not be able to carry them all in your backpack even if you gave most to your assistant there." Eustinian pointed at Jonathan.

"I'm not his assistant," Jonathan protested, but Eustinian wasn't listening. The young man's interest in the maps was quickly waning due to the poor reception he was receiving and he soon found himself wanting to leave rather than look at any map this Eustinian character had to offer.

"Tell me, Master Faelwyn, do you wish to have a current map, or perhaps one that shows Tanglewood as it used to be? I have maps dating back eons. Of course, the originals are not for sale, but I do have a handful of careful reproductions that I could part with for the right price."

Ruben smiled wide. "I should like two maps," he said. "One of Tanglewood as it is today, and one from the founding years, back when the council in Gwyndoltai was whole, before the drow exodus."

Eustinian's eyebrows flared and his eyes widened, but he recovered quickly and nodded as he pulled his spectacles down to wipe them on the hem of his shirt. "A collector of exquisite taste, I see," Eustinian said. "And what, may I ask, is the purpose for which you want these maps?"

"As you know, I have a very large office in Lehemat. I should like to decorate my wall with them. I have an entire miniature library in my office devoted to Tai culture and history. I think these maps will be the capstone of my collection."

Eustinian beamed and slapped the counter before him. "A scholar and a mage, most excellent. How could I refuse such a request?" Eustinian turned around and bent low behind the counter. He soon came up with four rolled maps in his hands. He set three to the left, and unrolled the fourth across the black leather mat on the counter.

"This one is a fine specimen, drawn by my predecessor only two centuries ago," Eustinian said. "It depicts Tanglewood as it stands today."

Ruben stepped close and examined it closely. Eustinian produced a magnifying glass from a large pocket in the front of his shirt. Ruben thanked him and continued studying the map.

"It is wonderful, but may I perhaps look at the others as well?"

"Certainly, certainly." Eustinian carefully rolled the map and then pulled a second out of the pile and opened it.

"Ah!" Ruben exclaimed as he examined the map, bending close to it with the magnifying glass. "This one is perfect."

Eustinian clapped his hands together and smiled. "I created this one. I spent more than a decade surveying the forest and capturing every relevant detail on the map."

Ruben nodded. "It shows. Do you have something to put it in that will protect it while I travel?"

"Land or sea?" Eustinian asked.

Ruben shrugged. "Perhaps a bit of both."

Eustinian nodded. He ducked under the counter and came up with a beautiful canisters. "The inner layer is made of cedar, the second layer is made of Tanglewood pine, and the outer layer is goat skin. This is the case I would use."

"Wonderful," Ruben said.

Jonathan stepped closer to look at the map. The sting of Eustinian's insults had faded enough that he was once again curious to see the map, though he was growing impatient with Ruben and the cartographer exchanging agonizingly gushing pleasantries. As he examined the map, he saw a small set of initials in the left bottom corner. The image triggered something in his memory and he suddenly knew where he knew the name from.

"You once made a map of the Murkle Quags, didn't you?" Jonathan blurted out.

Eustinian's smile disappeared and he peered over the brim of his glasses down at Jonathan. "My boy, I am certain I don't know what you are talking about."

Ruben turned to Jonathan with a kinder expression, explaining, "The elves didn't take part in our wars with the trolls. You ought to know that."

Jonathan shook his head. "Then you made the map before the trolls attacked," Jonathan pressed. "I know I have seen your initials before. They were on a map hanging on the wall at Fort Sym."

"Young man, what business would I have down in the quags?" Eustinian replied evenly. "Do I look like the sort of young elf who can stomp through the muck and survive a scrape with wild trolls?" Eustinian shook his head and puffed air angrily. "Hardly the sort of thing an elf of my position would do."

Ruben placed a hand on Jonathan's shoulder, but the young man was not about to let it go.

"I know what I saw," Jonathan said.

Eustinian pulled his glasses off and stared at Jonathan with his gray eyes. "Listen and listen well, I have never been, nor do I intend to ever be in the Murkle Quags. Elves keep to their own, and that is far beyond the reach of our lands. Besides, you ought to know that the only map of the Murkle Quags worth discussing is the one made by your grandfather."

Jonathan opened his mouth to argue, but Ruben squeezed harder on his shoulder. A tingling rolled through his shoulder, up his neck, and into his jaw. Jonathan was unable to form any additional words.

"My apologies," Ruben stated. "Sometimes he gets a little over anxious. He is still young, even by human standards."

Jonathan bristled at the insinuation, but it did lighten Eustinian's mood. The elf was smiling once more and turning away with a finger in the air as he hummed to himself. When he was sufficiently far enough away from them, Ruben bent down and whispered to Jonathan.

"I believe you, but we'll discuss it later. Trust me."

Jonathan looked up to Ruben's blue eyes and saw a sincerity there that convinced him to agree with the mage. Jonathan nodded, and closed his mouth. Ruben pulled his hand away, and the tingling left Jonathan's body.

Eustinian returned a few moments later with a single roll. "I have here an exquisite replica of the first map ever made of Tanglewood Forest after each of the main elven settlements were founded. Is this what you were looking for?"

The elf carefully unrolled the map and Ruben bent down to study it. He began listing off cities as he pointed to them. "Tirnog, Telward, Tyrwyn, Gwyndoltai, Neez, Tomyn, and Sierryn. It even has the dwarven kingdom of Shuldern drawn on here," Ruben said with a smile. "I notice this is made by another cartographer. Have you any replicas made by your own hand?"

Eustinian shot a wary glance to Jonathan, and then shook his head. "Unfortunately, I have not had the time to do as many replicas as I would have liked. Perhaps in a decade or two."

Ruben pursed his lips and nodded with a slight sigh. "Shame, I would have liked to create a set from the same cartographer, but no matter. Can you arrange for payment through Lehemat College of Mystics?"

Eustinian frowned slightly, and then nodded. "For you, Master Faelwyn, I can arrange such a thing. However, might I ask for a small deposit?"

Ruben nodded.

"Two hundred gold should suffice, and the balance I shall arrange with the college," Eustinian said.

Jonathan blanched. Two hundred gold was a ridiculous sum of money for almost anything, especially for a pair of maps drawn on old paper. The young man was almost disgusted when Ruben pulled a small purse from the right side of his belt and pulled out four large gold coins.

"These are each fifty-crown coins," Ruben said.

Eustinian lifted one up into the light and then smiled. "Pleasure doing business with you. Now, if you don't mind, I must return to my duties." Eustinian gestured to the door.

Jonathan wondered what duties Eustinian was talking about. After all, he had been lazily tying his shoe when they had first come in. There were no papers or other items indicating a work in progress anywhere in the room either. However, the stern look Eustinian shot Jonathan as Ruben turned away was enough to confirm the boy's suspicions. Eustinian Fink didn't have duties he needed to see to, he just didn't want Jonathan in the building any longer.

Jonathan turned to follow Ruben, but his mind was abuzz with questions. Why would Eustinian lie about the map at Fort Sym? Jonathan was sure it was the same signature. Something about it made the elf extremely angry, and Jonathan was itching to unravel the mystery.

Ruben pushed the door open, and the bell sounded their exit.

Once out on the street, Ruben pulled Jonathan over to the side.

"This wasn't just about maps, was it?" Jonathan asked.

Ruben shook his head. "I haven't told the others, but Raven spoke to me a little about his suspicions. He said that he was almost certain elves started the war between us and the trolls."

"Why would they do that?"

Ruben shook his head. "He didn't know, but he knew of the same map you saw in Fort Sym."

"Do you think Raven came here?" Jonathan pressed, pointing his chin at the cartography office.

Ruben shrugged. "Don't know, and Eustinian doesn't seem the type to divulge information willingly."

"We should tell the others," Jonathan pointed out.

Ruben nodded. "Now that you have confirmed the initials are, in fact, those belonging to Eustinian, we will. Come on, let's catch up to them."

"Do you know where they were headed?" Jonathan asked.

Ruben nodded again, and the two hurried through the crowds in the street.

*****

Eustinian took in a deep breath as he watched Ruben Faelwyn huddle with the young Haymaker just outside. They were up to something. The elf knew they didn't believe his lie about the map in Fort Sym. This was bound to have serious repercussions.

Once the pair disappeared in the throngs outside, Eustinian bolted the door and placed a sign letting others know the office was closed. He went into the back room and grabbed his velvety, blue brown over cloak. He fastened the silver brooch and then exited through a small door in the back of the office. His feet fell nimbly upon the alleyway as he hurried along through the winding pathways and thoughts of the young Haymaker kept running through his head.

The boy and mage couldn't possibly be alone.

No, a pair like that would need help to make it through Tanglewood Forest, Eustinian knew, especially now.

A chill ran down his spine as he thought of the possibilities. Only one seemed like a logical fit.

The Ghosts of the Quags were with them, and they were looking for Raven.

Eustinian Fink quickened his pace, keeping his nose down and his hood drawn up over his face. He nearly jogged to his destination, his feet only restrained by Eustinian's aversion for drawing attention to himself.

When he finally arrived at the manor, he ducked around the side and seized a brass knocker. He thumped the door four distinct times, and then waited. A sliding, thin panel of metal was pulled aside and a pair of green eyes peered out at Eustinian.

"Let me in," Eustinian grumbled. "Quickly, before I am seen."

Bolts scraped and then clicked on the other side of the door. It had only barely opened when Eustinian pushed it the rest of the way and barreled through.

"The master is busy," the doorman said.

"I must speak with him now," Eustinian replied evenly. He turned and glanced at the door. When he saw the doorman moving too slowly, he slammed the door shut himself. "Go, now!" Eustinian barked.

The doorman nodded and turned to leave the parlor.

Eustinian tapped his foot nervously, biting the nails on his right hand as he waited. After some time, the doorman returned, and gestured for Eustinian to follow him.

Eustinian moved quickly, following the other elf through a dimly lit corridor of red marble with mahogany wainscoting. Portraits of elves and forest scenes blanketed the walls, with occasional doors breaking the monotony. Eustinian didn't look at any of the portraits. His heart was thumping wildly, and his stomach was churning in knots. He wrung his hands as the two of them approached the final door on the left side of the hallway. The hallway itself ended with a seven foot tall, oval mirror in a golden frame. Eustinian wiped the sweat he noticed from his brow and then took a steadying breath as the other elf knocked gently and opened the door.

The doorman stepped in first, cleared his throat, and then announced, "Master Cartographer Eustinian Fink, to see you my lord."

Eustinian waited in the doorway, pausing with his head bowed reverently for a moment until he was permitted to enter.

"Come in, Eustinian, it is always nice to see you."

The doorman bowed and exited the room.

Eustinian walked inside and the doorman pulled the door closed behind him. Eustinian took three steps into the room, stopping just before large, rectangular rug began. On the opposite side of the rug, a great desk of rich cherry wood was situated with books and baubles cluttered atop it. A smoking beaker sat on a round, stone pedestal off near the one candelabra in the room that was lit. There were, in fact, six candelabras in the large room, one in each corner and two flanking the desk, but only the one in the far right corner was in use.

Behind the desk another elf with long, flowing white hair sat with his back turned to Eustinian. He was hunched over, moving as though he were writing something on a piece of paper on a table behind the desk.

"Wouldn't you like more light?" Eustinian asked to break the silence.

"Sometimes I find the darkness more soothing, don't you think?"

Eustinian frowned at the response. "I suppose it can be, master," Eustinian replied.

The elf cleared his throat and called out over his shoulder. "I doubt you have disturbed my work to discuss my candles. Come, tell me what is bothering you."

The other elf turned his chair to the left ever so slightly and looked toward Eustinian.

The cartographer had never before been in the master's personal study. He had always dealt with his servants, or lower ranking members of the family, but never with the patriarch himself. He couldn't quite make out Larkyn's face in the dim light behind the thick locks of white hair.

"Go on," Larkyn commanded. "Speak."

Eustinian nodded nervously and reached up to scratch his head. "It's about Raven, my lord."

"Raven has been dealt with," Larkyn replied evenly.

"T-true," Eustinian said. "What I mean to say is that others have come looking for him."

"How do you know this?" Larkyn asked as he turned the chair back around to the right and continued working on whatever it was he had been doing before Eustinian arrived.

"Another wizard has come. He came into my office."

"Did he ask about Raven?" Larkyn pressed.

"No, but he wasn't alone. Jonathan Haymaker was with him."

"Haymaker… I see." Larkyn sat upright, with his back still facing Eustinian. He took in a deep breath, shoulders rising and then pausing before he exhaled loudly. "It would seem as though that particular family might be your undoing."

Eustinian paused. His hands trembled and his voice caught in his throat. The words were stuck, but he knew he had to force them out. Better that Larkyn hear from him directly. "Jonathan Haymaker knows about the map in Fort Sym."

Larkyn's head dropped down and he groaned. "Eustinian!" Larkyn called out. "This must be dealt with quickly. We cannot let them poke around and investigate your involvement."

Eustinian dropped to his knees when Larkyn slapped the table with his hand and stood up. The cartographer kept his eyes on the floor and fought the urge to flee when he heard Larkyn's footsteps approach him.

Thump-thump-thump.

Eustinian's breath froze as a pair of black, curve-toed boots stopped just a few feet in front of him. He kept his eyes down and opened his mouth.

"I thought we could stop them," he said. "Perhaps if we find out where they are sleeping, we can take them."

"Eustinian, I forgave your failure when you had your map stolen from you in the Murkle Quags. I even helped you by sending trolls to kill the soldiers that had found you so that no human would know of your involvement. You cowardice, and ignorance I have overlooked, but your pride has come to haunt me. Had you not been so insistent on placing your initials upon the map, none would be the wiser about your involvement."

"But master, no one guessed the truth for more than two centuries, surely there must be a way to rectify this."

"Two centuries of luck do not justify the two recent incidents. First, Raven walks into your shop to ask you about your map, and now you have Jonathan Haymaker. You do know he is the one who killed the troll king, do you not?"

Eustinian nodded.

"Who was the wizard with him?"

Eustinian paused, shaking his head slightly.

"Who was it?" Larkyn pressed.

"Ruben Faelwyn," Eustinian answered truthfully.

Larkyn sighed. "Now the Lehemat College of Mystics is involved. Do you know what this means?"

Eustinian felt a strange, rough cord slither around his arms and shoulders. Magical tendrils wrapped around him and forced him to stand erect. A cold limb pressed Eustinian's chin up and for the first time, he laid eyes on his master's face. Fear and horror turned to confusion though, for he recognized the elf before him, and it was not his master.

"You are not Larkyn," Eustinian said.

The other elf grinned wickedly. "Astute observation."

Eustinian opened his mouth to speak again. "Why, you're—" a strong, barbed cord gagged his mouth and the rest of the words were muffled into a garbled mess.

"Yes, I am," the elf said. "Come with me, I have another task for you to complete." The elf waved his hands and the large rug rolled itself up and the floor opened into a stairwell. Eustinian tried to scream as he was dragged down by the magical cords squeezing and constricting his body. Breathing became difficult for him, and his bones stung, as if on the verge of snapping. When they finally reached the bottom of the stairs, Eustinian's eyes shot open wide when he made out the form of a very large troll standing beside a handcart.

"Take this one to the altar. He has but little magic, unfortunately, but his life force shall strengthen the enchantment nonetheless." The elf turned and smiled at Eustinian. "I trust you can at least die without messing up something else." He smiled with his wicked grin and then looked to the stairs. "I have other matters to tend to. If you'll excuse me."

Eustinian barely heard the words. His eyes were now fixed on the troll's big, toothy grin. The troll lumbered toward him, and Eustinian then saw a long, dark tunnel extending out to the west for as far as he could see.

A solid *thunk* hit Eustinian's head, and his vision turned to black.

*****

Captain Ziegler sat with his arms folded across his chest and a brooding frown on his face. Everyone was silent while the captain thought about their next moves. The information Ruben and Jonathan had just relayed to them about Eustinian and the other map was something Ziegler had obviously not expected.

Jonathan had a few options of his own he was considering, but he didn't dare speak them aloud. Between interrogating Eustinian, sneaking into the mage's council chambers looking for disciplinary records, or confronting Larkyn, none of the choices seemed overly exciting. He glanced over to the raven-haired Miranda. She was staring at the floor and swinging one leg off the side of a large bed. She had hardly said more than a word since he and Ruben had returned.

"I can go to Eustinian's office," Jason spoke up.

Every head in the room turned to him.

"You would go alone?" Ziegler asked.

Jason nodded. "He hasn't seen me. He doesn't know me."

"But you are human," Bull put in. "You'll stick out the same as any one of us."

"If we had more time, we could worry about that, Bull," Ziegler said over his left shoulder. "The truth of it is the fact that we are very much out of time. If Eustinian is involved, he has already been tipped off to our presence, and he knows what we are looking for. Whatever we want to do, we have to act now, before the enemy has time to regroup."

Jason pulled a forest green cloak from his backpack and put it on, pulling the hood up over his head. "With your leave, then," he said.

Ziegler nodded. "Very well, Jason you go to the cartographer's office. Miranda, Bull, and Moose will come with me to Larkyn's manor."

"You're going to approach him openly?" Ruben asked. "If he is involved, that would not be wise."

Ziegler scoffed. "I don't tell you how to run your department at the college, don't tell me how to run a stealthy operation. The two of you had better get down to the wizard's council. Look for the disciplinary record Friil spoke of. If you find it, then meet us at Larkyn's home. If you aren't there by sundown, we will leave and regroup here." Ziegler stood and put a finger up in the air. "Nobody is to get here any later than nightfall, am I clear?"

Everyone nodded.

The room turned into a chaotic mess of commotion and then emptied before Jonathan had let his assignment sink in. He was paired with Ruben to infiltrate and elven wizard's council. Ruben had a piece of paper, the one Friil had given to Ziegler, about the task, but he didn't know the first thing about elf wizards.

"Should I wear a cloak or something?" Jonathan asked.

Ruben grinned. "They won't fall for disguises or deception," he said.

Jonathan nodded and looked around, realizing his brother was already gone. "What is the plan?"

"Sneak in, take the record, and sneak out."

Jonathan frowned. "Have you ever done something like that?"

Ruben shook his head. "No, not really. Not unless you count sneaking into the cupboard to steal cookies when I was seven."

Jonathan slumped onto a bed. "Do you have any magic that can make us invisible?"

Ruben shook his head.

"Can you make us look like elves?"

"No, and even if I could, elves have a knack for seeing through illusions. That wouldn't work on them."

"Do you have a map of the building?"

Ruben shook his head and handed the paper to Jonathan. "No, it just has instructions for how to find the hall of records, and shows the types of runes we are looking for."

"Can you read Taish?" Jonathan pressed.

Ruben nodded and smiled slightly. "I am slow, but I can read it well enough."

Jonathan stood from the bed and read the paper more carefully, hoping that by looking at it a map might magically appear. He was not so fortunate as that.

"We should get moving," Ruben said.

The two of them left the room on the third floor of the Gilded Pike Inn and made their way down to the main floor of the building. The atmosphere here was nothing like the spectacle in Sohn had been. There were several patrons, but they were all finely dressed and keeping to themselves for the most part. A small band played various stringed instruments, strumming soft, melodic harmonies through the air. Soon the two of them were outside and walking through the streets once more.

They walked through the winding streets for more than twenty minutes before they came to a tall, cylindrical building made of black, heavily pocked stone and shimmering blue glass.

"This is it," Ruben said.

"Is there a back door, or a side entrance perhaps?" Jonathan asked as he surveyed the singular door in the front. It stood open, but there was a tall guard there holding a winged spear and scanning all the passersby.

"Come, I will use my position to get us into the building," Ruben said. Jonathan followed Ruben as the wizard walked toward the door. As Jonathan had feared, the guard stepped in front of them and leaned his spear out to the side, blocking off the entrance.

"Have you an appointment?" the guard asked.

Ruben smiled and bowed graciously, flaring his left arm out and bending low before coming up. "I am Ruben Faelwyn, from the College of the Mystics in Lehemat. I have come on holiday and wanted to come inside and peruse the records."

The guard stood stoic, his green eyes unblinking beneath his golden brow. "A thousand apologies, but if you do not have an appointment, then I must ask you to make one."

"And how do I do that?" Ruben asked.

The guard arched a brow. "If you do not know, then you must not be welcome."

Ruben balked and glanced to Jonathan. "I don't understand, are you saying that because I have to ask how to make an appointment, you won't tell me?"

The guard nodded.

"Well that's absurd, how does anyone do something for the first time without asking for instructions?"

The guard was silent. He lifted his spear and stamped the butt of the weapon on the flagstone walkway leading to the door. In answer to his gesture, the door slammed shut.

Jonathan turned and walked away. It took a few seconds, but eventually he heard Ruben puff in frustration and turn to catch up with him.

"Where do you think you're going?" Ruben asked.

"We tried your way, but it didn't work, now it's my turn."

"Oh and what are you going to do, wait until the changing of the guard?"

Jonathan smiled and nodded toward a coffee house two buildings down. "Trust me." They went to the coffee house and sat down inside. A fine young elf maiden came to them and began placing saucers with biscuits and small, white porcelain cups with gold leaf along the rim before them.

"What brings the two of you to Telward?" she asked.

"He's on holiday," Jonathan said as he pointed to Ruben. "This is my master, Ruben Faelwyn, from the College of the Mystics in Lehemat."

The young elf maiden smiled wide and turned her attention to Ruben. "A wizard?" she asked.

Ruben blushed slightly and nodded.

"My master would like his coffee black, no sugar, and with a hint of mint and lemon."

Ruben looked at Jonathan with a curious expression on his face that seemed to be asking the very same question the young elf maiden voiced only a half second later.

"Mint and lemon in coffee?" she asked.

Jonathan nodded emphatically. "That's how he likes it. He's a bit eccentric, but sharp minds have a reputation for peculiar tastes!"

The elf maiden nodded. "And what shall I get for you?"

Jonathan shook his head and fumbled around, patting his sides and making a show of looking on the floor under the table. "Master, it appears I have left your papers back at the inn. I will hurry and get them before your coffee is finished. I'll be right back."

"What inn are you staying at?" the young elf asked.

"The one down that way," Jonathan said, gesturing in the direction of the council building and hoping there was another inn nearby. "It's the, you know the one right, it's nearby with great rooms and…"

"The Worewal?"

"Yes, the Worewal," Jonathan said. "I will be there and back with the papers shortly. Enjoy your coffee." Jonathan then bolted out from the coffee shop, leaving Ruben sitting there with a bill to pay and a puzzled frown on his face. He skirted around the back of the building and then went for the one he was after. He had noticed a short, long house that stretched from behind the coffee shop all the way up to the back of the council tower.

After ensuring no one was nearby to see him, he scaled the wall and clambered onto the roof of the one story building. He moved to the center of the roof and then hunched over to maintain a low profile as he hurried toward the tower. He knew the coffee wasn't going to hold Ruben forever, so he had to move fast. At least now he wouldn't have to try sneaking around *with* Ruben.

He ran silently across the long roof, lowering himself to a crouch when he came close to the tower so he could study the windows facing him. As luck would have it, there was a large window that was open, and facing the roof. He leaned over to his right, but he couldn't even see the entrance from this point, let alone the single guard that had stopped them. He took in two steadying breaths and then he ran for the open window and leapt through.

He somersaulted across a thick rug when he landed inside. He looked up and saw a mostly rectangular room. The outer wall with the windows was slightly curved, of course, but the other walls were straight and parallel to each other. Live plants hung from the ceiling, with vines and leaves spreading down low. Several of the vines held strange, white globes that illuminated the room with a bright light. Behind him was a small, round table beside a singular, simple chair. To the left of that was a long bookcase that lined the wall. It was chocked full of tomes and scrolls.

Jonathan pulled the paper out once more and read the directions again. "Once inside, take the stairway in the center of the building down to the lower level. The archives will be in four sections. You must go into the section marked with an…" Jonathan turned the paper to the side and stared at the Taish rune as though it were some sort of strange vomit retched up from the pen from which it was drawn. It may as well have been, for all the sense it made to him. Still, he memorized the image and then shoved the paper into his pocket.

He rose to his feet and went for the doorway. He poked his head out into the hall and noted an elf pacing across the hall some forty yards to his left. To his right there were several more doors on the outer side of the hall, but there was only one opening on the opposite side. He decided to go for it.

Out into the hall and across the carpeted floor he ran, tip-toeing as much as his haste would allow. He stopped at the corner of the opening and then slowly peered around to take a peek. What he found pleased him greatly, so much so that he laughed at the ease with which he was infiltrating an elven mage tower.

There, right around the corner, were a grand set of stairs. They spiraled up and down the center of the tower, with landings at each floor and a giant tree growing along the middle. Jonathan ran to the stairs and glanced both up and down. Seeing no one else nearby, he started downward.

The only problem came as he rounded the tree trunk and came near to the first floor landing. He froze and backed up the stairs two steps when he saw a pair of elves standing just a few feet away. He knew there was no way he could get past them without being seen. He hoped he could wait for them to leave, but to his horror, one of them started walking closer to the stairs.

Pit-pat, pit-pat.

Jonathan silently backed up the stairs but then his stomach turned to stone when he heard voices from above. Next was the sound of many feet on the stairs above him, and they were coming down.

Thimp-thump, thimp-thump-thump.

He knew he only had moments before the elves would all come around the vast tree and he would be sandwiched in the middle. He did the only thing he could think of, he moved to the tree and grabbed a thick, green vine to help slow his descent as he slid down to the lower level. The vine held sturdy enough, but the bark was somewhat rough and he managed to scrape his elbows and hands just enough that he let go about four feet above the lower level, and fell the rest of the way. He landed on a mossy patch of ground, which helped muffle his fall, but it did little to spare his pride. He pulled himself up and stepped over a short railing separating the lower level landing from the area around the tree.

He walked through an archway of black stone into a strange hallway. Unlike the upper levels, there was not as much light here. Sconces were placed along the walls every fifteen feet or so, but instead of the bright, white orbs above, he now saw pale red things that looked like smooth stones. The peculiar instruments hummed low as they emitted their soft light, but Jonathan didn't mind it. If anything, the humming would help him mask the sound of his walking, and the softer, dimmer light might help him conceal himself better.

He walked around the hallway, passing the first section on the left for the symbol on the door did not match the one on the paper. The next section also didn't match. Jonathan was about to rethink his plan, but then he found the third section had a symbol upon the door that matched perfectly.

He reached for the black door's golden handle, and pushed it open. He slipped inside and closed the door behind himself. He then turned to survey the area, expecting to see bookcases or perhaps large desks, but nothing could have been further from the truth.

A long aisle split the large, wedge-shaped room down the middle. Flanking the aisle were thin tables without chairs. Atop the tables were strange, metal bowls set upon tall stems of gold. Beyond the tables were racks of shelves that rose all the way to the ceiling. Where Jonathan would have expected to find paper scrolls, or perhaps large books with handwritten records, he found stones and spheres of metal instead.

He pulled out the instructions from Friil and glanced at them again. "Go to the fourth row on the right, and look for the record on the second shelf from the floor marked with an..." Jonathan again turned the paper and memorized the Taish symbol he was looking for. He walked down the aisle and counted the rows. Then, he ducked between two tables and pointed with his finger as he passed over a sphere of glass, another of jasper, and a third made entirely of gold. When he came to the orb with the matching symbol, he frowned. It was a large onyx stone.

"How is this supposed to help us?" he asked aloud. He took the stone in his hands and shook it up close to his ear. Nothing rattled. He turned it over in his hand, gripping it in various places and trying to twist it open. Again, nothing happened.

Jonathan looked back to the strange bowls on the tables and then an idea came to him. He moved to the nearest table and placed the sphere into a bowl. A green light emanated from the golden stem, up into the bowl and flowing around the stone. The onyx quivered, and then began to hover in the air over the bowl by several inches.

A melody began playing from the stone. The note was low, and drawn out long and methodically. First pitching up, and then down. It was like a melodic pendulum swinging back and forth. Humming up, and then humming down. After a few repetitions, a softer, higher note sounded and the stone began to spin. The melody continued to play for several seconds, and then the stone was still and the green glow disappeared. The onyx stone became clear and a scene played out inside.

A handsome, black elf stood before a desk behind which three other elves sat. They spoke to him in Taish, and he stood silently. Because he could not understand the words they spoke, Jonathan tried to study the scene with his eyes to determine what was happening. As he concentrated, the orb seemed as though it pulled him into the scene through a veil of swirling black mist. Suddenly he found himself standing beside the handsome drow, walking around him and able to study the scene without interrupting it. It quickly became apparent that the drow was on some sort of trial. His wrists were connected by shackles, but more than that, his fingers were each restrained with silver sleeves that were chained tightly together as well.

His mouth was not gagged, but a circlet of metal was fastened around his neck also. As Jonathan looked carefully, he saw that there were chains connected to the stone floor beneath the drow. He turned to the other three and studied them as they spoke in what may as well have been gibberish for all Jonathan cared. They were all Vishi'Tai elves, or high elves. Each had golden hair and sharp, angular features. They wore robes of gold and had small books in front of them that they occasionally glanced to while speaking.

Then, one of them finally said something that Jonathan understood. Amidst the jumble of incoherent syllables and strange sounds, one of them said the word "Larkyn," and pointed directly at the drow. Jonathan spun around to see the drow, who he now understood was Larkyn, and watched as he hung his head low.

Jonathan turned back to the three elves and saw one of them pull something from inside a wooden box. His eyes shot wide when he saw the very same amulet the troll king had worn.

"No," Jonathan said. "Nebenuk said that was hidden away a long time ago. How could Larkyn have found it? And if he had, how did he lose it?"

Jonathan turned around and walked toward the image of Larkyn. "What happened, did you give it to the troll king? Is that it? But now you want it back?"

Suddenly, one of the other elves rose from behind the table and spoke in a deafening voice. He spoke the name, "Larkyn," several times and then he sat back down. Only then did Jonathan notice the onyx sphere sitting upon the table. No sooner had he looked upon it, then he was dismissed from the vision and standing back in the archives where he had been moments before.

The onyx gently lowered to rest in the bowl and there was neither light nor sound coming from it anymore.

Jonathan reached for the stone and turned it over in his hands. Perhaps Ruben would be able to make more sense of it than he was. Maybe that was why Ziegler had wanted Ruben along in the first place. Jonathan went to put the stone in his pocket, but it was too large. As he looked around at his clothes, wishing he had brought his backpack, the door to the room began to creak open.

# CHAPTER 8

Jonathan ducked into the row quickly, not wanting to be discovered. He peered through the space over the rocks on a lower shelf and watched as two figures came in and closed the door behind themselves. They both wore blue robes that flowed out with each step. They were speaking in the same language that the elves in the scene from the onyx orb had been, and they were coming ever closer.

Quickly, Jonathan scurried to the outer edge of the row and then ducked around the back side just as the pair came around to the side he had been on. Keeping his eyes on them, he inched backward toward the exit while the pair walked into the row. His heart nearly froze when the pair stopped right where Jonathan had taken the onyx sphere from.

One of them bent down and Jonathan caught a glimpse of a long nose under a set of golden eyes framed by silver, long hair. Those golden eyes flicked up and instantly locked on Jonathan. A shiver of fright ran up the young man's spine.

The elves didn't speak, they just broke into action. One ran left and the other went right.

Jonathan bolted for the door, but the first elf was upon him before he had made it more than ten yards. He grabbed Jonathan and threw him into one of the long tables. The edge of the hard wood dug into Jonathan's hip and he nearly cried out from the sharp pain. Then, his eyes caught a glint of something in the elf's hand. Jonathan looked up to see a curved dagger coming at him. He did the only thing he could think of, He ducked to the right and then came up and threw the onyx sphere at the elf. The stone struck Jonathan's assailant in the base of his throat. Something snapped and the elf grabbed at his chest, wheezing and coughing as he stumbled backward and fell, striking his head on a solid shelf on the way down. His body twitched and his eyes lost their shine as his last breath groaned out of him.

Jonathan barely had time to gather his wits about him before the second elf closed in on him. The elf wiggled his fingers and then a great force knocked Jonathan down to the floor. He bounced three times along the floor as the magical wind continued to drive him back until finally he was pinned against another table.

The elf closed in. Jonathan had nothing to fight with anymore except for his hands. The elf pulled a dirk from under his robes and came in fast. Jonathan turned to run, but the magic pushed him down again and held him face-down upon the floor.

Jonathan closed his eyes, preparing for the worst.

*Kaslam!* Something echoed loudly in the room.

Zhiiiist, ka-splat!

All at once the magical force disappeared and Jonathan was able to push himself up. When he did so, he saw Ruben running toward him.

"You shouldn't have come alone," he scolded as he rushed in to help Jonathan up.

Jonathan glanced over his shoulder to see a smoldering corpse lying several feet behind him. A large, charred hole was burned through his chest and wide, shocked eyes stared into the ceiling.

"What did you do?" Jonathan asked.

"Saved your life," Ruben replied as he tugged on Jonathan's arm. "Did you get the record?"

"There," Jonathan said as he pointed to the first elf. Ruben hurried and took the sphere from the ground and tucked it into a satchel at his side. "Come on, we have to get out of here."

Ruben was half dragging him through the hallway outside. Behind them, Jonathan heard a commotion of rushing steps down the stairs and shouting voices. They were about to be trapped by a multitude of angry elf wizards.

The two of them ran around the circular hall until they came to a strange metal grate at the end. Ruben pulled it free and then shoved Jonathan inside. A moment later he entered and replaced the grate.

"Keep moving!" Ruben whispered harshly. He pushed Jonathan down a long, dank corridor. Jonathan couldn't quite tell what they were running on. The floor was firm, but not entirely unyielding like stone. It also made slight squishing sounds with each step, as if there was water inside. Finally, as the last of the light from the hallway stopped piercing the darkness in the tunnel, Ruben stopped them and crouched low, pulling on Jonathan to bring him to a squatting position.

"Where are we?" Jonathan asked.

"We are on one of the tree's roots. Now, be quiet and let me concentrate."

Jonathan closed his mouth, wondering how they were going to get out of the mess they were in. The shouting was coming closer to the grate, and he could see the lights growing brighter and brighter with each passing second. Then, just as someone grabbed the grate, Ruben reached out and grabbed hold of Jonathan. A warm, fluid sensation washed over him and then his vision turned black.

Jonathan's head and ears felt plugged, as if a thick, viscous liquid was running through his every orifice and vein. His nose was filled with the scent of sap, and his head began to throb terribly. His limbs felt solid as stone, and his heart struggled to pump within his chest. He could not breathe, there was only the terrible agony of his burning lungs, yearning for air and fighting to move.

The constriction around his body grew tighter with each passing moment as something grainy and moist pressed against his skin. He felt as though he was stuck inside some great tube that was collapsing with him inside of it. Then, just as he was about to give up hope, the daylight broke through the blackness around him. The pressure released and the suffocating liquid drained from him until he was lying upon the green grass next to a large pine tree in the middle of the forest. The smell of tree sap still permeated his very being, but he was free of the terrible agony that had moments ago threatened to crush him into oblivion.

"We can't rest, we have to move."

The voice sounded as though it came from some distant plane, or a dream perhaps. Jonathan could barely make his lower jaw move, but he could not form a response. Even had he been able to, his mind lost focus only seconds after the voice had spoken.

Something gripped Jonathan's arm and squeezed it tight.

"No," Jonathan groaned. Fear wormed into his heart as he feared he would have to endure another round of whatever that magic was, but then Ruben appeared in front of him, eyebrow drawn into a tight knot and face red and stern. "Ruben!" Jonathan exclaimed weakly.

"Wake up!" Ruben said.

Jonathan felt a sharp, stinging slap across his face. His senses came back to him and he shook his head.

"We have to move, *now*!"

Jonathan and Ruben ran deeper into the forest.

"What was that?" Jonathan asked as they sprinted through the trees.

"Druid magic," Ruben spat.

"You're a druid?" Jonathan asked. That was the last thing he expected Ruben to say. Since when could a druid control lightning? Druids worked with nature and the elements, but usually only the earth-bound elements. Lightning was never something they could control, or at least not as far as Jonathan knew.

Ruben grabbed Jonathan suddenly and shoved him up against a tree. "Because of you, two elves are dead. I could have gone in without getting caught!"

Jonathan shook his head. "No, it wasn't like that, they were after the record!"

Ruben's grip eased up and he studied Jonathan's eyes for a few moments. "Are you sure?"

Jonathan nodded. "I was hidden. They didn't know I was in the room. They went straight to where I had picked the stone from, and then when they saw it was missing, they came after me."

"They thought you stole it," Ruben said through gritted teeth. "They were right!" Jonathan pushed Ruben with both hands, but it didn't accomplish as much as Jonathan had hoped. The wizard barely moved a few inches before tightening his grip on Jonathan's shirt.

"Listen, they pulled weapons without asking anything."

"How would you know?" Ruben pressed. "Do you speak Taish? Would you have understood their questions?"

Jonathan shook his head. "They didn't speak. They pulled knives on me and came after me. I tried to run, but they caught me. One of them threw me into a table and then tried to stab me. I had no choice but to defend myself. If they had only wanted the record, they could have easily taken it before you arrived. You tell me, what did you see the second one doing?"

Ruben's anger faded with that last question and he released Jonathan. He thought for a moment and then nodded. "I have never killed anyone before," he said softly.

"You killed that giant shark in the waters, and you slew those two wood sprites in the forest," Jonathan pointed out.

Ruben nodded. "Creatures and monsters yes. I have killed a few of those, but never a person." He looked up to Jonathan. "Sorry. I know we were supposed to get the record, and I knew that would have its risks. I just never thought…"

Jonathan nodded. "I understand. Just, tell me, can the elves do what you just did?"

Ruben looked back the way they had run and shook his head. "We are three miles outside the city. They won't think to look out here just yet."

"How did we travel three miles?" Jonathan asked incredulously.

"Too long to explain now, but let's just say that I can use magic to travel through trees. They have to be large, and they have to have the right energy, but I can make it work."

"If you can do that, then why not always travel that way through the forest?"

Ruben shook his head. "It's like running, it tires me out very quickly. More importantly than that, I can't normally travel with others."

"But you just traveled with me," Jonathan pointed out.

Ruben nodded. "That was the first successful time," he said as he took in a great breath and put his hands over his head. "I'm still not entirely sure how I did it, to be honest."

Jonathan blinked. "That was your *first* time with someone else?"

Ruben nodded again. "I have tried with parakeets before, but they always end up getting stuck inside. I haven't even wanted to try tree-walking for months after my last attempt." Ruben shrugged and slapped his hands down to his sides. "I guess the gravity of the situation helped me break the barrier."

"I could have been stuck inside the tree?" Jonathan asked, unable to focus on anything else.

"It was either that or die by elven wizards," Ruben said. "I did what I had to do."

Jonathan whistled through his teeth and shook his head. "Let's not ever do that again then, agreed?"

Ruben nodded and laughed.

"How did you even know the tree was there?" Jonathan asked after a few moments.

Ruben smiled wide. "The waitress at the coffee shop. We got to talking about the mage tower and she told me. She was the one who told me of the northern root that runs out from under the tower in a long tunnel and drinks from a deep, underground pool of waters flush with magical energy. That's when I thought perhaps I should try using the spell again. Of course, I had no idea how I would find you, but I knew that I had to try and get into the archive."

"What do we do now?" Jonathan asked. "They're going to be looking for us."

Ruben nodded. "I have enough energy for one more time. I'll use the spell to come out near the inn. There was a large oak tree there. I'll bring the others out here to meet you."

"How do you know where we are now?" Jonathan asked.

Ruben grinned and pointed to the trees. "When I walk inside a tree, the trees are my eyes. I saw exactly where we were going, and I can easily make it back here."

"I thought people were born with one type of magic," Jonathan said.

Ruben's smile disappeared. "My father was a druid. My mother was a Lisei Priestess. They each followed the life paths that matched their magical skills. Normally, a child will get one type of magic or the other. However, in my case, I was granted both types. I guess that is one of the reasons I was promoted so quickly in the college." Ruben smiled and huffed as his eyes lit up. "I know for a fact that is the reason why I was betrothed to Miranda."

Jonathan narrowed his eyes and tilted his head.

Ruben nodded understandingly. "Don't get me wrong, I have since come to like her very much. But, the genesis of our betrothal was partly a broker between powerful wizard families, as is our custom, and partly an experiment I suppose. Seeing as Miranda has her father's gift of fire magic, I suppose everyone is hoping that we will bear children who can wield three types of magic equally well. It's silly I suppose, because there are plenty of records of powerful wizards and sorcerers throughout Terramyr that can wield many kinds of magic, but on our peninsula, such is not the case. But, I should get moving. I don't want the elves to figure out where the others are and get to them first."

Jonathan simply nodded and Ruben disappeared into a tree, walking into its trunk and looking as though the tree absorbed him into itself like a tall, human-shaped drink of water.

*****

The next couple of days were a whirlwind of running north through the forest. Not only was the party worried about being chased from Telward, but Ziegler had reported that Larkyn had eluded them, leaving Telward a few hours before they had arrived to call upon him. According to the steward at the manor, Larkyn was on his way to Inghali, an elven city which most elves pretended did not in fact exist, for it was easier for most of the so-called enlightened elf races to ignore the sand elves and the debauchery they allowed in their ancestral homeland.

The group ate little, and slept less. They worked their way through the dense forest until half way through the fourth day, they arrived upon the southern shore of a massive lake that was more like an inland sea.

The southern banks were lined with tan sands, small, smooth pebbles, and bits of driftwood and seaweed layered up where waves had deposited them over the years. The lake was nearly fifty miles wide east to west, and twice as long north to south. Bull was the first to move toward the beach, where he promptly cast himself down upon the sand with a loud groan and sprawled out to relax.

"Don't get too comfy, Bull," Ziegler said. "We need to find the fishing villages around here, and see about getting a boat."

"Another boat?" Jason asked. "Why not stick to the trees and the cover of the forest?"

"A small fishing vessel can travel upwards of thirty miles an hour, given favorable wind conditions," Ruben put in. "At that rate, it would only take us a few hours to navigate to the other side."

"I'm up for anything that doesn't involve more running," Bull huffed from the ground.

"Are you tired, Bull?" Jason quipped.

Bull stuck a finger in the air. "I ain't tired, I just can't feel my legs."

They all shared a laugh at that.

"Come on, the sooner we find a boat, the faster we can all rest our legs," Ziegler said.

Moose walked over and stretched a hand down to Bull. Bull took hold of the offered hand and a second later the mountainous warrior had yanked Bull up into the air and onto his feet.

The group walked around toward the east, where Ruben was certain there was a small village.

"According to my map, there is a fishing village named Vizendel."

They kept to the beach, rather than make their way through the dense forest, for there were no roads shooting off the main northerly causeway that led alongside the western bank toward Inghali. Along the way, Jason picked up a few rocks and skipped them out onto the lake. Moose shrugged and decided he would play along. He grabbed a slightly round rock the size of Jason's fist and hurled it out to the water. It flew up in a high arc and landed in the lake more than one hundred yards from where they stood.

"You're supposed to skip the stone," Jason said. "It takes finesse."

Moose shrugged and pulled out another cigar. "I was going for distance, it requires strength."

Jason grumbled something that even Jonathan couldn't understand, and they all kept moving along. Far too soon for Jonathan's comfort, Ziegler even picked up the pace and everyone was once again jogging. He had long ago forgotten about the ache in his side. If anything, he now had a full-body ache that rumbled along with him as closely as his shadow. Much like Bull, Jonathan was beginning to go numb from it all. It was all he could do to keep his eyes on Ziegler and keep pace with everyone else.

It was sundown before they reached Vizendel.

The small fishing village was nothing like the grander cities of the elves. These were simple wooden houses and a few buildings near wharfs that had definitely seen some better days. Barnacles and algae grew along the posts, and had even reached the top side of the docks in places. There were four small sail boats tied to the docks with thick, discolored ropes, and a few barrels lined the wharf near a wooden storehouse of sorts that had several large fish hanging by the tail from a wooden post near the front door.

What Jonathan didn't see, however, was movement.

Where were the elves? None were on the docks, in the boats, or even walking between the houses.

The gardens near each house were overgrown with weeds and wildflowers. Birds busily pecked at berries and vegetables while there were none to shoo them away.

"Something isn't right," Ziegler said.

Everyone in the group went for the knives they kept in their backpacks. Jonathan readied his bow.

A raven squawked in the trees above.

A door opened and an elf walked out from the third house on the right. A black smock covered the front of his tan trousers and off-white shirt. His hair was long, braided into a single plait down his back. In his right hand he held three fish tied together at the tails. He looked up to the group and his eyes went wide. He started shaking his head, but to Jonathan's surprise the elf didn't say anything. Instead, he tried to wave them away frantically while nodding to the woods.

"What is he doing that for?" Bull grumbled.

"Keep your eyes peeled," Ziegler said.

The elf kept waving at them, hurrying across the street and glancing nervously to the woods.

As the group inched closer, a wind fluttered in from the north and carried with it a familiar stench.

Jonathan's heart began to thump faster and he put an arrow to his bow string.

Moose was the first one to say what they were all thinking. "Trolls are here," he said.

Just then the door to the house on the right exploded open and two trolls jumped out. Their ugly, green noses were flared and their yellow teeth were bared beneath matching mohawks of red hair. They shouted something and fired bows without additional warning.

Moose caught one arrow with his backpack and then dropped the bag to throw his knife. The blade whirled end over end until it sunk into one of the trolls' neck and the creature fell to the ground, screaming and hollering.

The second arrow went wide, missing everyone.

Miranda and Ruben answered simultaneously. She sent a fireball and Ruben fired a bolt of purple lightning. The poor troll didn't stand a chance. The fireball struck his forehead and the lightning shot through his heart.

Bull sprinted up to the troll with Moose's knife stuck in his neck, grabbed the hair in one hand, yanking the head up and back while he dug his knee into the troll's spine, and then he worked quickly to plunge his knife into the troll's heart. A second later he released his knife and pulled Moose's knife through the troll's neck, severing the head. He tossed the dismembered head to the street and then turned to enter the house.

"Moose!" Bull called out.

Moose was already on his way inside. The hulking man made the door in four steps, pulled Bull's knife from the headless troll, and then stomped inside. A moment later, the entire southern wall of the house exploded and two trolls went flying out amidst a shower of broken boards. Jonathan lifted his bow, seeing that neither of those two trolls were mortally wounded. He fired his first arrow through one troll's eye as he rolled along the ground. Jonathan's second arrow pierced through the second troll's heart.

Miranda added another fire spell for good measure, and then the battle turned into a hell storm.

Doors opened all around them and trolls poured into the street.

Ruben brought down lightning upon three trolls emerging from a house with swords, frying them instantly. Miranda blasted another with a fireball that ripped through the troll and then exploded in the doorway he had emerged from.

Jason dropped his knife and ran for a sword that one of the trolls had dropped.

Jonathan turned to cover his brother. He fired three times, dropping three trolls. Jason bent down to scoop up a sword and then made quick work of a fourth troll by severing its head.

Screams went up in the village, and the party spun around, looking for the source.

"There!" Bull said as he emerged from the demolished house he had just cleared with Moose. He was pointing across the way to the storehouse with the fish hanging in front. A large, heavily muscled troll exited the house and had two she-elves, one in each hand by the throat. He roared violently and then the sound of snapping necks filled the air. The elves twitched and then their lifeless bodies were dropped to the ground.

Jonathan stared in horror, but then he noticed a troll archer coming out from around a corner to the right. He sent his arrow just in time, for the troll was about to fire as well. Luckily, Jonathan's arrow struck a moment before the troll released his shot and the troll fell to the ground while his shot jerked up and over the village.

Jonathan reached back for another arrow, but then he noticed a troll barreling down toward him. The snarling creature had a spear in hand, and was coming in hard. Jonathan grabbed for an arrow, but his fingers fumbled and he missed. Just before the spear reached him, Moose came around on the side, snatched the spear behind the head and yanked it up. The troll went with it, swinging his legs and growling ferociously, but Moose jerked the weapon away and sent the troll flailing through the air. A second later, Moose threw the spear and pierced the troll's heart. The troll fell lifeless to the ground with a sickening tha-bump.

Jonathan looked up to Moose, who simply winked at him and smiled. Only then did Jonathan realize that the man was still smoking his cigar.

"Jonathan, rooftop!" Jason called out.

Jonathan snatched an arrow, this time without fumbling, and turned to see a pair of archers lining up. They were both preparing to fire. Ruben and Miranda were engaged with their backs to the archers, fighting a group of six trolls. Ziegler was hacking his way toward the hulking troll standing over the two dead elves and roaring. Bull and Jason were busy fighting hand to hand.

If Jonathan couldn't take both trolls in one shot, someone was going to be killed by the second troll archer.

Jonathan jumped to the left, then spun to the side and pulled his arrow back as quickly as he could. He lined up the trolls and then fired, whispering a small prayer to the gods for help. The arrow flew straight and true while Jonathan stood motionless, staring in an attempt to steer the missile with his eyes. He was relieved only when the arrow cut the string of the first archer's bow and then continued onward to sink into the second archer's neck. The first archer screamed as his arrow fell to the ground when the bow limbs snapped into place and cracked. The second archer jerked to the side and his shot sailed down to strike some other hapless troll fighting in the road, striking it in the forehead.

Jonathan pulled a second arrow, and then a third, driving through the two troll archers' hearts before moving on to find new targets.

Jonathan looked up to see the hulking troll disappear into the storage building and then reemerge with another victim. It was a male elf, this time. The troll held him up over his head, and then he swung the elf by his ankles and dashed his head against the building before tossing the limp and broken body to the ground.

Jonathan drew an arrow and fired on the hulking troll, but it looked up and snatched the arrow from the air just inches before it would have pierced its heart. It sneered at Jonathan and then it produced a brass staff. Flames erupted from the staff and flooded the building. Screams and shrieks filled the air. The hulking troll barked some sort of orders, and the dozen or so trolls still alive turned to retreat. The hulking troll then spewed the magical flames on the ground, creating a hedge of fire between him and Ziegler.

Ruben peeled away and sent a lightning bolt at the large troll, but the troll raised its staff and somehow managed to deflect the bolt. It ricocheted back and struck the ground near Ruben, throwing him to the side as it exploded in a puff of dirt, stone, and smoke.

Moose and Bull took down two more trolls, Jason caught one himself, and Miranda blasted two more. Jonathan turned his bow on the others and was able to bring down another pair of the hideous creatures before they all vanished behind the wall of flame.

Ziegler sprinted forward, leapt through the barrier, and disappeared behind the flames as they resealed the barrier behind him.

"Captain!" Bull shouted as he rushed forward. At that moment, the firewall bowed out and exploded. A wave of white, fiery air blasted out toward the party. They all dove to the ground and covered themselves as best they could. Jonathan felt the sting of the fire as it rolled over him. When the danger passed, Jonathan jumped up to look for Ziegler.

He was relieved to see the captain was safe, but he couldn't revel in the feeling for long.

Captain Ziegler took the head off of two more trolls, and then he turned his attention to the burning building. He grunted and shouted as he swung a large sword at the wall, breaking through the panels and boards. Black, thick smoke billowed out from the opening, but Ziegler didn't stop. He hacked away at the wall and then dropped the sword to use his hands to rip the building apart. Once there was a hole in the wall big enough, Ziegler dove into it. Jonathan and the others ran to help.

Moose pulled at the opening, ripping nearly half the wall down on top of them in the process. A great cloud of smoke blasted them and Jonathan had to duck and put a hand to his face to keep from choking.

"Captain!" Bull shouted again as he rushed in.

"Here!" Ziegler called out from the smoke.

Moose also dove in, and a moment later the three of them emerged with four elves. They were coughing and sputtering. Moose and Bull slapped the elves lightly on their faces. Miranda offered them water, and Ruben moved in to listen to their breathing.

Jonathan stood there, helpless. He didn't know what to do. He was no physician. He watched helplessly for a moment, until his brother nudged him on the side.

"Give them water, like Miranda is doing," Jason said as he held out two water skins.

Jonathan nodded and went to work. He knelt beside a she-elf. Her skin was covered in soot. Her hair was partly melted to her left shoulder and the left side of her face. Bull was kneeling on her other side. He took one of the water skins and began pouring water over the melted patches of hair. The she elf slowly turned her head and her green eyes looked up to Jonathan for a moment before turning dull. Her body heaved and convulsed as she took in another desperate breath.

"No, you don't have my permission to die," Bull snarled. "Move back, Jonathan," Bull said. The bald warrior then moved to the elf's chest. He placed a hand over her heart and then leaned down to listen to her breathing. He took in a breath and then put his mouth over hers. Jonathan could hear the exchange of air and the elf's chest rose slightly. Bull came back up, took another breath, and then pressed his mouth to hers once more. When he came up the next time, he stopped and flattened his hand on her chest. He moved two fingers to the side of her neck and shook his head angrily. "No, no, no!"

Bull gave another breath and then began giving compressions to her chest as well. He looked up to Jonathan. "Hold her feet up," he said.

Jonathan didn't question the man. He moved to the elf's feet, grabbed them by the ankles, and lifted them up a foot off the ground.

"Keep them there!" Bull ordered. He continued to alternate between giving breaths and compressions for several minutes. The black smoke swirled around them, and the heat was becoming unbearable.

Moose tried to convince Bull to move the elf further away, but Bull pushed him away, refusing to stop his efforts to save her. Jonathan stood and watched helplessly. Soon, the others gathered around them, but no one said anything to Bull. Jonathan watched as Ruben called a wind to push the smoke back, but everyone else was still, watching Bull work as his face and bald head grew redder and redder.

Finally, he fell backward, exhausted and out of breath.

Moose bent next to him. "Bear would be proud," he said. "You did your best."

Bull shook his head and rose to his feet. He pushed his way out of the crowd and yelled at the sky while kicking clumps of dirt with his foot.

Moose looked to Jonathan and silently motioned for him to put the feet down. Then, the large man removed his cigar from his mouth and extinguished it in his hand before tossing it to the side. Jonathan swore he could see tears welling in Moose's eyes just before the giant warrior turned to watch Bull.

There was nothing they could do to save her.

Jonathan looked around then, hoping to see at least a few other survivors. Unfortunately, he saw only bodies lying upon the ground. The group had been quick to rescue the elves, but the smoke and fire had killed them even quicker.

Jonathan felt a numbness enter his stomach and his shoulders drooped heavily. He had been through war before, and had seen others die. His friend Sami had died in a collapsing building right in front of him. The scout Rourke died while saving Jonathan's life. Even Bear, a veteran Ghost of the Murkle Quags, had been slain in front of him. Yet, these were the saddest deaths he had ever witnessed. These were peaceful elves. They fished for a living, and never would have bothered anyone or anything. They were likely even devoid of magic, or else they might have succeeded in defending themselves from the trolls before Jonathan and the others ever came to Vizendel.

"This is our fault," Jonathan said. "If we hadn't come…"

"No," Moose said. "The trolls were here anyway. They would have killed the villagers sometime regardless of our arrival. At least this way, the villagers are avenged."

Jonathan nodded and then looked up to find Ziegler, wanting to know what their next move was, but then he realized that the large captain was nowhere to be seen.

"Where's Ziegler?" Jonathan asked.

Moose jumped up and went to the building, but Ruben grabbed his arm before the mountain of a man could reach the blaze.

"He's on the water!" Ruben shouted.

"Alone?" Jason asked.

The group ran toward the docks, Moose shouted for Bull and they all jumped into a sailboat to catch up to their captain.

"Bloody fool!" Bull grumbled as he untied the boat and jumped in.

"Wind, now!" Moose shouted at Ruben. Ruben nodded and raised his hands. A mighty wind came down and launched them all forward with a jarring jerk that propelled the boat out into the open water.

Jonathan went to the front of the boat and watched as Ziegler sped toward another boat. "We need to go faster," Jonathan said.

Ruben replied, "That's the best I can do!"

Jonathan shook his head. They would never be able to reach the captain before he caught up with the others. Beside the hulking troll with the magic staff, there were five more troll warriors on the second boat.

"Curse his fool headedness!" Bull spat.

"Why didn't he wait for us?" Miranda asked as she moved up behind them.

Bull grunted and sighed. "After we ended the war with the trolls, Ziegler came to live with me and my family. I introduced him to my wife and son. Well, one night, my son asked about Ziegler's family. I would have thought the captain wouldn't have said anything, but he did. He recounted his real name and told my son about the incident just over thirty years ago when his wife and two daughters were killed by a troll raiding party in a small village that used to stand to the northeast of Battlegrym. He told us of the spear stabbed through his shoulder and showed my son his scars. He said that the soldiers came, but only after the village was burning. Apparently some of the townsmen had lit the blaze to chase away the trolls. It worked, but nearly everyone had been killed before the flames grew big enough to send the monsters running."

"Ziegler told us the same things," Jonathan replied.

Bull nodded. "But he told my son more than that," he said. "He told my son about a massive, hulking troll that gathered people into a small church and began killing them. He also told my son that the fires started by the townsfolk to scare the trolls away got to that church before he could. His wife had died by the sword, but his two daughters died in the church. The big troll with the staff looks an awful lot like the one Ziegler had described to my son."

"But this troll wasn't afraid to use fire," Miranda pointed out.

Bull shrugged. "Perhaps the monster relishes the irony. I'm not sure if the troll recognized Ziegler, but I know the captain recognized him."

Jonathan looked out across the waters once more, watching helplessly as Ziegler's boat closed in on the trolls.

*****

Captain Ziegler steered his vessel toward the trolls. There were six of them upon the other boat, but only one that he was focusing on. His eyes could not take themselves from the tattoo on the troll's left shoulder, the black eyes set wide alongside the narrow, hooked nose, and that foul red hair pulled into a braid. It was the same as he remembered. The troll looked as though he hadn't aged a day since that horrible massacre those thirty years ago. Ziegler, on the other hand, was obviously older, with gray in his hair and wrinkles creasing around the corners of his eyes. However, he also had much more experience. He was no longer the young man he once was. He was the commander of the Ghosts of the Quags.

Oh, how he had longed to find this particular beast in the Warrens, but that day had never come. Ziegler had assumed the creature dead, until today. A fire rose inside the man and his heart slammed inside his chest, demanding retribution for the lives the troll had stolen from him.

In his mind's eye he saw his children and wife once more. They were playing, swinging each other around in a field of daisies. They stopped and turned, laughing as they looked to him. Ziegler smiled back, and then he pushed the image away. He reached around his back and pulled a dagger from a sheath hidden under his waistband. His boat jumped and bounced over the small waves in the lake as he sped toward the trolls.

The hulking leader turned and smiled at Ziegler once more. He pointed to the man and drew a yellow nail across the green skin of his neck. The troll then turned and shouted orders to two of the others. The trolls drew their swords and dove into the water, directly in Ziegler's path. The human captain held his course, hoping the boat would smash the would-be assailants. Unfortunately, they used hooked knives to pierce the hull on the sides and climb into the vessel with him. So fast were they that Ziegler wasn't aware what they were doing until they had clambered onto the deck with him.

Ziegler let out a feral yell and rushed forward. The first troll raised his sword, but Ziegler's rage amplified the man's strength. He lashed out with his left hand and punched the troll before it could swing the weapon.

The troll's jaw broke and two teeth exploded out to the side, along with a bit of dark blood. Ziegler then came in with his dagger and put two thrusts into the troll's heart before launching a savage front kick that forced the troll overboard.

Ziegler then turned to the second troll. The troll came in fast with the sword, but Ziegler lifted a nearby barrel and let the hollow container take the brunt of the attack. He then leaned into the barrel and pushed the troll backward. His right arm hooked around the barrel and he drove the blade of the dagger through the troll's left temple. The troll collapsed to the deck.

The captain reached down and grabbed the corpse, and then tossed it into the water as well. He didn't want any additional weight slowing his pursuit.

The large troll turned with a wicked sneer and pointed his staff to the water.

Surely he wasn't going to set fire to the water, was he? Was that even possible?

The answer became frightfully obvious as the magical flames flowed out to rise upon the surface of the water.

Ziegler rushed back to the rear of the boat and tossed the last few barrels over the side in an effort to speed his pursuit, hoping speed would prevail over the magical flames. The boat seemed to fly as the wind picked up from behind. The bow lifted out of the water and the ride grew very choppy as the vessel started to skip across the surface of the water. Ziegler ducked down and held on as he approached the magical fire. The flames swirled and danced around the boat, some bending down to the deck and others pushed aside by the wind around the boat.

He managed to sail through with only a few patches of the boat lighting on fire, but thankfully the sail was intact. That was all that mattered to Ziegler. He could see from the troll's disappointed face that he had not expected Ziegler to cross through the flames with the boat. The distance between them was closing quickly now. The troll pointed his staff at the boat and attacked the hull with flames, but it didn't matter now. In a matter of seconds the two boats would collide.

Ziegler reached down and took one of the troll swords and then he turned and ran to the bow. Flames grew around him, turning the hull into a sizzling mess of flames and gray smoke as the water below fought with the magical flames to keep the boat from being destroyed. Ziegler made it to the front rail just as his boat launched upward and came down atop the aft section of the vessel the large troll was on.

Ziegler leapt into the air, flying unharmed through the tops of orange and red flames that stretched up to swipe at him.

An unfortunate troll was steering the other vessel when Ziegler's boat came down on top of him, crushing him and smothering him in fire. Ziegler touched down two seconds after the boats collided, avoiding the jarring impact altogether and using his forward momentum to somersault toward two other troll warriors. He sliced a leg off at the knee on his left and came up with his dagger to the heart of the troll on his right. Ziegler head-butted the dead troll to aid in removing his dagger and then he wheeled around on the injured troll.

A new leg was beginning to bud on the end of the severed stump, but Ziegler was not about to wait until the fight was fair. He shoved the blade of the sword through the troll's chest and then jammed the tip of his dagger through the top of the troll's skull in a hammer-strike.

Ziegler turned to see the hulking troll snarling at him.

"You remember me, don't you?" Ziegler spat. "You attacked my home. You killed my wife."

The troll breathed heavily and then formed a single word in Common Tongue. "Pig," he snarled.

Ziegler shook his head. "She was an angel!" he roared. The troll lifted his staff to attack, but Ziegler closed the distance between them and kicked the top of the staff out to the side. Yellow and white flames shot out to the left, narrowly missing Ziegler. He lashed out with his dagger and cut off three of the troll's fingers. The troll hollered and dropped the staff on the deck.

A savage, massive, green fist came in hard and slammed into Ziegler's chest. Ziegler flew backward three feet and slammed into the base of the mast. The troll bent down, his fingers already growing back, and grabbed the staff once more.

Captain Ziegler snarled and charged in again. He leapt onto the troll's back, wrapping his left arm around the monster's neck and raising his right hand to strike with his dagger. The troll, however, was quick enough to reach up and grab Ziegler's right hand before it came down, stopping the attack before the knife could ever reach his head.

The troll then used his one free hand to angle the staff at Ziegler.

The captain saw the attack coming and released his choke hold to grab the shaft of the staff with his left hand while still trying to drive his dagger downward with his right. The two then struggled for dominance over the staff as flames spewed out around them. The boat caught fire and soon they were two forms battling inside a ring of flame and smoke as the boat began to tip and lurch in the water.

Ziegler struck out with a kick to the troll's groin. The troll's knees slackened, but it did not lose its grip on the staff. Its other hand squeezed tightly around Ziegler's wrist until the bones crunched and then cracked as the joint was broken. Ziegler cried out in pain, and dropped the dagger.

The troll released Ziegler's injured wrist and used the now free hand to pummel the man's ribs and stomach with heavy punches. Ziegler took the hits and struggled with the staff. He knew he had to get the weapon away from the troll, and somehow manage to kill the beast before it jumped into the lake and swam away. Ziegler's anger fueled his muscles and he pushed with all of his might, driving the troll back three steps until the flames licked at the back of the troll's legs and he began to suffer burns that charred his green skin.

The troll hollered wildly and redoubled his efforts to push Ziegler backward.

Ziegler had hoped for exactly that response. Holding the staff with his left hand, he dropped down and swung under the troll as the hulking creature drove forward. Now off balance, it was a simple matter to kick the troll into the flames that had been behind Ziegler. His boot connected with the troll's rump and the beast flailed and stumbled into the fire face-first. Ziegler slowly rose to his knees, huffing and puffing as he watched the fire roil around the troll, but then to his horror the troll jumped up and turned around once more.

The nasty, jagged teeth were bared in a wicked smile and the troll came rushing toward Ziegler once more.

Ziegler rolled to his left, scooped up the dagger in his left hand, and then spun around to drive the blade deep into the troll's chest. The heat of the flames enveloped Ziegler and the fire forced him to close his eyes, but he felt the dagger pierce the creature's skin and slip between the ribs. A moment later the heat faded away and the troll fell over backward.

Ziegler stood over the dead beast and spat upon him. Then he casually reached up and slapped the budding fires on his shirt until they died.

"May the fires of Hammenfein torment you for the rest of eternity," Ziegler said.

The boat then lurched backward and spilled him and the troll's corpse into the lake. A great hissing sound went up all around him as the flames fought against the cool waters. Smoke and steam erupted everywhere, and then there was a heavy force slamming into his back and head. He gasped for air, but felt only cold water enter his mouth and throat as the weight on his back drove him down into the depths of the lake.

# CHAPTER 9

Jonathan helped tie down the boat when they reached the northern shore of the lake. He and Jason dragged a large log over to the bank as an anchor point, though Jonathan was doubtful they would ever use the boat again. Still, Ziegler assured him that it was better to conserve supplies than waste them, for one never knew what the future might bring.

The captain had been ghostly quiet after Moose had fished him from the water. He had been unresponsive at first, but Bull's technique of giving breaths and compressions had brought the captain back to consciousness within just four rounds. Other than complaining about a sore chest and a broken wrist, the captain said he was feeling better than he had in years. Luckily, Bull was able to construct a solid splint for Ziegler the night before. That, at least protected the injury, but Jonathan knew it would do little to dampen the pain until it was entirely healed. The captain's battle with the last trolls had been a terrible thing to watch.

Each time Jonathan looked out to the gently tossing waves, he still saw the flaming boat capsizing with Ziegler on it, dumping him down into the lake and then slamming on top of him. It was a miracle that he had survived - a testament to just how tough Captain Ziegler was.

When Jonathan finished with the boat, he joined with the others in making camp for the night. The sun had dropped fully behind the horizon only half an hour after Ziegler's fight with the troll on the boat. Even had the sun still been up when they reached the shore, it seemed none of them were in the mood for continuing the journey without a break. They all sat silently, gazing at the fire and eating their meager meals before breaking off for sleep. Moose insisted he take the first watch, citing Ziegler's bad wrist as a good reason for the change in traditional roles. When Ziegler agreed without an argument, Jonathan knew that the day had been a very rough one for him as well.

When the morning sun broke upon the camp, Jonathan stood and looked to the north. It was a strange sight to see, for the Nahktun Mountain Range came right up to the eastern shore of the lake here. The brown and rugged peaks jabbed at the sky with their rocky spires and threatening cliffs. This mountain range, Jonathan knew, marked the boundary between two very different worlds. On the west side, one would find the kingdoms of men and elves, but on the eastern side of the range one would discover a terrible valley shrouded in eternal darkness. It was the place where the first great wars had taken place. A realm where the very gods who had created Terramyr had clashed and swept up the mortal armies along with them. So many had perished, and so much blood had been spilt that the land itself was cursed now, a place where only nightmares could survive.

Bull must have seen Jonathan staring at the mountains, for he came up and placed a hand on the young man's shoulder. "It's said that one can find the gateway to Hammenfein beyond these mountains."

Jonathan nodded. "I have no desire to delve into the four levels of hell," he said honestly. "It gives me the chills just looking at this side of the mountains."

Bull shook his head. "Don't worry your pretty little head about it. The range is hundreds of miles wide, and it stretches from the southernmost shore to the northern edge of the continent. The mountains will keep the evil back. Besides, most of them can't abide the sunlight. Their nightshroud, or whatever you call those thick clouds that blot out the sun from their lands, stop where the eastern edge of the mountains begin. We're safe enough here."

Jason stepped up on the other side and agreed with Jonathan. "Safe or not, I'll be happy when we put this area behind us."

Jonathan nodded.

Bull shrugged. "I, for one, am happy to be out of the forest. It will be nice to be able to see dangers from afar."

Jonathan looked to the north and nodded his agreement. Tanglewood Forest still stretched to the north from here, but they were outside its eastern edge. The rest of the way to Inghali they would be traversing through valleys of grassland.

Ziegler was calling for them to move out just a few minutes later. If Jonathan had had any hope of a slower pace given Ziegler's injuries, he was sorely mistaken. Not more than ten minutes from the shore, the captain set a grueling pace that he said was a jog. To Jonathan it was definitely a run. His feet thumped and plodded along the grass. Fortunately, the going was much easier than before. Aside from a few hares and several herds of deer, the party saw no other creatures along the way, though they did enjoy several fine meals of roast venison thanks to Moose's expert hunting and trapping skills.

When they arrived at Inghali, Jonathan was surprised to see a sprawling city made almost entirely of tents. With the exception of a large, round building in the center of the settlement, there wasn't a single structure that couldn't be torn down and packed away for a nomadic trip. There were horses and oxen all throughout the city, as well as several chickens and geese.

Jonathan's first glimpse of a Pes'Tai, or sand elf as they were called in the Common Tongue, was a unique delight. It was a beautiful she-elf, slender and well-toned. She wore a burgundy silk vest without sleeves. A golden design of flower petals was embroidered along the left side of the vest. Her long, black silk trousers flapped gently in the wind as she walked. Upon her right hand she wore a very thick glove of leather, upon which sat a hawk with blinders over its eyes.

She looked at Jonathan and winked, smiling at him before turning to walk away toward some other point in the city. Jonathan couldn't help but notice how her clothes hugged her curves as she walked. He watched her disappear around a large tent that sprawled out across several hundred square feet, and then turned his attention back to his group. At that moment, he caught a hint of the glare Miranda was shooting his direction before she saw him catch her and turned away.

He drew his brow in close, wondering why she should care if he was impressed with another woman. After all, she was betrothed to Ruben.

Still, as he looked at her, he couldn't help but remember how he had felt with her hand in his that one time back in the Warrens.

*Stop!* Jonathan told himself. He shook the image from his head and took in a breath. It was pointless to think about - a childish fantasy even. He needed to concentrate on the task at hand. He was here to help find a friend's father, and rescue him. He repeated the word "friend" in his mind a few times to beat it into his brain. Unfortunately, in the process he had missed the fact that the group had stopped and Ziegler was giving instructions.

He walked right into Moose's back.

"Jonathan, get your head out of the clouds. What's wrong with you?" Ziegler chided.

Jonathan shrugged and smiled sheepishly, but he couldn't think of anything to say.

"As I was saying, we need to be alert here. Pes'Tai like to fight, and they don't particularly like outsiders wandering through their city. We are here to find Larkyn, and then be on our way."

Jonathan, trying to be helpful to make up for his blunder moments ago, pointed to the large building in the center of the city. "How about there? It's the only permanent structure here." There hadn't been much in the travel guide about Inghali. It was listed only as a place to avoid if possible, though it didn't say why. The book had noted that the Inghali kept amazing horses capable of running farther and faster than most other species known upon the face of Terramyr, but there was only one note regarding the city itself that Jonathan could put to use. The scholar had made a note guessing that the singular permanent structure in the otherwise temporary city made of tents was a governmental structure, a meeting place of sorts for the nomadic clans to gather in and conduct business.

Unfortunately, the scholar had been wrong when he made that guess.

Ziegler shook his head and didn't even bother turning around to look at the building. "That's the Inghali arena. That is the last place we need to go." Ziegler tipped his head forward and glared at Jonathan just long enough that the young boy understood he was to keep quiet. "Now, our sources tell us he came here to hire mercenaries."

Ruben nodded and commented, "That fits with the disciplinary record as well. He has been reprimanded in the past for using mercenaries as house guards. He has also used them to enforce house rules." Ruben held up the onyx stone as if to show the source of his information.

"What's so bad about that?" Bull asked. "I wouldn't mind having a few mercs around to keep my boy in line at times." Bull snorted at the joke, but he was the only one laughing, so he clammed up and gave a half-hearted one-finger salute with his index finger.

"There were reports of the mercenaries assaulting civilians," Ruben said. "That is what's wrong with it."

"Right," Ziegler said. "And now that we know he is behind these kidnappings, I am betting he is using them for far more than just enforcing proper etiquette at the dinner table."

"There was also a mention of necromancy," Ruben said, hoisting up the onyx sphere once more. "The three elves couldn't prove the allegation, so that one was thrown out, but it still raises a concern for us."

"So, Ruben, where do we go if we want to hire mercenaries?" Ziegler asked. "That's where we'll find the fetcher. Then, we can ask him all the questions we want."

"Unless he has an army," Ruben pointed out.

Ziegler nodded his head to the side and shrugged. "Yeah, I suppose that might delay things a bit. So, if there is no army, then we interrogate him right here. If there is an army, we follow them to wherever they are going and try to figure out whether he knows where Raven is."

"Right, and then we kill him anyway," Bull put in, slamming a fist into his left palm for emphasis. "We can't let him get away with what he had done in Vizendel."

Ziegler nodded. "Patience, Bull. We'll strike when the timing is right."

"Um, guys," Jonathan said as he looked up and saw several groups of heavily armed elves on horseback approaching. "We might be in trouble."

They all looked up and saw not just one group, but five approaching from several directions at once.

"This is not good," Ruben said.

"Easy boys," Ziegler said. "I'm sure we can talk them down."

The groups came in close and then stopped in such a way that Jonathan and the others were pretty well hemmed in. Jonathan studied each group and saw that despite the similarities between them all, each group had particular characteristics that set them apart from the others. One group was dressed in fine silks with golden beads sewn into their right sleeves, a second was dressed in leather and suede, with large scarves wrapped neatly below their chins and strange, pointed leather helmets with horse hair protruding from the top. The third group had not a bow or sword among them. Instead, they each carried large halberds with long, curved blades. These elves each had a symbol of a dragon sewn into their shirts over their left breasts. The fourth group was like the first, dressed in fine silks of many colors, but instead of gold beads they had tattoos on their faces, something Jonathan would have never expected from elves. The last group were all dressed in black trousers and burgundy vests. Several of them carried hawks upon their right arms and had bows slung over their shoulders.

Jonathan immediately recognized the woman in the front of the group. She looked down upon him and smiled again. Despite himself, Jonathan smiled back at her.

"These are five of the most powerful houses in the Pes'Tai nation," Ruben said in a gasp. "Their decision here will determine our fate."

Ziegler inched closer to Ruben. "Which one is the most powerful?"

"What?" Ruben asked breathlessly.

"Which group should I address first?" Ziegler asked. "If I tell them we are on holiday…"

The woman smiling at Jonathan pointed at him and said something. The group froze.

Jonathan blushed and smiled wider. "Sorry, I don't speak your language," he said.

The woman smiled at him and nodded.

From the group on the left, one of the elves pointed at Miranda and said something.

Then one of the elves with the facial tattoos pointed to Moose and said something else.

"I don't like this," Bull said. "Feels wrong."

All at once, the tension broke and there was a flurry of commotion. A thick, blueish-green bubble appeared around each of them and the elves all converged on them. Jonathan tried to reach for his bow, but the bubble slowed his movements and he hardly did more than lift his right hand three inches before a pair of elves were on him. He could hear muffled shouts and screams. A strange odor filled the bubble he was trapped inside of and then he lost consciousness.

Jonathan woke several hours later, lying upon a long pillow and covered with a red blanket made of silk. He blinked his bleary eyes. He looked up and realized he was inside a tent. Glancing left, he saw a curtain of canvas just two feet away, forming an interior wall of sorts. He turned over and was surprised to see the golden-haired she-elf sitting upon a square pillow on the dirt. She was watching him intently with her green eyes, still smiling at him. The hawk was now resting upon a wooden perch off to the side, tilting its head down at Jonathan warily and staring at him with its golden eyes.

"What happened?" Jonathan asked. Gathering his wits he threw the blanket off from him and noticed that he was now in different clothes. Someone had dressed him in black trousers like those of the young elf, except his had a red silk stripe running down the side of his leg. He looked to his chest and saw that he was wearing a white vest that fastened with leather strips fastened through a series of silver eyelets up the middle. He looked back to the elf. "Where are my clothes? Who dressed me?"

"You should not address me," the elf said in a pleasantly melodic voice.

"What?" Jonathan asked.

Before he knew what was happening, the flap behind him was pulled aside and another elf, this one a male, strode toward him and slapped a thin piece of wood over his bare forearm.

"OW!" Jonathan yelled as he crawled back from the elf with the wooden switch.

"A slave should learn his place," the she-elf said.

Jonathan turned to regard her with wide eyes. "Slave?" he echoed.

The switch came down again on his arm, this time crossing over the first welt. "OW!" Jonathan shouted. He was not about to take this lying down. He jumped up to his feet and drove a powerful uppercut into the elf's chin, knocking his head back. The elf recovered quickly and raised his arm to hit Jonathan again with the switch, but Jonathan ducked low and kicked out to sweep the elf's feet. The elf jumped nimbly in the air and then came in with a kick of his own. Jonathan leapt to the side and grabbed a handful of dirt before coming back to his feet. He concealed the dirt in his left fist, waiting for the elf to approach him again.

The elf raised the wooden switch and sprinted toward him without saying a word. Jonathan reacted fast, tossing the sand with his left hand. The cloud of dirt struck the elf's eyes and Jonathan moved in to the side, pummeling the elf in the left side of the face twice before yanking the switch from his hand and whacking him across the neck and back with it. The blinded elf shrieked and yelped, furiously rubbing his eyes and trying to get away from Jonathan.

A kick to the stomach sent the elf to the ground and Jonathan struck him once more with the switch for good measure. A quick glance ensured the female elf was still sitting quietly where she had been moments ago, and then Jonathan bolted out for the opening. He threw the flap open and took one step outside, just catching a taste of freedom, before another elf appeared before him. Before Jonathan could react, the elf knife-handed the side of his neck, kicked in his knee, and then elbowed him in the throat. The poor boy was on the ground, coughing and sputtering in less than a second.

A pair of hands wrapped around his arms and dragged him back into the tent, dropping him on the pillow he had woken upon.

"You have spirit," the she elf said. "I knew I liked you."

Jonathan struggled to push himself up from the ground and glared at her. "When I can breathe again, I will kill you."

The elf giggled and held a hand to her mouth. "Come now, let's not confuse courage with idiocy. I am Elantra, the mistress of house Eofuld. I command magic that you could not possibly comprehend. You may have earned your spot as master slave, but you will never pose a threat to me."

"Master slave?" Jonathan echoed.

Elantra nodded and pointed to the cowering elf who was still rubbing his eyes. Only then did Jonathan notice that the elf was dressed in the same clothes as he was. He looked up to the two who had carried him inside, and saw they were wearing clothes much like Elantra's.

"These are my younger brothers, Herin and Desin. They also serve as my bodyguards." Elantra rose to her feet and pointed to the other slave. "Miran has served well as my master slave for more than thirty years. It shall be exciting to see what a new master slave shall bring to my servants. Perhaps you can infuse them with your vigor, and help them serve more fervently." Elantra smiled and stepped closer to him.

Herin and Desin reached down and pulled Jonathan up to a standing position.

"As master slave, you may address me, but it is still not wise to do it too often, for I have the power of life and death over you."

"I will run," Jonathan promised. "First chance I get, I will run and there is nothing you can do about it."

Elantra turned her head and narrowed her green eyes on him. "Because you are human, I will overlook the outburst, for now. I will give you a demonstration, and then you will understand."

Jonathan grit his teeth.

The two brothers released their grips and backed away from him.

"Go on, try to run," Elantra said. She gestured toward the opening with his right hand and smiled.

Jonathan figured it was a trap of some sort, so he remained in place.

"Don't want to obey? Pity. So then I will demonstrate my power in another way."

Elantra placed her hands upon her shapely hips and narrowed her eyes on him. "Slave, fetch me my wine."

Jonathan's feet turned and moved without him trying to move. He grunted and protested, but his body would not listen to him. It was obeying her command. He walked over to a slender table that had been behind the flap before the other slave had opened it, and he found a decanter of wine and also a silver goblet. He brought them both to Elantra and then bowed before her.

"Slave, fill it half way," Elantra said.

Jonathan did as instructed, despite the fact that in his mind he was trying to regain control of his body. He then offered the wine to Elantra. She smiled and took it from him, watching him with delighted eyes as she drank deeply from the goblet. When she finished, she handed him back the goblet and then tilted her head. Inside Jonathan's mind, the order to put the wine away was heard loud and clear even though Elantra's lips didn't move. His body was quick to do as it was told, and then he returned to stand before her.

Elantra laughed wickedly and then Jonathan felt he had control over his body back. He looked around and brought his hands up to his face.

"You see?" Elantra said. "There is nothing you can do except I allow it."

Jonathan looked over to the other slave and then back to Elantra.

"You are wondering about him?" Elantra asked. "He will still be my slave, but you will be in charge now. It is our custom, when a new slave is captured he may challenge the master slave. If successful, then the challenger becomes the master slave, and receives along with that responsibility all the pleasures and privileges that entails."

"What pleasures does a slave have?" Jonathan asked before his mind could stop his tongue. He closed his eyes as soon as the words left his mouth, but there was no taking them back now. He didn't dare open his eyes until he heard Elantra laughing.

"As master slave, you shall accompany me to all festivals. Other slaves must remain in the tent, tending to their stations. Also, you shall have some power to direct the tasks of other slaves, though you will need to learn the order of my house first. And finally, the master slave has a special responsibility to his mistress."

Jonathan frowned as she stepped in closer to him. "You see, it is customary for the master slave to help the mistress form new slaves. Only from the loins of the strongest slave shall new slaves be born. As you have defeated the previous master slave, you have proven that your offspring shall be superior to his. In this manner, I can ensure that my slaves are the strongest and best possible."

Jonathan balked at the idea. Was she insane? Was this perhaps some strange nightmare? Maybe he was still trapped in the magic bubble somewhere and needed to wake up. He reached down and pinched his arm, twisting a fold of skin just to be sure.

Elantra raised her brow at him. "Curious response," she said.

"I won't do that with you," Jonathan said.

Elantra scoffed and shook her head. "With me?" A laugh escaped her mouth and she had to cover her face with her left hand. "You really know nothing about our customs do you?" She shook her head and dismissed her brothers. "No, I am speaking of joining with the female slaves to form new slaves. I could not possibly be joined with a slave, elf or otherwise. Such a thing would be beneath my station." She turned and reached for her leather glove, which was several feet away upon a small box next to the wooden perch.

Jonathan felt his body compelled to retrieve the glove. He did so and then found himself gently sliding it over her arm and tying the laces.

"Come, we shall go to the arena. I suspect there will be exciting fights tonight."

Jonathan stood rigid as the hawk leapt onto Elantra's arm.

For the first time since he woke, he realized he had no idea where any of the others were.

Now that Elantra spoke of the arena, his heart was gripped with fear.

As they walked out from the tent and made their way toward the large building in the center of the city, Jonathan remained one pace behind and two paces to the left of Elantra. Where before he might have admired her form, now he loathed her with every fiber of his being. If not for the two brothers walking behind him, he might have tried to strangle her before her magic ended him, but he knew he wouldn't ever get close to her with them right there. He had no choice but to follow her for now.

"What do you call the big one in your group?" Elantra asked suddenly as they walked past a queue of elves waiting to enter the large, round building through a set of wide gates.

"Moose," Jonathan answered involuntarily.

"I shall place my bet on him, I think," Elantra said. "He will be fighting for House Brind. What is the bald man's name?"

"Bull," Jonathan said, wishing all the while he could hold his tongue.

"He is an angry one, but I think he will not defeat the one you call Moose."

"They are going to fight each other?" Jonathan asked.

Elantra shrugged. "Possibly. It depends on how the preliminary matches turn out. The one you call Bull was claimed by House Relyn. If the two house champions do equally well tonight, then it is possible they will need to fight each other."

"When you say fight, what do you mean?"

Elantra turned on him with a suspicious eye. "I mean they will fight to the death. Once every lunar cycle, the five great houses meet and send their champions in to fight for title and glory."

"What of Ziegler and the others?" Jonathan asked. "Where are they?"

Elantra shrugged. "I don't deal with wizards. I don't recall who took the wizard and the young female mage. The one with the broken hand was taken as a slave, but he will not be put in the arena."

Jonathan suddenly had a terrifying thought. Was Jason also destined for the arena? Would he have to fight Bull or Moose?

"Then there is the one that looks like you but has darker hair."

"Jason," Jonathan said without being compelled. "He is my brother."

Elantra turned and studied him for a moment. She took in a slight breath and then shook her head. "I believe he was taken slave by House Hendir. I can't be sure, of course, but I think that is the family that ended up with him."

"Will he also fight?" Elantra shook her head and Jonathan nearly doubled over as he sighed with relief. "Where is he then?"

Elantra frowned. "House Hendir is not known for its hospitality. I like you, so I won't lie to you. Your brother will be set to work in the mines owned by House Hendir. Most slaves don't survive such work for more than a year or two. There is great wealth to be gained for Hendir, but the mines are cursed with a toxic gas that builds up in the miners' bodies until they die."

"Can you buy him then?" Jonathan asked. "I will do anything, I will give you anything you desire."

Elantra's face turned cold and she shook her head. "Such questions are not appropriate. I already own you and everything you possess. To insinuate otherwise is to shame yourself before your mistress."

Jonathan felt a strange tingling come over his face and his mouth closed, unable to open and utter the words he was yearning to speak.

He followed Elantra through an ornate door made of brass, down a narrow corridor that led to stone steps, and up to a large balcony overlooking a circular pit with a dirt floor. Jonathan could see blood stains in the dirt, as well as five different tunnels sealed with a metal portcullis. For now, the arena was empty, but he doubted it would remain peaceful for long. Crowds were gathering in the lower levels, some standing and some sitting. Several balconies, each similar to the one he was in, were also beginning to fill on the upper levels as well. Try as he might, he didn't see Miranda, Ziegler, his brother, or anyone else from his group.

"Sit," Elantra said.

Jonathan's body moved to sit in a high-backed wooden chair beside her that was situated close to the rail and raised up enough that he could see the entire arena.

"Your friends have been chosen for a great honor tonight," Elantra said. "If they fight well, they will win much glory."

Had his lips been able to part, he would have told her that he wanted nothing to do with the arena, much less to see his friends try to kill each other.

*****

Moose sat in a strange, dark cell. His arms and legs were tingling, but not quite asleep. He turned his head to the side, stretching the stiff muscles and exhaling the tension. He turned his head to the right, and there he saw a tall elf with a tattoo stretching across his left cheek and down his neck.

"What do you want with me?" Moose asked in his deep voice.

The elf smiled.

"You are here to fight."

Moose shook his head and spat on the floor.

"Oh, you will fight, my giant friend. If you refuse, then I will force you."

Moose patted his sides, looking for his cigars. If he had found one of them he would have happily lit up in front of the elf and then drowned the weakling in a thick cloud of smoke.

"If you don't decide to fight on your own, then I can force you."

"Force me?" Moose echoed.

The elf nodded. "Each elder of the five great houses is imbued with a special kind of magic. We can compel our slaves to obey us."

"I am not your…" the words caught in Moose's throat and his mouth shut involuntarily. His legs pressed into the floor and he stood up straight, arms at his sides and head turned to face the wall in front of him.

"As I was saying, I can compel your obedience. I do, however, prefer to see you fight of your own accord." The magic hold on Moose left him, and the large man was free to control himself once more. He turned to face the elf, who smiled back at him. "You have been given a great honor. You have been chosen as the champion of our house. Do not let us down."

"You intend for me to fight other men?" Moose asked. "Or am I to fight elves?"

The elf shook his head. "There is only one other man in the arena tonight. The others are all Kratii, or lizard men as you might call them. This shall be a fun night." The elf smiled and pointed to the opposite wall. "Fight well."

Moose turned and saw the stone wall of his cell swing open, leading to a long, upward sloping tunnel. When he hesitated, he felt his legs move him toward the tunnel. He surveyed the scratch marks and blood stains in the stone and shook his head. This was not how he had expected his visit to Inghali to end.

As he walked to the metal gate at the end of the tunnel, a second portcullis closed a few feet behind him, ensuring he wouldn't flee back toward his cell. He looked around then, realizing that he had no weapons.

Then, a tall elf riding upon a large animal that looked like a crab emerged and began cantering around the edge of the arena floor. From his strange saddle he waved at the crowd in the stands as they cheered. When the crab took him to the center of the ring, the elf threw down a spear, a sword, and an axe. Then he tapped the crab and it turned to remove him from the arena. Moose watched as the gate closed off the tunnel the elf had used and the elves in the stand began to chant something in their language.

The portcullis in front of him opened then and the crowd broke into frantic cheering and shouts.

Across the arena, Moose could see another form enter from a tunnel exactly like the one he stood in.

It walked on two legs, but was most definitely not human. Its head was adorned with thick spikes, and it had a long snout for a mouth. A massive, powerful tail stuck out from the creature's back and his two large feet were tipped with claws that Moose could see even from such a distance. The green skin on the Kratii warrior shimmered in the waning light of the sun. It was running for the weapons.

"Enter the arena, or I shall make you," the elf said from behind.

Moose turned to see that the elf had followed him up the tunnel, and was standing just behind the portcullis.

The seven foot tall human nodded and reluctantly entered the arena.

Gasps and cheers rippled through the crowd upon seeing him. Even the Kratii stopped to look at him. It was obvious most of them had not expected him. Moose glanced around and noticed that there were four pillars in the arena along the outside rim. He followed them up with his eyes to see that they held up large beams that in turn supported balconies with many elves upon them.

He then returned his eyes to the lizard man, who was now picking up a spear and trying to size up Moose. Moose walked confidently into the arena, watching the Kratii warrior carefully. The lizard hissed and snarled, baring sharp teeth inside its snout and blinking translucent lids across its eyes.

Moose broke into a jog, heading directly for the lizard. The elves in the stands began chanting in unison. The lizard warrior waited, and then it whirled around full circle and launched the spear. Moose had expected that. He caught the spear, then sprinted in toward the Kratii. By the time the lizard man bent down to scoop up the sword and then had straightened up, Moose swung the spear and broke it over the Kratii's head. The lizard went down and a gash oozed blood. Moose then kicked the sword away from the lizard and turned to walk away.

The crowd began to boo and jeer. They pointed at the Kratii, but Moose saw no honor in killing the poor creature. In all honesty, it hadn't been a fair fight. Then, despite his feelings, his body turned around and he walked back to pick up the axe.

The crowd cheered once more, dancing around in the stands and shouting ecstatically.

Moose glanced around as best he could, but he couldn't see the source of the magic controlling him. He moved toward the Kratii, raised the axe with one hand, and then brought it down upon the helpless creature's neck.

The audience roared with cheers and began chanting a word he did not understand.

The magic left his body and he threw the axe in disgust. Then, another portcullis opened and two more Kratii emerged. These Kratii were already armed. One held a long trident, and the other wielded a pair of scimitars. They glanced to each other and then emitted strange clicking noises before they fanned out to advance on Moose.

"Khefir curse you all," Moose swore. He turned to see the portcullis he had emerged from close. The elf with the tattooed face stood behind it with his arms folded across his chest. It was now painfully obvious to Moose that he could either fight his way, or the elf would control his every move. If he had any hope of surviving long enough to figure out a plan to escape, he would have to please the sadistic elf. "By my father's house I shall kill you for this." Moose then bent down to pick up the axe.

The crowd cheered wildly.

Moose ran toward the lizard with the two scimitars, figuring that warrior would not be throwing either of his weapons. The lizard grinned and sprinted in to match Moose's speed. He raised one scimitar high and the other he held out to the side. Moose raised his weapon over his shoulder as if preparing to come in with a chop, but that was not his plan. He was more than two feet taller than this lizard man, and that gave him several advantages, one of them being much longer legs.

He could see the other lizard rounded his run to flank him, and that is exactly what Moose had expected. His time in the Murkle Quags had taught him well, and tonight he would show these cursed sand elves exactly who they had brought into their midst. He ran full tilt, staring directly into the scimitar wielding lizard's eyes. Then, just before they reached each other, Moose led with a powerful front kick that landed on the lizard's chest before it knew how to react. The muscle and soft tissue pressed inward under the force of Moose's foot, and then the sternum broke inward and the lizard's chest collapsed as it flew backward through the air. Before it had even landed, Moose wheeled around on the trident wielder. He launched his axe, which spun gracefully end over end until it decapitated the second Kratii. The lizard had been running so fast that the headless body finished two more paces and then tumbled down to slide closer to Moose.

The giant man reached down, grabbed the trident, and then walked over to the first lizard, who was gasping for breath and raking the dirt with its claws. Moose whispered an apology and then drove the trident down into the lizard's chest, stopping its heart.

The crowd roared even louder, if that were possible, at the victory.

Moose turned and glowered at the elf with the tattoo. "What else?" he asked over the din of the arena.

The elf pointed behind him. Moose turned and saw another portcullis open. This time there was a strange, furless beast that emerged. Its skin was leathery and cracked. Its chest was wider than a horse's, and its legs were thicker than a bull's. It wore a leather harness and attached to that was a sort of chariot. Atop the chariot was a Kratii with a bow.

Moose launched the trident with all the strength he possessed. It flew straight and true, hitting its mark before the Kratii had fully emerged from the tunnel. The lizard was struck so hard that it flew back and slammed against the closed portcullis in its tunnel. The crowd roared with delight as the strange beast galloped around the outer edge of the arena. At first, Moose thought perhaps the animal was scared by the death of its rider, but he soon realized it was circling around to attack him. Its four powerful legs tore the dirt apart as it raced toward him, cutting a corner so sharp that the chariot broke free from the harness and allowed the beast to run even faster. Its stunted snout opened to reveal canine-like fangs and Moose knew for sure that this challenge was only half over.

He waited for the animal to lunge, and then he stepped to his right. As the animal sailed by, Moose punched with his right hand. He felt two of the animal's ribs crack and the strange beast snarled before it landed and then turned on him. Moose stepped to his left this time as the beast came up on its hind legs to swipe at him with deadly claws on its front paws. Moose reached up and grabbed it just behind the paws and held the beast up on its hind legs. It snapped with its jaws, but never came close to biting Moose. The beast was strong, stronger than anything Moose had ever fought before. It bore down on him with its weight, trying to crush him to the ground and thereby gain the advantage. Moose growled and grunted with effort, pushing the front legs up and keeping the beast off balance. He launched out with a kick, but the beast's body was angled away from him just enough that he missed.

The beast roared, slinging thick, foamy slobber out of its mouth as it watched Moose through angry, hungry eyes. Moose knew he couldn't keep the beast up for ever. They each jerked to this side and that, trying to catch the other off balance. The continued to dance their deadly routine as they crossed over one of the dead Kratii. Moose smiled then.

He had a plan.

He jerked the beast to the right, it countered to the left. He pushed the beast forward, and it pushed him back. He repeated this three more times until he had positioned himself right where he needed to be. The blood-soaked axe was now under his right foot. He slipped his toe under the handle, just below the head of the axe, and then kicked it up and into the air to the right. He jerked the beast right, but not with his full power, just enough to get it to pull left. As soon as it moved left, Moose let go and punched the beast for good measure, then he turned and went to catch the axe before it fell.

Everything turned silent. Time slowed. The axe fell only slightly as Moose went for it. Every movement seemed to take an eternity to complete, that is, until he wrapped his hand around the shaft, and then everything sped up. Moose whirled around with all of his might.

The axe blade caught the beast as it lunged for him, slipping into the beast's open maw and hacking the head in half, with the lower jaw hanging limp from the bloody mess of bone and flesh, while the top half of the head spun away to land in the dirt.

The beast's body slammed into Moose and dropped him to the ground, but he was not hurt. He let go of the axe and pushed the monster off of him and then rose to his feet amidst thunderous applause.

The elf with the tattoo on his face then entered the arena and gestured for Moose to join him.

Moose obeyed his new master, not willing to see what kind of magical control the elf might be capable of if publically humiliated by disobedience. When he arrived, he found the elf smiling at him.

"I have never seen anyone slay a sand hound like that before," he said. "Usually they try to use a bow and keep their distance." The elf turned and motioned for Moose to follow him back down the tunnel.

Moose remained silent as they walked back toward the cell he had woken up in before.

"In any case, you have qualified for the final round, so you have pleased me."

"What is the final round?" Moose asked.

"All champions must go through the same trials you just faced. Those house champions successful in the preliminary round go to the final round, where they must fight all other champions simultaneously. The last champion alive wins the tournament."

Moose grunted. "Then I will be free?"

"Free?" the elf repeated as he turned around to look at Moose. His cold blue eyes looked the giant warrior up and down incredulously and then he shook his head. "No, then we take you into battle, and you help us fight the Kratii."

"If you can enslave enough Kratii for your arena, why would you still be doing battle with them?"

The elf nodded knowingly. "We have the upper hand in battle, of course, but the Kratii can procreate much faster than we can. Indeed, they are like bugs. Quash a colony and four more take its place. We compete for the same lands, and they are a scourge, a blight, upon the face of Terramyr."

"Funny, I don't see the Kratii enslaving you for sport."

A terribly heavy force fell upon Moose then and crushed him down to his knees. His very bones felt as though they were bending, on the verge of snapping.

"I can end your life, slave. It would be wise for you to remember that."

Moose grunted, and then the force was lifted from him.

"You will win the championship tonight, and thus you will win for me the right to lead the five houses into battle against the Kratii for a time. Should you die in battle, then I will appoint a new champion in due time. Should you live, then there will be another tournament to see if you are still fit to be called champion." The elf sneered at Moose then and glanced to his massive arms. "I should hope to get at least a year or two out of you. In that time, I shall gain much honor for my house." The elf then pointed to the bench. "Go, rest until I return."

Moose sighed and walked to the bench. He sat down and the elf with the tattoo left the cell. The stone wall closed and the noise from the arena was fully blocked. The giant man sighed and leaned back against the cold, stone wall and closed his eyes. He had no idea the surprises the night would bring.

# CHAPTER 10

Moose sat alone in his cell for about an hour before the elf returned. He spent the time hoping that Ziegler would figure out a way to come and free him from the prison he was in. He couldn't understand how these elves had the kind of magic they did. It was unnatural, and Moose detested everything about it. He prayed to the gods, and to the demigods, hoping someone would hear him and send him help. When he finally heard footsteps coming toward his cell, he almost dared to hope that it was his captain, coming to free him at last. He looked up, hoping and wishing for it to be one of his comrades.

It wasn't.

The tattooed elf had returned, and this time he wore a large smile on his ugly, tattooed face and he gripped the bars of the cell excitedly. Moose stood up to hear what his instructions were.

"Only three other champions passed the preliminary round," he said with a wicked cackle. "That means you only have to kill three other champions."

Moose nodded resignedly.

The elf continued on, saying, "This time will be different. You will walk to the center of the arena, where there will be five swords resting upon the ground. You are to pick one up, and then salute all five houses. The head of each house will be watching from his or her respective balcony. Afterward, a trumpet will sound and you will walk back to the tunnel you emerged from, this helps the audience build up their anticipation, see? And then you will hear another trumpet. On the second trumpet, you will charge the center and slay the other champions. Do you understand?"

Moose nodded.

"And, don't even think about going soft on me again. I will waste no time in forcing your cooperation, do you understand?"

Moose nodded again. "Kill them all and bring honor to you, my master," he said. "I understand."

The elf sneered and nodded, then he gestured to the stone wall and it started to open.

"I will go up and take my seat now."

Moose walked up the tunnel and stood quietly at the final portcullis. The second portcullis dropped behind him and the one in front opened. He emerged to tumultuous applause. He glanced at the other champions. The one on his left was a brown colored Kratii. He was large, but still at least a foot shorter than Moose. The next champion was a green Kratii with a yellow torso. He was heavily muscled and had large fangs protruding from his snout. Still, Moose was confident he would be walking away from this fight with ease. Then he saw the fourth champion and his heart sank.

"Bull," he whispered aloud to himself.

No, he couldn't fight Bull. There had to be a way out of this. He couldn't let these deranged elves force him to slay Bull. At that moment, Bull saw him and he nodded sadly. It was obvious to Moose that Bull was in the same predicament.

Moose approached the center where the swords were arranged upon the dirt. The moon had risen and was shining in its full glory down into the arena. Bull smiled up at Moose.

"They got you too?" Bull asked.

Moose smiled. "They can control us, make us fight," Moose said.

"I know," Bull said. "I tried to fight the spell, but my body acts on its own if I don't fight."

The two Kratii clicked and clacked, but didn't speak.

They bent down to pick up their swords. Moose and Bull did the same.

"I won't fight you," Moose said.

"We won't have a choice," Bull replied. "There's nothing we can do."

The Kratii turned and saluted each house. Bull and Moose turned and did the same. As Moose went through the motions of saluting each house on the balcony, he formed a plan.

"Bull, listen," the houses each have one leader who can use the magic that controls us, right," he said quickly.

"Yeah, so?" Bull asked.

"So my house is sitting in the balcony above my tunnel, where is yours?"

Bull replied quickly, "The ones who control me are in the balcony adjacent to your tunnel."

Moose smiled. "Do me a favor then," Moose pleaded. "When the trumpets sound, fend these Kratii off of me while I try something."

"What are you going to do?" Bull asked as he saluted the last of the balconies.

The first trumpet blew.

"Just trust me," Moose said. "Do what you can."

"I will," Bull promised.

The four champions walked back to their starting positions. Moose eyed the pillar next to his tunnel. The balcony his master was seated in hung over the pillar, and over the tunnel. It was a long shot, but it was worth a try. He moved into position next to the pillar and turned around. He raised his arm and offered a final salute to Bull, who was standing on the opposite side of the arena.

The second trumpet sounded and the crowd rose to their feet and cheered.

Moose tossed his sword to the ground and turned to the pillar. He wrapped his massive arms around it, clasped his hands together and pulled against it with all of his might. He knew the Kratii would come for him first, he had his back to them and was an easy target. His only hope was that Bull would reach them before they got to him. A crack rippled through the pillar and the balcony above shifted dangerously. Moose grunted and pulled, the pressure building in his arms, back, and face.

"GAAHHH!" he yelled as the stone pillar cracked again and began to come along with him.

He then heard the deadly snarl of a Kratii warrior closing in on him. He glanced over his shoulder and saw the brown lizard sprinting for him. The thought crossed his mind to give up and reach for his sword, but he couldn't turn back now. He had to try and kill the masters who could control him and Bull.

A second later a sword spun through the air and sunk deep into the neck of the brown lizard and the warrior was knocked to the side before he could reach Moose.

"I'm here!" Bull gasped.

The next Kratii jumped toward him, but Moose turned away, trusting that his friend would shield him just a few seconds more. The stone above cracked again, and a huge hunk of marble fell to the ground beside Moose. A second later the bottom third of the pillar popped out and the balcony began to tumble down. Moose turned and pushed Bull out of the way as two balconies came crashing down fifty feet to land in a jumbled mess. Most of it fell into the arena, but there were large hunks of the balconies the crushed audience members in the lower level.

All at once there was a slight tingle in Moose's neck as a magical power grabbed hold of him. He turned and reached out with his bare hands to finish the second Kratii, who was standing stunned at the sight of the collapse. Then he turned to Bull.

Bull looked at him quizzically, and then turned his attention to the heap of rubble. Moose ran for Bull, but Bull outpaced him, running toward the tattooed elf, who was half buried in the rubble, but was stretching his arm out toward Moose. The bald-headed warrior drove his sword down into the elf's neck and through his chest, killing him and breaking the spell on Moose.

Moose instantly regained control of his body and the tingling in his neck vanished.

"Archers!" Bull called out and pointed up to the other balconies.

Moose nodded and ran for the pillar opposite the one he had just collapsed. An arrow struck him in the left shoulder, but he didn't stop. He kept his eyes on the next pillar, determined to bring the arena down on the sick elves that lorded over it. He managed to reach the pillar, but only after another arrow struck his right thigh. The burning pain ripped through his body, but he didn't let it stop him. He barreled into the pillar, cracking it just under the weight of his body. Then he grabbed it like the first and began pulling.

Another pain stabbed into his lower back, and two ripped into his buttocks. Another struck the outside of his right thigh and he could feel the strength leaving his body.

"Don't pull, push!" Bull shouted from behind.

"What?" Moose bellowed over his shoulder.

"PUSH THE PILLAR!" Bull shouted again.

Moose switched directions and pushed into the pillar with everything he had. A moment later, Bull lunged into the pillar as well, adding his strength to Moose's. Together, they brought the second pillar down. They tumbled to the ground as hunks of marble fell all around them. They looked up and saw the connecting beams, which had depended upon all four pillars to hold up the balconies, were now crumbling and cracking. The other two pillars toppled out into the arena and the two stalwart warriors shared a proud smile as the arena collapsed all around them.

Then, a great shadow was cast over them as a heap of rubble and stone fell on top of them. Some of the impact was absorbed by the piles already heaped up around them, but what force wasn't diverted by the stone nearby was enough to crush them. Moose felt his legs and right arm break under the weight. He cried out in pain, as did Bull. Moose's breathing became shallower, and his sight began to blur.

The last thing Moose remembered after the building had collapsed was the sound of Bull breathing out for the last time. Moose looked up to the moon through the tiniest of cracks between all of the rubble that had smothered him and he smiled at it.

"Take me home Nagé, for I have finished my fight," he said. His hand went to his side to find a cigar, but then he smiled when he remembered that the elves had taken those from him. He offered a half snort, and then his body went weak and he succumbed to his wounds.

*****

Jonathan felt a mix of delight and horror as he saw the first pillar crumble under Moose's strength.

Elantra rose from her seat, obviously stunned by the display of strength.

"We have a saying where I am from," Jonathan told Elantra. She turned to look at him with an open-mouthed stare. Jonathan smiled. "Never taunt a moose, for it will destroy your entire house, even if it breaks its back to do so."

Elantra snapped her fingers and Jonathan's mouth was forced shut.

Jonathan then saw Moose running toward his balcony, and he realized that Moose was not about to stop until the entire arena was demolished.

Elantra saw Jonathan's gaze and turned back around. She snapped her fingers and shouted to her brothers. "Shoot him!" Elantra's brothers retrieved bows from the back wall of the balcony and then ran forward to fire at Moose.

Jonathan tried to step forward, but the magical force held him in place.

Elantra moved in close and held up a finger. "You will watch your friend die!" she sneered.

Jonathan struggled against the spell. He brought up all of his rage, all of his anger, and all of his fear, and focused it just on moving his hand. He could see Elantra's eyes taunting him, but he tried anyway. Elantra's brothers pulled back their arrows and took aim. Jonathan started yelling within his mind. It grew louder and louder until his right hand formed into a fist and his arm launched up and punched Elantra in the face. She gasped and was knocked into her brothers just as they released their arrows. Jonathan seized upon the freedom. He grabbed the chair in front of him, picked it up, and rammed Elantra with the legs, pinning her and her brothers against the railing of the balcony. One of the legs caught Elantra in the throat, and Jonathan heard a strange crunching sound. The brothers then pushed back, knocking Jonathan to his rump, but Elantra was already finished, it seemed, for she was desperately gasping for air and none would come to her. She clutched at her throat, wide eyed and gaping like a fish upon land.

Her brothers turned to Jonathan and advanced on him.

Jonathan turned and saw the hawk fluttering its wings and squawking loudly with the blinders on. He kicked the perch out toward the brothers, buying himself just enough time to run out and down the narrow corridor. He heard loud shouting behind him and then a terrible, thunderous crack rippled through the hall. The building shook and screams of terror erupted all around. Jonathan tumbled down the last few steps and out the doorway just as the corridor collapsed behind him. Smoke and dust billowed out into a large cloud in all directions. Jonathan immediately thought of Bull and Moose. They were still inside. He watched helplessly as hunks of stone and wooden beams continued to rain down to the ground for several seconds.

There was nothing he could do for them, he knew, but he stood and watched anyway, hoping that they would walk out from the rubble, laughing and shouting as they always did. Just this once, he wanted to see Moose come out and light up one more cigar.

No matter how long he waited, Moose never did come out.

Worse than that, sand elves were running in from all around the city now. Amidst crying and wailing, Jonathan could clearly hear shouts of anger. He turned to see several fingers pointed at him, and he knew he had to run. He turned and sprinted up toward Elantra's tent.

Several elves gave chase.

Jonathan ran for all he was worth, letting out a scream in the process, but the elves were closing in fast. They wore the same clothes that Elantra had been wearing, and he knew they were from the same house. If they caught him, they would surely kill him for the death of their leader and her brothers.

Then, from a tent to the left, Ruben stepped out and aimed his hand over Jonathan's head. A triple blast of lightning shot out and blasted the pursuers. Ruben then waved frantically for Jonathan to join him in the large tent.

Jonathan smiled, relieved that he had at least found one other member of their group, but his jaw nearly hit the floor when he went inside and saw the truth of the matter. Ziegler, Jason, and Miranda were all inside the tent. There were four elves bound and gagged around the center pole, and twenty feet beyond that was a tall, slender elf snoring loudly beneath a plant that looked something like a petite tree.

"It's a kavelder tree," Ruben said, pointing to the miniature tree. "It is highly prized among druids for its medicinal properties."

Jonathan screwed up his face, dissatisfied with the lackluster explanation.

"It aids those who have trouble sleeping. The pollen in the small flowers is very potent. I was able to release it and then free myself from the restraints they had me in."

"Restraints?" Jonathan asked. "The one who took me could control me with her mind."

Ruben looked at him blankly. "I have never heard of that before," he said flatly. "Are you sure?"

Jonathan nodded. "Very sure."

Ruben shrugged. "Well, I drugged this one and his helpers. Then I scoured the city for the others. I brought them all back here. There are seven horses out back as well. Then I heard the commotion outside and we took cover, until I heard you scream that is.

"Thanks," Jonathan said.

"Don't mention it," Ruben replied with a smile. "Have you seen Moose and Bull?"

Jonathan's shoulders slumped and he nodded sullenly. "They were in the arena," he said.

Ruben blanched and glanced to Ziegler.

Captain Ziegler stood up and limped toward the tent flap. He poked his head out the flap. He grunted and then turned back to face the others. It's just us now then," he said.

"We can check the rubble," Jason offered.

Ziegler shook his head. "We can't fight off the rest of the city. We need to use the chaos to cover our escape."

Jonathan stepped forward and approached Ziegler. "If it helps, Moose and Bull died collapsing the arena on the sand elves. Moose pulled out a support column by himself, and then he and Bull collapsed another one. They were very brave."

"And they slew some very powerful, wicked clan leaders," Ruben offered.

Ziegler nodded and took in a breath. "Let's go. We ride for Gwyndoltai."

"What about Larkyn?" Jonathan asked. "He could still be here."

Jason shook his head. "No, the elves that took me, I was able to talk to them about Larkyn. They told me that he passed through earlier and hired some mercenaries, then left for Gwyndoltai."

"Why would they tell you that?" Jonathan asked.

Jason smiled and pulled out a dagger. "By the time Ruben found me, I had already freed myself. In the process, I interrogated the leader as best I could. Turns out, Larkyn was a regular through here. He was known by most of the elves."

"Enough talk!" Ziegler snapped. "Get on the horses and let's move!" The captain cut a hole in the back of the large canvas tent and then mounted the first horse and kicked it into a gallop.

Jonathan and the others hurried to catch up.

They rode furiously, dodging a few disoriented elves who were running amuck in the streets and shouting while they pointed to the collapsed arena building.

The party spurred their horses faster, maintaining a terribly grueling gallop as they left Inghali and then reentered Tanglewood Forest only twenty minutes later. At that point, they had to ride in a single-file caravan, but Ziegler still didn't ease the pace. Jonathan's horse grunted with nearly each breath and the hooves pounded the dirt relentlessly as a moist lather built up along the horse's neck and along the saddle.

If there was one thing that proved correct that had been written in Jonathan's travel guide about the Pes'Tai, it was that they had the most famous horses in all of Terramyr, renowned for maintaining top speeds for more than a day if necessary. That is what made them such a formidable force on the battlefield and open plains of Scale Valley, which stretched north from Tanglewood Forest's edge to the seas northward.

After another twenty minutes the horses seemed to hit their stride well and continued onward through the night. Ruben maintained several light orbs overhead, with a few of them a couple dozen yards in front of the group so they could ride easily. After the group had covered sixty miles of forest road, Ziegler slowed the pace to an easier trot.

No one dared ask if they would make camp and rest at all that night. Jonathan glanced over his shoulder, knowing that there could easily be a group of elves coming after them by now. They would need to push as far as the horses would go.

They rode until daybreak, and then they stopped near a cool stream to allow the horses to drink and nibble upon the grasses and clover near the brook. Jonathan only then realized that he no longer had his pack, nor his metal bow he had received from the elves as they crossed the waters to Telward. In fact, he was still wearing his slave garb. He furiously opened the laces on the front of his shirt and threw it on the ground in disgust.

"Pick it up," Ziegler said.

Jonathan wanted to tell him what the shirt signified, but he didn't dare disobey the man. His face was hard, jaw set and eyes colder than they had ever been before. Jonathan bent down and picked up the shirt, reluctantly putting it back over his torso.

He watched Ziegler as the large warrior spun around, scanning the trees and undergrowth carefully. Captain Ziegler then removed his shirt and draped it over a branch. Jonathan once again saw the numerous skull tattoos covering the warrior's arm and side. There was one tattoo for every lost Ghost who had died in the Murkle Quags under Ziegler's command, Jonathan knew. The newest one had been inked onto the captain's body after Bear had been killed during their battle with a gigantic troll in the Warrens. Captain Ziegler walked over to Ruben. "You said you had some of our backpacks, did you find mine?" he asked.

Ruben nodded, turned back to his horse and retrieved Ziegler's bag.

Ziegler sighed and took the pack into his hands. He flipped open the top flap and reached inside. He pulled out a strange contraption that looked like a needle with a sort of tube or canister above it. On the lower side there was some sort of lever or trigger mechanism as well. It took Jonathan a moment to realize what it was, but as soon as he figured it out, his eyes welled with tears.

Ziegler stood in the center of the group as they all watched him sanitize the needle with a match, and then he put two new tattoos onto his body. His skin welted, turning red and raising a bit as Ziegler worked, but the man did not make a sound. He continued until the work was complete, and then he put the device back into his backpack. He rubbed a thumb over the tattoos and closed his eyes as his head fell low.

"Brothers Moose and Bull, may you rest in peace here beside Bear. Gods willing, I shall see you both again soon." He raised his head and took his shirt down from the branch before marching over to his horse and saddling up. He pulled his shirt on and then looked at Jonathan and the rest of them. "Time to move," he said.

Jonathan's body moved slowly with exhaustion, but after watching Ziegler's strange ceremony to honor Bull and Moose, he was not about to complain. The rest of the group seemed to feel the same, for they all wore grim, determined expressions on their faces and went to obey their captain's orders.

They rode another hundred miles that day before they made camp and allowed the horses to rest.

Jason sat next to Jonathan while they shared some bread Ruben had managed to swipe from his captors and stuff into a bag. Miranda sat alone, leaning her back against an oak tree and staring further down the road toward Gwyndoltai. Ziegler disappeared into the forest, and Ruben sang a song as he held a water skin in his hand.

Hold now
Your journey here must end
Volganor is calling
Your fate the Gods attend

Hold now
Stand fast as legends born of yore
Mingar now is calling
From across Zintara's shore

Now you can sleep
Forget toils and battles apace
Now you can sleep
All your troubles now fade away
Safe in hallowed halls
You shall never again weep

Hold, can't you see
The gods have found you?
Enter their hallowed hall
Across the sea
A rainbow rises
Nagé has come to carry you home

Jonathan listened intently to the words as he finished his bread. He thought of Moose and Bull, and allowed his tears to flow over his face quietly. Ruben repeated the song three times, and each time Jonathan felt his sorrows lighten and his eyelids grow heavier.

The young boy had no idea that Ruben was not only singing, he was casting a spell over the camp. After the third repetition of the melancholic song, Jonathan, Jason, and Miranda has fallen into a deep sleep. There, in the dim light of Ruben's singular magic orb floating in the air above the camp, the wizard brought his hands up to his face and sobbed into them as he rocked back and forth. Neither Jonathan, nor the other two in the camp were any the wiser, for the sleeping spell had put them into a sound rest that could not easily be broken. Even the horses had fallen into a restful slumber, allowing their muscles to recover from the relentless pace of the journey.

The only witness to Ruben's tears was Ziegler, who stood stoic and fast several yards away, and watched the wizard from the shadows of the night.

Early, golden rays broke upon the forest in the early hours of the morning to find the camp fully rested and ready for the day's travel ahead of them. They mounted their horses and Ziegler again led them at a gallop though Tanglewood Forest. They kept pace at one hundred miles per day, stopping only at night to rest, and arrived at Gwyndoltai upon the seventh day from the time they had fled Inghali.

If Jonathan had been in awe of Tirnog and Telward, he was now entirely speechless upon seeing Gwyndoltai. The great, founding city of the elves was more breathtaking than any city or natural wonder he had ever seen before. The descriptions he had read in his travel book could never have done it justice, either. A great ring of elevated aqueducts circled the outer walls of the city, bringing life-giving clear water to vines and flowers that crept up white marble columns and stretched across the arches that supported the aqueducts. Vineyards and orchards spread out from there in a great ring of emerald leaves and painted blossoms. Beyond that, and protected by what appeared to be several inner rings of walls, was an extremely tall, alabaster tower that rose up until the spire disappeared into the clouds themselves.

Even the air smelled of sweet honey as they dismounted their horses and began to walk along a road paved with large, flat stones and bordered with a fence made of silver rails and golden posts. Jonathan would have normally expected Ruben to talk about the history of the city, but the wizard was uncharacteristically quiet, keeping his eyes to the road and walking just behind Ziegler.

The great walls of green and black marble rose up in a ring before them, standing fifty feet high and filled with fountains fashioned into eagle heads that spouted the water down to the aqueducts below that would in turn carry the water to the outer ring and feed the lush plants. Jonathan could see two other roads that he imagined would have looked like spokes on a wheel, driving a direct line to the inner rim of Gwyndoltai. No one was on either of the two roads that he could see, and Jonathan had to wonder whether anyone was in the city at all, for he didn't see anyone working the fields, vineyards, or orchards either. As they drew closer to the open gatehouse, Jonathan noticed a plaque set upon the right side that was written in Common Tongue. From the words written upon it, he learned that the road they were using was the only allowed entrance for those who were not elves, and wished to enter Gwyndoltai. It also cautioned against entering any of the other sections of the city.

Ruben finally broke his silence and asked Ziegler to stop the group. Then he turned to address them. "Gwyndoltai is a very traditional city. We must behave here." He turned and pointed to the sign Jonathan had just read. "The other sections this sign speaks of are the ancestral homes of the various elf races. The Vishi'Tai, Svetli'Tai, Sierri'Tai, Tomni'Tai, Korr'Tai, Pes'Tai, and Nizhni'Tai all have sectors in this city that are considered their personal holy lands. Under no circumstances are we to enter any of those other sections, or we will be imprisoned without any degree of leniency or mercy."

"What section are we going to enter?" Jason asked as he pointed to the open gate.

Jonathan was about to answer, excited to talk about the large capitol city of the elven nation, but Ruben beat him to it.

"This is a hanging garden. The elves use this section to allow outsiders to enter their first city. Further in, there will be another gate, where we may make supplication to enter the second circle. From there, we will have to ask to gain entrance into the third circle. However, with the disciplinary record, and our suspicions, I think we have a good chance of getting in, if you let me do the talking. The center of the city is for the council chamber, and usually one must be a king or queen to gain entrance there. However, it is still possible that the council will hear our concerns via a proctor speaker, and then give us the help we seek."

"Why should they help us?" Jason asked. "I mean, we have had to fight in nearly every elven city we have come to. Why would the council help us now?"

Ruben nodded understandingly. "If we were accusing a Vishi'Tai, then perhaps we would be facing an insurmountable challenge, but we have evidence against a drow, and the council no longer looks upon them favorably."

"We stand a better chance here than anywhere else," Ziegler put in. "Let's go in and find out whether they have seen Raven."

The group walked through the large gates and Jonathan's mouth fell open at what he saw. In the large, wedge-shaped section of the city that was bordered by two walls leading toward a second circular wall, was a veritable jungle of large flowers, pools with fountains, and small buildings that appeared to be no larger than houses back in Holstead, but were made of fine granite and marble, with silver and gold accoutrements. He looked up to see a plant as tall as a tree, but its trunk was like that of a large flower, green and supple. Great leaves fanned out above him and swayed gently back and forth as higher up there were red and orange blossoms that looked to be at least half as large as he was.

Birds were busily flapping about, flying in and hovering near the flowers as they dipped long, hooked beaks in to drink of the nectar before flying off to another flower. In the gardens here he could see a few elves working, trimming hedges or cleaning the mosaic tiles surrounding the various pools. He couldn't help but wonder about how amazing the other sections of the city must look if this was the way the elves took care of the one section intended for guests that must come only rarely, since in Jonathan's lifetime he had never heard of the king, or anyone else for that matter, traveling up to Gwyndoltai to speak with the elves. All of that was handled by messenger birds, or at most a small envoy sent from the elven cities.

It took nearly ten minutes to walk to the inner gate. This one was closed, and Ruben was forced to ascend a small series of marble steps and then pull upon a brass chain to ring a bell.

Several minutes later, a tall elf with discerning, blue eyes came to the gate with his arms clasped behind his back. He wore a velvety black jerkin with red clasps up the center. Over that he had a long, flowing black coat that was slender at the waist, but flared out behind him. Golden trim was sewn into the sides, and the collars stood up and stopped just below the elf's angular jaw. His pants were black as well, made of silk and tucked into highly polished boots of black leather. The whole ensemble was an extreme counter point to his bright eyes and long, silvery hair which flowed freely behind him as he moved.

"What is it you wish, traveler?" the elf said in a dry, stale voice.

Ruben bowed his head. "I am Ruben Faelwyn, from the College of Mystics in Lehemat. I have come to seek advice regarding the disappearance of one of my colleagues."

"The council is not in session today. It is Aelwyr's Day, a day of rest and celebration. I am surprised that you didn't know that, being from the College of Mystics as you claim."

Ziegler took a determined step up the stairs, but Ruben held out his hand.

Ruben then continued to converse with the elf at the gate. "Aelwyr's Day is not for another three days, according to the calendar set forth by the first council of Gwyndoltai."

The elf behind the gate smiled and bowed graciously. "A test, fine sir, to ensure you were what you claim to be." The elf then turned to a large chain of silver on his side of the gate and pulled it downward. A series of clicks and clanks reverberated inside the gatehouse as the portcullis was raised and held open. "I cannot assure you that the council will hear your inquiries, but you are free to move onward to inquire whether the proctor will carry your message for you."

Ruben bowed again, and the elf stood aside and gestured for the group to enter the next section of the city.

Jonathan noticed that the space between the walls was even thinner in this part of the city. They were heading toward the point of a wedge, it seemed, but that did not make this portion of Gwyndoltai any less resplendent than the other areas he had already seen. Grand manor houses sat in neat rows of cobblestone streets lined with flowering pear trees and winding magnolia trees in full bloom with their whites, purples, and pinks prominently displayed for all to see.

Jonathan marveled at the manors, noting that most of them looked to be empty, or at least there were no inhabitants of this sector that he could see out upon the streets. Unlike the first area, there weren't even any elf workers around, though Jonathan knew they must regularly come through, as the buildings and roads all sparkled and shined in the bright light of the sun.

It took another ten minutes for them to reach the next gatehouse, which consisted of great double-doors made of some sort of red wood that Jonathan didn't recognize, supported with black metal hinges and plates. A smaller door was built into the large door on the left, which would allow for someone to pass through without the giant set of larger doors needing to be moved out of place.

Once again, Ruben bounded up the stairs and pulled upon a brass chain hanging on the wall nearby. A loud gong sounded, its tones echoing behind the massive doors and lasting for several seconds before fading into the silence once more.

It took much longer than the elf at the first closed gate had taken to appear, but eventually someone did come and open the smaller door. This elf was nearly seven feet tall, with his golden hair pulled into a high knot above his head and draped down his back like Jonathan had seen done with horse tails for parades. He stood in grand, red robes with silver runes sewn into the chest and emerald vines sewn into the tops of the sleeves down to the wrists. His skin was slightly tanned, and his eyes were black as night. He smiled at Ruben and nodded when the wizard bowed his head.

"Ruben Faelwyn," the elf said unexpectedly. "I see you have finally arrived."

Ruben glanced back to the group and frowned. "I'm sorry, have we met?" he said.

The elf smiled gently and shook his head. "No, but I met with your predecessor at the college a few decades ago. A pleasant wizard, as far as human wizards go. I have heard great things about you, and suspected you may come to Gwyndoltai at some point."

Ruben nodded. "I have come to seek a proctor to deliver a message to the council for me," Ruben said flatly.

The elf's smile disappeared and was replaced with a straight-lipped expression that stared back at Ruben from under an arched brow over the elf's black eyes. It was several moments before either of them spoke. Jonathan wondered if perhaps they might be communicating with their minds, for they seemed to stare at each other for a long while. The elf's black eyes narrowed, and then flicked out to the group. They scanned each member of the party in turn, and then rested upon Jonathan.

"He will deliver the message," the elf said as he pointed to Jonathan.

Jonathan felt a nest of snakes hatch in his stomach and his throat went dry.

"If I may," Ruben began as he bowed his head. "Jonathan does not understand your customs."

The elf shook his head. "I will go with him, but the boy will deliver the message to the council."

Ruben bowed again and then backed away. Everyone turned to Jonathan expectantly.

He walked up the stairs and Ruben removed his leather satchel and held it out for him to take. Jonathan nodded, knowing that the disciplinary record was inside. He then followed the elf in red robes. He was so nervous now that he did not take notice of the grand, towering mansions around him now. He tried to think of how he would word what he needed to say. Would the council listen to him? Did they know about Inghali? Was he walking to judgment?

The door behind him closed with a deafening echo, sealing him off from the others. The elf in the red robes walked quietly and quickly toward a final wall. Through the closed portcullis, Jonathan could just make out the base of the astonishing tower that rose up to touch the clouds. The baby snakes in his stomach seemed to grow as he looked at the door in the tower. Now they were like full-size vipers slithering around in his gut. His face went flush and he nearly turned to run back to the others.

Before he was even ready for it, the portcullis opened and the tall elf in red robes ushered him to the door in the base of the tower. The elf produced a key and unlocked the outer door, then pulled it open and motioned for Jonathan to go inside. The young man walked in and found himself in a type of mantrap. Another heavy door stood only a few feet away, closed and locked. The elf in the red robes stepped in and pulled the door behind them closed, locking it with his key before knocking on the next door.

A small panel in the door slid away and a pair of green eyes peered out at them.

The elf behind the door said something in Taish.

The elf in red robes answered and the panel slammed shut.

A moment later, Jonathan heard a series of clicks and metallic scrapes, then the door opened inward.

Jonathan entered a wide hallway and saw a pair of guards with robes like the one who was escorting him to the council chamber. The only difference was that each guard held a spear and had a long scimitar hanging from a sheath on their waist. They eyed him warily and he did his best to keep his eyes forward, pretending not to notice them.

When the hallway ended, there was a great room with a black and white marble floor. Along the edges of the room were several staircases that led upward. Jonathan looked up to the ceiling and saw a large, strange orb of gold glowing and giving light to the room. From where he stood, it didn't look attached to the ceiling, or anything else for that matter.

"Come," the elf in red said as he pointed to a staircase nearby. Jonathan followed him upward and studied the golden orb, looking for the chain that surely had to connect it to the ceiling, but he never saw one.

"Hurry please, the council is very busy today," the elf said.

Jonathan nodded and rushed to catch up. When he reached the second floor he turned left to follow the elf through a doorway that led into another chamber in the center of the tower. This one had a floor of green marble. Several golden orbs, like the one on the first floor, but much smaller than that, floated near the circular wall-like sconces, bathing the room in a warm light that helped ease Jonathan's nerves somehow. There was a large, circular table in the center of the room, and in the center of that was a floating image that Jonathan stared at for several minutes. It floated above the table a few inches, gently turning on an invisible axis. He stepped closer to study it and then realized that he was looking at some sort of magical map. Continents and oceans slowly turned on the image in front of him, as though someone had drawn a map upon a ball of some sort.

"It is called a globe," a voice said as a door to the left opened up. A tall elf walked into the room. He had long, white hair, skin that matched the hair, and purple eyes that studied Jonathan intently.

The next door on the right opened, and another elf walked in. This one was much shorter, about five and a half feet tall actually, with golden hair, evenly tan, golden skin, and red eyes that seemed to burn like fire. This elf did not speak, but moved to the table and stood behind the chair nearest him.

Jonathan then glanced at the table and realized it was a continuation of the city's design. Golden strips marked each wedge-shaped portion of the table for the race belonging to the corresponding city sectors outside. Three chairs were positioned at each wedge, except for his section, which had only one chair, making for a total of twenty two seats around the table. Jonathan stood respectfully, waiting for others to enter the room and take their seats. Two more tall elves joined the first with white hair. A few moments later, two more golden-skinned elves entered and flanked the first golden-skinned elf.

After a while, the second door on his right opened and another elf did enter. He was the same height as the golden-skinned elf, but had wider shoulders. His skin was a strange greenish-brown that reminded Jonathan of the forest. The elf's black, beady eyes flicked up to the boy and then the elf offered a single nod before taking his seat at the table and reaching up to scratch the left corner of his mouth. No other elves came to join him.

Jonathan couldn't help but notice the contemptuous glances the other two elves shot at the third when he sat down.

"The council is now complete," the tall elf with the white hair announced. "Please be seated."

Jonathan waited for them to move first, and then he stepped around his chair and took his place at the table. He glanced around to the four empty sections of the council table and wondered where the others were.

"I will lead the meeting," the tall elf with the white hair announced. The shorter elf with golden hair nodded, but the elf with the dark skin simply yawned and dug under his left thumbnail with his right index finger. "First, let us discuss the matter of your status," the elf spoke as he looked to Jonathan.

Jonathan frowned and stared back blankly.

The elf with the white hair pointed to Jonathan's clothes. Then he remembered he was still wearing the slave clothes Elantra had given him.

"How did you come to escape from the Pes'Tai?" the elf with the white hair asked.

"It's a long story," Jonathan said.

"Summarize it, then," the shorter elf with dark skin said.

The elf with the white hair glowered at the other for speaking out of turn, but the elf simply shrugged and went back to cleaning his thumbnail.

"I was journeying with my friends when we were taken prisoner by the Pes'Tai in Inghali."

The elf with the white hair frowned. "Well, why did you go to Inghali? Everyone knows they take outsiders as prisoners and slaves."

Jonathan shook his head. "We didn't. We were told that someone else we were looking for was there, so we went to find him."

"Who? Another slave?" the elf asked.

Jonathan shook his head. "A drow by the name of Larkyn."

The elf raised his right brow and leaned back in his chair as he took in a breath. "That is interesting indeed," he said. "We will speak of Larkyn in a moment, but first, tell me how you escaped the Pes'Tai."

Jonathan nodded. "Two of my friends were chosen to fight in the arena. I was with Elantra…" he tried to think of her last name, but frowned when he couldn't. "Sorry, I don't remember her last name."

"Eofuld," the greenish-brown elf said as he moved his thumb up to bite on the nail.

"Must you do that here?" one of the other white-haired elves asked.

The greenish-brown skinned elf sighed and folded his arms reluctantly.

"Go on," the leader of the council said.

Jonathan nodded. "To make it short, my friends were able to collapse the pillars supporting the balconies in the arena, and the building fell down."

"This was during the fight?" the leader asked.

"Yes, it was during the last fight with the champions."

"The arena would have been full," the golden-haired elf commented.

"Only a few made it out, I think," Jonathan said.

"You being one of those few," the leader surmised. "Impressive. And your friends?"

Jonathan shook his head. "They were buried in the rubble."

There was a silence in the room as the elves across the table turned to speak quietly amongst themselves. Jonathan glanced to the greenish-brown skinned elf, but then looked away when the elf arched a brow in such a way that almost made it feel like a threat.

"We never rejoice in the bloodshed of our kin," the council leader said. "However, we are not surprised that the debauchery the Pes'Tai are so infamous for has finally brought upon them a terrible judgment. It will take them a long time to recover from losing the leaders of the five houses. Likely, they will scatter in the winds now, or perhaps turn to fighting amongst themselves for supremacy instead of continuing their never ending campaign against the Kratii in Scale Valley.

"You should know that you are safe now. The Pes'Tai abhor the inner forest, and will not venture into Tanglewood to follow you. They left the council long ago, eons before you were ever born, and it is prophesied that they shall not return to the heart of Tanglewood until the end times, which are still thankfully a long way off from now."

Jonathan nodded as if he understood, but the elf's words did little to comfort him.

"Now, what is your business with Larkyn?"

Jonathan reached into the satchel and removed the onyx sphere, setting it upon the table.

"How did you come by one of those?" the elf asked.

Jonathan ignored the question, and instead explained everything he knew about Larkyn and Nebenuk's amulet. He told them about how he found the amulet on a troll king in the Murkle Quags and that Raven suspected it was forged with elven magic. He told them of the trolls that had taken over Vizendel and the disappearances. He told them that Raven had gone to find the truth behind the amulet, but had never returned. The more he spoke, the deeper the frowns became on the elves' faces. They listened to him with great focus, and then when he finished, they sat silent for several minutes until the leader of the council reached out and held his hand with the palm facing the sphere.

As if obeying some unspoken magical command, the sphere flew up and landed in the elf's hand. He turned it over, looking at its sides and then he let go, allowing it to hover in the air before him. He spoke words that Jonathan couldn't understand and then the sphere began to glow, only this time it had silver and blue light running through and around it. The sphere then opened and swallowed the entire room, complete with the table and all of the elves in the council.

A moment later, the same scene Jonathan had watched before played out on the center of the table as the spinning globe momentarily faded away so as not to obstruct the disciplinary record. When it was finished, the orb turned dull and the room was as it had been before the leader had activated the orb.

The leader turned to the first golden-skinned elf that had entered the chamber and sent the sphere magically floating to him. "Isylian, do see that the record is kept in our vault here, for safe keeping."

The golden-skinned elf nodded and tucked the sphere away in his robes.

"I think I have seen enough," the leader said. "Allow me a moment to confer with my other council members, and then we shall issue our verdict."

Jonathan balked at the word "verdict" and wondered what that meant. Were they deciding about telling him where Larkyn went, or were they deciding on a punishment for the catastrophe in Inghali?

The golden-skinned elves conferred amongst themselves while the white-haired elves whispered in their group. Again, the greenish-brown skinned elf sat quietly, twiddling his thumbs and yawning.

A moment later, the other elves all turned around and faced him once more.

"Have the Svetli'Tai council members come to a conclusion?" the leader asked.

The golden-skinned elf with the fiery red eyes stood up and nodded. "We vote to help the boy in his quest."

The white-haired elf nodded and turned to the greenish-brown skinned elf. "Has the Korr'Tai councilman come to a decision?

The elf turned to look at Jonathan and nodded. "I agree, we should help."

The white-haired elf tapped the table a couple times with his finger, obviously disturbed that the single Korr'Tai councilman was not standing and observing proper etiquette. He glared at the elf for a moment, and then finally rose to deliver his verdict as well. "We also agree that we should help you."

Jonathan smiled and nodded happily.

The leader continued. "Larkyn often visits his ancestral home in Tomyn. If you wish to find additional clues to your friend's disappearance, we suggest you look there. However, do not confront him if you can avoid it. He has a reputation for hiring mercenaries as guards, and is extremely ill tempered. He will not lose any sleep over murdering you and your friends.

"Furthermore, if you find Nebenuk's amulet, the council must ask you to return it to us. It is our duty to protect such items, and we must ensure it does not fall into the wrong hands again."

Jonathan shook his head and blurted out what he was thinking. "But, if Larkyn already stole it from you, how will you ensure no one else can get it?"

The Korr'Tai on Jonathan's right slapped the table and let out a belly laugh. "I have decided something else," he said with a great smile. "I like this human!"

"Be silent!" the leader bellowed, his words bouncing off the walls in a lasting echo. He then turned to Jonathan and nodded his head once. "I admit, mistakes have been made, but if Larkyn stole the amulet, you can bet he had help from a nefarious source. It is not unheard of for the drow to dabble in the darker arts, or perhaps seek help from demons. You undoubtedly saw this yourself while watching the disciplinary record, for the three elders there chastised Larkyn for working with necromancy."

"If he is as bad as all that, why don't you send a patrol or something to help us find him and bring him to justice?" Jonathan pressed.

The elf drew his brow into a tight knot and glanced at the others before responding. "Perhaps if you had proof that Larkyn was behind these disappearances, we might have more of a cause to act in that way. Or, perhaps if you had proof that he did in fact take your friend, Raven, or even if you could get him to admit that he was working with the troll king who had the amulet. But as it is, there is not enough evidence."

Jonathan sighed, feeling utterly defeated. What good was the council? All they had done was given him a clue to help find Larkyn, but they wouldn't do anything themselves. He shook his head and began to push his chair back from the table. He was done.

"We can take them to Tomyn," the Korr'Tai said as he stood from his chair.

Jonathan froze and turned back to the elf.

"I have many warriors here with me. I can lend them to the boy if the council is unwilling to act officially. This way, it will appear as though my warriors are helping to escort a group of travel-weary humans southward, ensuring their safety through the woods."

"He has a point," the Svetli'Tai council member named Isylian said. "Or, perhaps we could send one of my patrols with them. I have more scouts at my disposal."

The leader nodded. "Very well, but let's send a mixed escort. Three of my warriors shall accompany however many you both wish to send. I cannot spare more than that, however, or it will look as though the council has decided, rather than a couple of elven nobles."

"Agreed," Isylian said. "I have nearly thirty warriors I can spare. I shall ensure that the elves we send are from my own personal retinue."

The Korr'Tai laughed and shook his head as he held his arms out to his sides. "I am the only Korr'Tai noble left, so I will join the boy along with seven of my warriors."

"Excellent," the white-haired leader said with a smile directed at Jonathan. "Then it is settled. We shall send warriors along with you under the guise of escorting you southward. As Tomyn is nearly directly due south from here, we can use the pretense as a perfect reason to construct a meeting between our warriors and Larkyn and his mercenaries. May the Gods watch over your days and the stars guard you in your sleep."

# CHAPTER 11

Within two hours, Jonathan was rejoined with the others and a group of forty elven warriors were with them. Koanin, as the Korr'Tai councilman was called, set the forty warriors around the group and charged them with ensuring that each human was protected for the duration of the trip. Afterward, he had his seven warriors follow him with gifts wrapped in green blankets carried in their arms.

Koanin walked before his soldiers and addressed Ziegler first. One of the warriors, dressed in leather armor that matched the leaves of the forest, handed Koanin something long, wrapped in a brown blanket.

"Unlike some of my elven cousins, I am not big on pomp and ceremony," he said. "However, I wanted to present you with gifts. It is improper that a captain should be without a suitable weapon. To you, I present Aeolfang, a longsword forged in Tyrwyn by the master sword makers."

Ziegler bowed his head and reached out to take the proffered weapon from Koanin. He removed it from its sheath and held it up in front of him. For the first time since news of Moose and Bull's death, Ziegler smiled. "It is a fine blade, many thanks."

Koanin bowed his head and then he turned to Ruben. A second warrior rushed forward with a small, wooden box. Koanin took the box from the warrior and then offered it to Ruben, opening the lid on its hinge and allowing the wizard to see inside. "Even the masters at the College of Mystics do not have a ring like this," Koanin said. "This is my father's ring. I find it appropriate that it now aid a druid in his work."

"How did you know I was a druid?" Ruben asked.

Koanin smiled. "Korr'Tai are closest with Tanglewood Forest, the trees told me." He nodded to Ruben and the wizard took the ring and slipped it onto a finger. "It will help augment your druid magic, and signifies to the trees that you are their friend. May it help you in your times of need so long as you stay close to the trees."

Koanin then moved toward Miranda and smiled. Jonathan expected another warrior to come up with a gift, but no one moved. Instead, Koanin stepped close to her and gently took her right hand in both of his. "It is rare, even in Tanglewood, to find a rose so beautiful. I have a special charm for you, my dear." Koanin let go of her hand and pulled up a silver chain from around his neck. Hanging at the bottom thereof was a large, purple stone. He smiled and then stepped behind her. Miranda moved her hair of the way and bent down slightly to accommodate him as Koanin fastened the clasp around the back of her neck. Miranda centered the stone on her chest while Koanin walked back around her and smiled. "This stone augments your focus, and helps you cast more concentrated magic."

Miranda nodded. "Thank you," she said.

Koanin bowed his head and then moved to Jason. A warrior rushed up with a slender, long item wrapped in a blanket. Even before it was unwrapped, Jonathan had guessed it was a sword. Koanin took the weapon in hand and pulled just a few inches out of the sheath so the sun could shine upon the black metal. "This is Drek'noyn, forged by the same masters in Tyrwyn, but it is made of a rare metal called Telarian steel. It is strong enough to withstand a dragon's breath, and will never lose its edge."

Jason nodded and took the weapon happily. He pulled it out of the sheath and the silver runes etched in the middle of the blade glimmered in the sunlight. "It is an honor," he said.

Finally, Koanin moved to Jonathan. He reached out and placed a hand on each of Jonathan's shoulders. His black eyes scanned Jonathan's clothes and he smiled wide. "First, let's get you some better clothes!"

The elves around them all laughed, and then a stout warrior came forward and presented Jonathan with square packet that had been wrapped in such a way as to make a forest scene appear seamlessly across the many folds that held the wrapping cloth securely in place. When Jonathan opened the packet he found that the forest scene that had been visible when the cloth had been folded had been replaced by a battle scene set among the young trees of an ancient Tanglewood Forest.

For a moment he almost forgot to inspect the clothing inside the packet. When he did look down, he found a set of black pants and shirt with a green leather jerkin that matched the color of the Korr'Tai warrior's armor. Jonathan took the clothes happily. The seven Korr'Tai warriors moved in and formed a screen around him so he could change clothes right on that spot without compromising his modesty. When he was done, the warriors walked away and Koanin had another item in his hands.

Jonathan saw an exquisite recurve bow.

"It is made of several layers of wood, as well as bone and even a thin layer of the same Telarian steel from which your brother's sword was formed," Koanin said. "It will serve you faithfully."

Jonathan beamed from ear to ear and thanked Koanin profusely.

Koanin smiled and then looked to his warriors. He shouted something in Taish, and all of the elves mounted their several steeds. The Svetli'Tai elves rode upon horses not unlike the ones Jonathan and the others had taken from Inghali. The Vishi'Tai elves rode upon elk with great, formidable antlers. The Korr'Tai leapt up onto the backs of large, spotted deer.

It was a strange group to be sure, but Jonathan was more than glad for the company. He was more sure now than ever that they would finally find Raven and pay Larkyn back for all of his treachery.

The group rode out at a quick pace that they could easily maintain as they took a narrow road to the south toward Tomyn. Ziegler and Koanin led the way for quite a while as the elf warriors encircled Jonathan and the others, bows at the ready in case they were attacked.

They traveled just over one hundred miles the first day, and then they set up camp for the night.

Koanin barked orders at the elf warriors, presumably setting up scouts and watch shifts, while Jonathan ate fruit and bread with his brother.

"You must have impressed them," Jason commented through a mouthful of peach.

Jonathan shrugged. "Actually I think Koanin just likes telling the other elves what to do," he replied with a shrug. The two of them shared a laugh and then devoured their food. They watched as the elves went about eating standing up. None of them made chairs from rocks or fallen logs, instead, they all ate on their feet and kept their eyes turned to the forest, scanning for dangers. When it came time for them all to sleep, the elves did that differently as well. The Vishi'Tai were on patrol first, so they went into the forest. The Svetli'Tai slept leaning on their horses, and the Korr'Tai climbed the trees and used their magic to wrap themselves in thick leaves.

Jonathan smiled at the Korr'Tai, admiring their command over the trees, and then he drifted into sleep.

The second day was much like the first, except that they stopped after fifty miles and had lunch near a small pond.

As Jonathan was eating his food, Koanin came and sat next to him, grinning wide and black eyes dancing happily.

"I should thank you," Koanin said as he slapped Jonathan on the knee.

"Me?" Jonathan asked. "What for?"

Koanin pointed to the pond and then took in a deep breath. "I used to come here and fish," he said. "But I haven't been outside of Gwyndoltai for more than three centuries now."

Jonathan stared at him incredulously. "You haven't left the city for three hundred years?"

Koanin shook his head. "No. I have been stuck in there ever since…" Koanin puffed and then he looked to the pond again. "I proposed to my wife here, just on the other bank of the pond," he said. "We came back here when we named our first child."

Jonathan smiled, not sure where the conversation was heading.

Koanin sighed and then his smile faded away. "My wife loved the forest," he said. "It's special to all of us Korr'Tai, but it was different with her. She really could speak with the trees. They told her things. She used to joke that she would likely turn into a tree when she died. Told me she would rise up next to this very pond." Koanin glanced at Jonathan with teary eyes and smiled nervously. "I wish she had," he said. "She went into the woods one night, called away by the trees again. I was away in Gwyndoltai at the time, otherwise I would have gone with her."

A silent pause ensued and Koanin fidgeted with his fingernail again and shook his head as he took in a few deep breaths. "She disappeared that night, never to be seen again. I came as fast as I heard. We searched for days. The other nobles gave up after a few weeks, but I kept looking. I knew that she wouldn't just vanish. She knew the forest too well."

"Did you ever find her?" Jonathan asked in a hushed tone.

Koanin sighed and shook his head. "I was heading southeast from here, deeper into the heart of the forest. That was when I had this strange feeling gnawing at my soul. It was as though a tree bent down and whispered to me, telling me to come to the pond. Hoping that perhaps my wife was helping me through the trees, I came back here. She wasn't here. I found my wife's necklace over there, right where she said she would turn into a tree. I don't know if she placed it there, or if someone else put it there to make me stop looking for her." Koanin took another deep breath and his head drooped downward. "Most of the Korr'Tai left Tanglewood nearly one thousand years ago. There weren't many of us left in the forest after that. Not nearly enough to defend ourselves." Koanin reached up and wiped the tears from his eye and sighed again. "I rushed home to tell my daughter that I had found the necklace, but when I reached the village, it had been destroyed. Everyone but the seven warriors you see with us today were dead. The only reason they were spared is because they had been with me, searching for my wife."

"Who attacked the village?"

"I never found out. There was no sign of the attackers anywhere. Except for one thing," Koanin said as he nodded and a smile crept back onto his face. "There were signs of necromancy in the village."

"How do you know that?" Jonathan asked.

Koanin explained, "When you are as in tune with nature as the Korr'Tai, you can feel the abominable magic. There are also ways to check for it. I followed my suspicions and confirmed that it had been used in the attack. From that point on, I remained in Gwyndoltai searching for any clues as to who might be using necromancy in Tanglewood Forest. For a long time, the investigation was entirely fruitless. Then, about five years ago I started finding a few reports. There was nothing I could act on, or else I would have done that, but I had a list of suspects narrowed down. Then, you showed up and brought that disciplinary record. That and news of Nebenuk's amulet were the missing pieces I needed."

"You think it was Larkyn?" Jonathan asked.

"Everything fits," Koanin replied. "Troll warriors, disappearing elves from other cities, and Tomyn just happens to be a city in ruins. No one lives there after the drow exodus. I had heard that Larkyn sometimes went there to visit family ruins and gravesites, but now that I know he has Nebenuk's amulet, I am sure he is the same one that attacked my village. Besides, Tomyn is due south from here, and my village is only twelve miles to the west of this pond. It can't be a coincidence."

Jonathan nodded. "I should tell the others," he said.

Koanin shook his head. "No one else needs to know. I only wanted to tell you as a way of thanking you. This has been a long time coming, and I am looking forward to finally ending the pursuit." Jonathan smiled and Koanin stood up and stretched. He turned around to Jonathan and smiled. "There is one more thing I should say as well."

"What's that?" Jonathan asked.

Koanin's eyes flared and his smile turned crooked as a spray of blood shot out from his neck. Jonathan cried out in horror as a bloody arrowhead protruded from Koanin's throat.

"We're under attack!" Jonathan yelled. He reached up and caught Koanin as the Korr'Tai noble fell forward. Koanin choked, his mouth moving in jagged twitches as his black eyes fixed on Jonathan.

"Larkyn…" Koanin whispered with his final breath.

"Larkyn has found us!" Jonathan shouted to Ziegler.

Captain Ziegler was up and holding his sword in his good hand. "Come over here, Jonathan!" he shouted from behind a spooked horse.

An arrow whizzed by Jonathan's head and the boy turned to sprint toward Ziegler. If not for one of the horses that ran between Jonathan and a second arrow, Jonathan would surely have been struck, but the horse caught the arrow instead and then reared up with a shriek before darting off into the forest.

Elf warriors were up and rushing around.

Jonathan took out his bow and turned to fire across the pond, from where the first arrow had been fired. What he saw was not a drow at all, but one of the Svetli'Tai scouts walking out of the woods, with his bow drawn and aimed at him. Jonathan hesitated.

Ziegler grabbed Jonathan and pulled him out of the path of the arrow.

"It's an ambush boy!" Ziegler yelled.

"The Svetli'Tai are attacking us!" Ruben shouted.

Just then a Korr'Tai warrior ran out onto a thick bough above in the trees and fired back on the attacker, catching him in the chest. A flurry of arrows went flying every which way and Jonathan could barely stand without running the risk of being struck by a flying missile.

He looked up to see Ziegler charging a Svetli'Tai warrior. The elf dropped his bow and shook his head.

"I am not against you!" he shouted.

A moment later an arrow struck the elf in the head and he fell over dead."

Ziegler ran toward the elf that had shot the warrior and ran him through with his sword.

"They aren't all bad!" Jonathan called out as an arrow *zinged* right by him and thunked into a tree. He spun around and fired his bow, taking down the elf that had fired at him.

Then, a tree branch moved down and scooped Jonathan up just as an elf warrior lunged in from behind. Jonathan looked down through the smaller branches as a Korr'Tai warrior rushed in behind the Svetli'Tai traitor and stabbed him in the back. The traitor looked up to Jonathan and screamed in pain.

"Master Larkyn will prevail!" the traitor said, and then he died.

Jonathan then nodded to the Korr'Tai elf below, realizing the elf had used his magic to make the tree scoop Jonathan out of danger. The elf offered a short nod and then disappeared into the forest.

From Jonathan's new vantage point, he could easily see everything happening near the pond. He moved into position and began picking off the enemy as he found them. Soon he had dropped three hidden archers hiding in the forest beyond the other side of the pond.

Four more Svetli'Tai warriors were killed by their own comrades in the next several seconds.

Ruben was sending lightning across the pond and blasting a trio of swordsmen that were on Jason and Ziegler's tail while Miranda was using her fire spells to attack and scare the enemy warriors' horses. Soon she had caused a full mess of stampeding horses and she and Ruben had to take cover while the animals trampled their way back out to the main road.

Jonathan pulled back and fired upon a Svetli'Tai archer climbing a tree, and then he turned to see another sneaking below him. He wheeled on the enemy and went for another arrow, but the elf sent a blast of magic the pulverized the branch he was situated upon and Jonathan went hurtling through the air. Everything seemed to slow as he flipped end over end. He saw the last of the Vishi'Tai elves slain by the sword of one of the traitors, and he watched helplessly as two Korr'Tai took arrows to the chest. He glanced to the side his brother was on just as Jason counterattacked a traitor that jumped out from the bushes. The elf was dropped and Jason moved on to help Ziegler finish off two more traitors. Then, everything sped up and Jonathan landed smack in the middle of the pond.

The water crashed in around him as he fell deeper into the pool. A couple of arrows plunked in after him, but the water stopped them before they could reach him. As his momentum slowed and he righted himself, he came nose to nose with a very large pike. He reached up and grabbed one arrow that had somehow managed to stay in his quiver and pulled it out. Good thing too, for the pike opened its mouth and came at him. Jonathan jabbed the arrow into the pike's mouth and up through its head. The three foot long fish jerked and twitched, and then turned belly-up and started to float to the surface slowly.

Jonathan glanced around, hoping the pond was not full of the dangerously territorial species and then swam to the top as well. Upon reaching the surface, he was reminded of the gravity of the battle raging around him as an arrow grazed his left shoulder, cutting it with a narrow gash that stung terribly. He cried out and began swimming as fast as he could pull himself through the water. He reached the bank where his brother was, and Jason reached down to pick him out of the water.

"Where's your bow?" Jason asked.

Jonathan shook his head and ran to the nearest corpse, pulling a sword up from the dead elf's hands. Jason then guided him to the edge of the woods where they could take cover from the onslaught of arrows that was now very much a one sided affair. Jonathan glanced up to the tree next to the one he had been in and saw the last few moments of the final Korr'Tai's life as he leapt from the branch and fired three arrows in rapid succession while in air. His targets were two Svetli'Tai elves armed with bows. They fired back and the arrows crossed paths in the middle. The Korr'Tai flipped in the air, narrowly missing the missiles sent for him, and then spun around to watch his victory.

The Korr'Tai's first arrow struck one Svetli'Tai warrior in the chest, but the second arrow caught the same elf in the right shoulder, causing the elf's hand to jerk upward. This motion put his hand directly in the path of the third arrow, which had been on its way to the second Svetli'Tai traitor's chest. Now, however, the first elf caught the third arrow with his hand and it stopped the arrow after it protruded half way through the elf's hand.

The second elf was now free to fire again, and he did. The Korr'Tai was hit twice in the chest before he landed on the ground.

Jonathan closed his eyes and pulled back around the tree, unable to watch anymore.

"How many are left?" Ziegler asked.

Jason was quick to answer. "About ten, I think," he said. "Miranda and Ruben are still alive, so that puts the odds at two against one."

"We've had worse," Ziegler commented.

Jonathan opened his eyes and saw his brother whispering something to Ziegler. They were planning how to attack the other elves, he knew. In that instant, his Memaw's words came back to his mind.

"You brought him back once, and you can make sure he returns again," she had said.

Jonathan turned and glanced out and saw one elf on their side of the pond, and seven more approaching from the other bank, with their bows drawn. He knew then that if Jason and Ziegler ran out, they would be shot. He glanced back to Jason, and then he smiled at his brother. He would make sure his brother got back home again, just as Memaw wanted.

He turned and sprinted out around the other side of the tree, drawing attention away from Jason and Ziegler.

"Get back here!" Jason snarled, but Jonathan wasn't listening.

He charged out from the edge of the forest and into the open. Seven bows turned across the pond to aim at him. The elf on this side had already fired. Jason dropped to his knees and slid under the first elf's arrow. As he slid across the damp grass and mud in his wet trousers, he looked up to see seven more arrows streaking toward him. He lurched forward, somersaulted and then used his momentum to leap into the air. One of the arrows bit into the side of the heel of his boot. Another drew a thin red line across the top of his thigh as it sliced over his leg, but no other arrows touched him. He came down on the ground, rolled once more to stabilize himself, and then sprinted for the elf closest to him.

The elf was pulling another arrow, but Jonathan let his sword fly at the warrior. The elf was able to duck, but in the time it took him to dodge the whirling sword, Jonathan was upon him, tackling him to the ground as another flurry of arrows flew toward him. Jonathan twisted to the side, using the other elf as a living shield as the other arrows came in. The elf's eyes went wide and his body turned stiff, falling awkwardly on top of Jonathan.

Then he heard his brother shout and yell. He looked out from under the dead elf to see Jason and Ziegler rushing out of the trees close to the other side of the bank. He smiled, for they had done exactly what he had hoped they would do, use his distraction to skirt around under the cover of the forest to get closer to the other seven archers.

Jonathan pushed the dead elf off of him and stood with the dead traitor's bow in hand. He fired once and took down an elf with a shot to the warrior's forehead. His second shot pierced another in the upper back, and his third caught an archer who was almost fully drawn back with his own bow and aiming for Jason. A second after that, Ziegler and Jason finished off the last four in a flurry of blood-stained swords that left two of the elves headless and one without an arm.

A crackle of lightning ripped through the forest off behind Jonathan and he turned with his bow drawn. Jason had said there were ten. That meant there could be two more somewhere. That thought was put to rest when Ruben and Miranda emerged from behind a large tree. Ruben smiled and waved.

"Got the last two!" he called out.

The group all converged on the western shore of the pond and checked each other over. From what Jonathan could see, they had all managed to survive without much more than bruises or nicks and scrapes.

"I didn't expect that," Ziegler said as he spat on the ground and sheathed his sword. "Jonathan, what was Koanin telling you before the attack?"

Jonathan glanced to Koanin and felt a pang of sadness come over him. "He was telling me that he thought Larkyn was responsible for destroying his village and his wife's disappearance."

"Then why didn't Larkyn call upon the council to act?" Ruben asked incredulously.

Jonathan shook his head. "It's a long story."

Ziegler cut in with a raised hand. "We don't have time for that. We need to reach Tomyn before Larkyn becomes wise to the fact that we survived his ambush."

"How do you know it was Larkyn and not one of the councilmen who sent the warriors with us?" Jason asked.

Ziegler shook his head. "Because one of the traitors was shouting about 'Master Larkyn,' during the battle. It seems that he has more reach than we suspected, and he bought some of these warriors off as well."

"But…" Ruben interjected. He shook his head and put a hand up to his neck. "But…" Jonathan looked to the wizard and noticed that he was sweating profusely from his forehead, and his face was turning redder. "I..um…" Ruben stammered. The man slumped to his knees and Miranda shrieked.

"There's a dart in his back!" she gasped.

Ziegler hurried around Ruben and inspected it while steadying the wizard with his left arm. "It's small," Ziegler said as he pulled it out and held it up. "It's only a few inches long, couldn't have pierced any organs here. It was too high for the kidneys, and too shallow to penetrate the ribs.

Jonathan watched as Ruben's eyes rolled into the back of his head. "Heart Spring," he said weakly.

"Heart Spring?" Ziegler asked. "Where is that?"

Jonathan rushed to the campsite where Ruben had been sitting. He rifled through the pack until he found the canister with the current map and then sprinted back, nearly breaking the lid while trying to open it. He dumped the map out onto the ground and unrolled it.

"East," Ruben said.

Jonathan scanned the map. He found Tomyn, and then followed the river to the northeast until he saw a large body of water drawn upon the map with the name Heart Spring written under it. "Here!" he said as he pointed.

"Tomyn is south," Ziegler pointed out.

Ruben went weak and his eyes closed.

Miranda took the dart and smelled it. "There was something on this dart," she said as she handed it back to Ziegler. He sniffed it and nodded.

"It isn't any poison I know of, but it is surely something foul."

Miranda pointed to the map. "Heart Spring is a place where people go for special healing. My father used to tell me about it when I was a little girl. He said that if you go and bathe in the waters there, the magic in the spring will heal whatever ails you."

Ziegler nodded. "Jason, round up five horses, and do it quickly."

Jonathan looked around for his bow that he had received from Koanin and went to retrieve it as well as a full quiver of arrows. By the time he had gathered what he was after, Jason had returned with the horses.

The forest was unforgiving as they moved eastward. There were no roads from where they were to Heart Spring. The horses, being accustomed to Tanglewood, were able to navigate the dense trees and undergrowth, but they could barely keep a light trotting pace. Still, it was faster than the group would have been able to do on foot, especially since Ruben was no longer conscious.

What they could have covered in a day on the open road, required three days and most of two nights to cover through the forest. Only when they neared the banks of the river did the traveling get noticeably easier.

Even then, Miranda still fussed over Ruben, riding near to his horse and praying over him. The trees did not grow along the sloping, grassy bank on the northern side, so the last ten miles were able to be taken at a much faster run. As it was, Ruben was barely breathing when they reached the large spring.

Jonathan watched from the bank as Miranda hurried to lead the horse carrying Ruben to the edge of the heart-shaped spring. The bubbling waters gave off steam as they foamed all throughout the pool. Without stopping, Miranda walked the horse straight into the water until she was up to her chest. By that time, Ziegler was with her, and helped her slide Ruben down and into the pool.

"He needs to drink some of the water," Miranda said.

Ziegler cupped some water in his hand and fumbled with Ruben's limp body until he had the man's head positioned back against his chest with the mouth slightly open. He dumped a handful of the liquid in and waited.

"More," Miranda said.

Ziegler scooped up four more handfuls, but nothing happened. Jonathan and Jason moved to the edge of the bank and watched.

"Maybe he needs to go in deeper," Miranda said.

Ziegler nodded. "Boys, come in and help me."

Jonathan and Jason jumped into the water.

The first thing Jonathan noticed was the pleasant heat. The water wasn't scorching, but it was hot and seemed to reach into the body and warm the muscles and bones too. Then, there was a terrible sting in his leg where the arrow had grazed him during the battle. He hadn't told anyone, but it had become slightly infected during their ride to Heart Spring. It wasn't serious, just some puss that built up around the deeper end of the cut, but as it touched the water and the liquid flowed into the wound, Jonathan felt a searing pain.

He pushed the sensation out of his mind. He had to help Ruben now. But just then, as he forced himself further into the pool, he felt something cool slide around his leg. Startled by the sensation, he stopped and looked down. Blood and puss was stripped away and new skin closed the wound before his eyes. Jonathan then smiled and rushed toward Ruben, confident the waters could heal him too if he could get into the pool a bit further.

Jonathan took Ruben from Ziegler and with Jason's help he moved him closer to the center of the pool. The ground beneath his feet dropped away sharply a few feet away from the center of the pool and he fell in up to his neck.

"Here!" Jonathan said.

Jason nodded and they both dunked Ruben down into the pool. Jason moved to pull Ruben up, but Jonathan shook his head as the waters healed the cut in his shoulder.

"Wait, give it time!" Jonathan said.

"We don't want to drown him!" Jason replied.

Jonathan shook his head. "He'll be fine. Trust me." Jonathan pulled away from Jason and he and Ruben slipped down deep under the surface. Jonathan watched through the clear water as Ruben's hair floated up and waved in the water. Then, a strange ribbon of green came up from the depths of the pool and swirled around Ruben. By that time, Jason had dived under the water to pull them out, but he too stopped when he saw the phenomenon.

Jonathan smiled at his brother and then watched as the green strip enlarged and whirled around Ruben until the man was spinning in the water. A thin trail of blood oozed out from Ruben's back and a golden spark flamed into life as the wound healed over. Then, Ruben's eyes opened and he started swimming for the surface. Jonathan and Jason followed.

The three of them smiled and laughed, and then swam back toward the others.

"You found it!" Ruben exclaimed. "How did you find it?"

Ziegler pointed to Jonathan. "He used your map, and we rode straight here from the pond."

Ruben turned and embraced Jonathan. "Thank you!" he exclaimed. Then he turned around and wrapped Miranda in a tight hug. She smiled and laughed and then he pushed her away, looked into her eyes, and bent down to kiss her passionately.

Jonathan's smile lost its fire then as he watched the two kiss. He cleared his throat and started to walk out from the water.

Travel to Tomyn. Find more Larkyn clues. Use abandoned places page for inspiration.

# CHAPTER 12

The group ate a full meal and then packed up and prepared to leave again. Ziegler took them down to the river, following a different source that sprung up from the ground nearby and ran down to join with a river that had started somewhere beyond Heart Spring. Ziegler, having made many different types of rafts during his time in the swamps of the Murkle Quags, instructed them how to build a raft. Then he looked down to his bandaged wrist and unwound the makeshift splint. He flexed his hand and bent his wrist each way before nodding and smiling.

"It looks as though Heart Spring did us all some good," he said. "Come on then, let's crack on."

Jason cut down smaller trees with his sword. As Koanin had promised, not even the trees could dull the Telarian steel's edge. Miranda, Jason, and Ruben were set with the task of making rope from vines and strips of pliable bark from some of the younger saplings. The job took them all the better part of a day, even with Ziegler's experience, but they were able to set out on the river a few hours before sundown.

In several hours, they had traveled well over fifty miles, thanks to the speed of the river. Then, as the sun was burning the sky with pinks and oranges, they pulled into an eddy as the river flattened and widened for a bit and made camp on the beach. They slept under the stars on the naked bank of sand, not daring to use any lights and risk alerting any of Larkyn's scouts that they were still alive.

Ziegler was sure Larkyn had to have sent patrols out after them by now, which was one of the reasons he suggested using the raft to reach Tomyn. It would hopefully be the last thing Larkyn would expect.

Jonathan was unable to sleep for much of the night. He lied upon his back and watched the stars, but couldn't take his mind off of the kiss Ruben and Miranda had shared. Try as he might to let it go, it bothered him, deeply. After a while he sat up and glanced around. Jason was snoring loud enough to wake the dead, and the others appeared to be asleep as well. Jonathan quietly stood up and moved closer to the edge of the shore. In the silvery moonlight, he found a few stones worth skipping and began throwing them at the water. He watched each one skip, counting the number of bounces before it disappeared in the water. He was on his fifth stone when someone came up beside him. He turned, expecting to see Jason or Ziegler, but he saw Miranda.

She smiled at him.

He offered a half-smile and returned to throwing the rocks.

"Can't sleep?" she asked.

Jonathan shook his head. "Anxious, I guess," he replied. "What about you?"

Miranda glanced back over her shoulder and rubbed her upper arms. "The same." She then looked to him and offered another smile.

Jonathan pointed to the sky and said, "Well, at least it isn't raining all the time."

Miranda laughed softly. "The Murkle Quags are definitely not a place I miss," she said. She bent down to grab a round, flat rock and then skipped it. It bounced seven times across the water, and then landed on the opposite bank.

"Well done," Jonathan said with a nod. He then wound up and tried to outdo her, but he angled his throw incorrectly and the rock shot straight into the water with a *ker-plunk!*

"Nice try," Miranda said as she knelt down to find more stones.

Jonathan just shook his head and waited for her to collect more rocks.

Miranda stood up and threw another stone. It made it to the other bank just like the first.

"Magic is cheating," Jonathan said.

"I only have fire magic," Miranda replied evenly. "That wouldn't help much in a rock skipping contest."

Jonathan smirked.

Miranda then stopped suddenly and turned to him. "It wasn't my choice," she said.

Jonathan's brows drew together in a puzzled knot. "What?" he asked.

"The betrothal, it wasn't my choice," she said.

Jonathan nodded quietly.

"I meant what I said, back in the Warrens, about wanting to visit you. I tried three times, actually, but my father caught me each time."

"He stopped you?" Jonathan asked.

Miranda nodded. "Said I wasn't allowed to marry anyone who couldn't wield magic. Said it was important to keep the lines going strong. When he was introduced to Ruben, well, he got the idea in his head that maybe we could even improve the magic lines. Ruben has two lines of magic in his blood, and he can use both. My father said I had to marry Ruben."

"And you don't get any say?" Jonathan asked.

Miranda shook her head. "It isn't so hard to understand is it? I mean, I heard that your brother was betrothed to his fiancé as well, matched by your grandfather and the young woman's father right?"

Jonathan nodded. "They seemed to work it out in the end though," Jonathan said as he glanced back to his snoring brother. "He didn't like her much before he left for the war, but afterward… things changed."

Miranda nodded and she glanced back to Ruben.

Jonathan looked over to the wizard and realized that things might eventually change for Miranda as well.

"I guess that is what I am hoping for too," Miranda said. "I am trying to make the most of it, because I don't have any other option really."

Jonathan thought about telling her to run away with him, but he knew how ridiculous that would sound. They were in the middle of Tanglewood Forest, with her fiancé, looking for her father. It seemed the fates were conspiring against him.

"I will always remember you," Miranda said.

Jonathan looked at her and smiled. He took her hand in his. "I have never stopped thinking of your," he said.

Miranda nodded and brushed her hair back with her other hand. "I guess, that's what I need from you," she said. "I need to know that you can be okay with this. It will always be hard, but if you could give me your blessing, it would make it easier."

Jonathan smirked and shrugged. What was he supposed to say? What could he say? She already knew how he felt, but she was asking him to let it go, to let her go. Jonathan looked down and wiggled his toe in the dirt. Finally, he nodded his head. "Yeah, I can do that," he told her. "I understand. It's out of your hands, and you should be as happy as you can be."

Miranda smiled and leaned in to give him a warm, soft kiss on the cheek, then she pulled away. "Thank you," she said. "I will always have you here," she said as she patted her heart.

Jonathan smiled sheepishly and then watched her go back to her bed roll. Then he turned around and picked up the biggest rock he could find and lobbed it across the river and into a large tree on the other side. *K-nok!* The sound was loud and sharp, but nobody in the camp stirred. He kept watching the river drift by in the darkness for hours, until at last his body temperature dropped and his muscles yearned for sleep, then he turned in for the rest of the night.

They were all up early the next morning and onto the raft before the fog had lifted from the river. The rapid waters carried them swiftly through the lush forest, winding around large rocks and shooting down steep stretches at almost terrifying speeds. There were times when they all bent low to the raft and held on as they dropped nearly vertically down long expanses that stretched for a mile or more before crashing into slower waters as the river leveled out once more.

At sunset they pulled in to shore again, and pitched camp for the night. They slept under a cloudy night, the first they had experienced since leaving Holstead, and woke up to a dreary, drizzling rain that soaked their bodies and dampened their spirits. Their remaining bread was ruined before midday, and they had even lost one of their backpacks with fruit when the raft unavoidably slammed into a rock jutting out of the waters.

To make matters worse, around midafternoon they neared a large waterfall and had to fight the current to bring their craft in to shore. They tried to carry the raft, but it was too large and the terrain was too slippery and dangerous with jagged rocks and thick trees at every step. At last they decided to send the raft down the waterfall and hope it survived the drop. Ruben and Ziegler waited at the top, while Jonathan and Jason hurried to get into position at the bottom.

Jonathan scrambled over a few mossy logs and then down the rocky sloe until he came to the bottom of the drop off. The waterfall was as loud as thunder up close. Water spray wafted on the air away from the waterfall and added to the still drizzling rain.

Jason pointed out a spot about fifty yards downriver from the bottom of the waterfall where the river looked slow enough to stand and try to catch the raft. The two rushed toward it and got into the water up to their knees. Then they watched the waterfall for any sign that the raft was on its way.

A few seconds later, Jonathan pointed as the raft tipped over the edge and flipped to crash down upon its top. The rushing water pummeled it from above and the raft turned over and over in the water beneath the falls.

"Should we go get it?" Jonathan asked.

"Are you nuts?" Jason shot back. "If the raft can't get out from under the current, how well do you think we would do against it?"

Jonathan shrugged. His brother had a point which seemed obvious now, but at the same time, Jonathan could see some of the rigging coming undone under the power of the water, and two of the logs had already separated away from the raft.

The others were half way down the slope when the raft finally broke free and floated down the river again. Jonathan and Jason moved out and grabbed hold of the craft, or what was left of it, and with great effort brought it into the shallows, and then pulled it up onto the bank.

"What a mess," Ziegler said when he came upon the wreck. "Still, easier to fix this then build a new one from scratch."

As before, Jason and Ziegler cut down some trees while Miranda, Jonathan, and Ruben cleaned off the limbs and fastened the logs together to make the raft whole again. Unfortunately, it took them the remainder of the daylight to do so. They spent the third night there, beneath the waterfall, and then resumed their journey in the morning. Fortunately, by the next day the rains had stopped and Ruben and Miranda were able to use their magic to dry out everyone's clothes and supplies.

They all clambered back atop the raft, and let the river carry them the rest of the way to Tomyn. They could just make out a tall tower, covered with ivy and overgrowth from lack of use, as they pulled into the shore for the night. They were careful to camp on the opposite bank that night, and cover their raft with branches and debris before camping further in the forest for good measure. Ziegler took first watch. Jason took second, and Jonathan took the final watch before morning.

Knowing they were so close to Tomyn, Jonathan was extra vigilant during his shift. He stood behind a thick growth of briars and used his vantage point to scan the river and the opposite bank for any sign of movement. He routinely walked around the camp, checking for enemies creeping up from behind. Fortunately, the night was quiet, and nothing happened.

The morning sun broke over the river with its warmth and birds heralded its arrival. Jonathan woke the others and they all prepared to cross the river. They crept through the forest for the last mile to Tomyn. Occasionally Ziegler would signal for them all to stop, but then he would resume moving forward without incident. It took them nearly an hour to cross the remaining bit of forest, but they made it to Tomyn silently, without raising any alarms.

Jonathan and Jason were sent around the large tower they had spied from the river, while Ziegler and the others continued forward. Jonathan found the door at the base of the tower already ajar, so he slipped inside and peered around. Some bits of what used to be wooden furniture littered the main floor, along with heaps of brick and stone that had fallen out of place over the years. A broken set of stone stairs wound its way to the top, but the remnants of the wooden platform at the upper level were barely more than a couple of boards held together by rusted metal.

"There's nothing here," Jonathan whispered.

"Let's move," Jason said.

Jonathan pulled out of the building and then the two of them moved quickly to catch up with Ziegler and the others. The entire city was overgrown with ivy and bushes like the tower. A few trees had even sprouted inside houses, tearing through the roofs and crumbling walls of stone out of their way over the years it took to mature. The main thoroughfare was little more than a few stones still poking out from the centuries of dirt and growth that now covered the road. Birds and deer inhabited a large structure to the left that appeared to be some sort of barn, for through the decayed outer wall they could still see signs of animal stalls inside.

"It looks deserted," Jason said.

Ruben paused and looked to them for a moment, then he smiled and pointed to the ring that Koanin had given him. "Maybe I can see what the trees know," he said with a smile.

Ziegler nodded and the group crept toward a large grove of aspens growing between two brick buildings. Ruben moved to the closest aspen and pressed up against its white bark. He then whispered some sort of incantation and closed his eyes.

Jonathan watched the wizard for a few moments, and then turned to peek around the corner of the building.

"Well," Ziegler said quietly. "What do you see?"

Ruben sighed and shook his head. "Sorry, I really thought that would work," he said.

Ziegler sighed and snapped his fingers. The group was back out in the street and moving through the city again. They passed by an old shrine to some deity, but the statue had long since been broken and was now unrecognizable. There were a series of houses after that, most missing their roof.

"Keep your eyes peeled for a set of windows," Jason said as he nudged Jonathan with his elbow.

"Windows?" Ziegler said. "What in Hammenfein do we need windows for?"

"*We* don't," Jonathan replied. "Jason needs a pair of windows to impress his soon to be father-in-law."

Ziegler grunted and offered a single nod. "Eyes sharp. They could be watching us right now."

They crept through building by building for over an hour, but never found any sign that anyone, Larkyn or otherwise, had been in the area at all. Still, they continued their search, scouring the city one house and abandoned building at a time.

Then, as they were crossing toward a rather large church, Jonathan whistled to the group and pointed at the crypt off to the side of the building. "Guys, look," he said.

"It's a crypt," Ruben said dismissively. There won't be anything in there except for caskets and cremated ashes."

Jonathan shook his head. "No, I mean look at the gate. The building is old and has ivy all over it like everything else here, but the gate has a new lock. Look, it isn't rusted or anything."

Ziegler motioned for everyone to be quiet and he moved around to the crypt while he held his sword at the ready. He gingerly reached up with his left hand and touched the lock, then he turned and nodded. He waved for the others to join him.

"Larkyn practiced necromancy right?" Jonathan said. "Maybe this is where he performs his secret magic."

"How big are drow crypts?" Ziegler asked Ruben.

Ruben shrugged. "Well, they are similar to ones you might find in Lehemat, so maybe a few rooms and a large chapel type room for the ceremony."

Ziegler nodded. He pulled on the gate, it didn't move. He pushed it, still it didn't budge. "We'll have to make a bit of noise," he said.

"Wait," Ruben said. "I have always wanted to try something."

"Ruben, we don't have time for any more foolish spells with the trees," Ziegler replied.

Ruben shook his head and stepped in front of Ziegler anyway. He bent low to the ivy climbing on the nearby wall and whispered something to it. The ring on his hand began to glow and a small offshoot grew out of the vine and crept along the metal gate toward the lock. It slipped the point inside, and then a second offshoot formed and helped apply torsion to the mechanism. A series of faint clicks sounded and then the lock turned and the gate opened.

"Well, I'll be a frog's uncle," Ziegler commented. "That was impressive."

Ruben beamed and then gestured for Ziegler to lead the way.

The group stealthily crept down the stairs and soon entered into what looked like a chapel. There were stone pews lined in four rows below a dais of gray stone that supported a pedestal made entirely of metal.

"Seems normal enough," Jason whispered.

Ziegler shook his head and pointed to the floor. "Footprints," he said.

Jonathan looked down and sure enough, there were easily visible footprints in the dust along the floor. The group followed the thickest trail down a narrow hall and then around a bend to a large, iron door. Unlike the gate above, this portal was unlocked. Ziegler gently pressed it open and the group walked inside. A strange, red glow emanated from a crystal floating above an altar. Jonathan could tell by looking at the stone on the floor and the walls that the altar did not match. It was made entirely of onyx, the same stone that was used to form the altar the troll king used.

"Something isn't right here," Jonathan said. Ziegler nodded and gestured toward two more doors on the opposite side of the room. Ziegler and Jason moved to stand watch at the doors, while Ruben moved closer to inspect the floating crystal.

Jonathan glanced back through the doorway they had entered and gripped his bow, ready to fire at the first sign of an ambush.

Suddenly, the door on the right opened outward. Jonathan jumped up against the wall and pressed into the shadows. Jason snugged himself up behind the door and Ziegler tiptoed away as well. Ruben and Miranda ducked behind the altar and watch Jonathan for their cues.

Jonathan strained against the dim light, but it didn't take him long to recognize what was entering the room. The creature was tall, with a mohawk of brown hair standing high over its ugly head. Its arms were muscular and lean, dragging something along the ground.

The troll bent down and then came up with its prize. To Jonathan's horror, an elf was placed upon the altar, bound at the wrists, knees, ankles, and around the upper arms. A thick gag muffled the elf's screams. The red crystal twirled in the air above the elf, pulsing now with throbbing light that waxed and waned as it revolved. The troll sneered wickedly and raised an obsidian dagger.

Jonathan didn't waste another second. He drew back an arrow and let it fly straight into the monster's heart. The troll looked up after the shaft dug deep into its chest, arm still poised over the intended sacrifice. It grunted and then fell backward. Jonathan looked beyond the troll and into the open doorway. There were iron cells in that chamber. He signaled to Ruben and Miranda. They rose up and began untying the elf on the altar while Jonathan moved into the open room with his brother.

"This is sick," Jason commented when they came to a pile of dead elves heaped into a grotesque pile in one of the cells. "Who would do such a thing?"

Jonathan shook his head. "We have to check the other doorway."

Jonathan and Jason returned to Ziegler, who was still waiting by the closed door with his sword poised and ready to strike at anything that came out. Jonathan reached for the door and pulled on the handle. It opened and a flood of bright light assaulted his eyes.

There was a commotion from within, grunting and shouting along with what sounded like furniture scraping along the stone floor. Jonathan blinked against the light and saw a large form standing up. As soon as he made out the mohawk, he put two arrows into the being's chest. Jason and Ziegler rushed in and finished off three more trolls.

"All clear!" Ziegler called out as the last troll's head rolled upon the floor.

"It's an office of some sort," Jason called out.

"Why would trolls need an office?" Miranda asked.

"Not the trolls," the scared elf said as Ruben removed the gag. "That's Larkyn's office."

"Larkyn?" Jonathan echoed as he turned around to regard the elf they had rescued. "Who are you?"

"My name is Deltys. I am a mercenary, or, I was."

"Mercenary?" Ziegler bellowed as he exited the room and approached the altar. He held his sword tip at Deltys' throat threateningly. "You worked for Larkyn?"

Deltys shook his head. "No, not really. What I mean is, he hired our group a short time ago. He came to Inghali looking for mercenaries. We signed on with him. He said he needed protection. Everyone has heard the rumors of Tanglewood Forest becoming more dangerous the last few years."

Ruben nodded and looked to Ziegler. The captain was not yet convinced, and kept his sword aimed at the mercenary's throat.

"Anyway, we came to Tomyn like he wanted. Then, one by one the others in my group went missing. Larkyn grew furious, said we needed to triple the patrols and be on our guard."

"Did he say what was after him?" Ziegler asked.

Deltys shook his head. "Nothing was after him. It was all a ruse. He hired us to lure us here for his dark magic. By the time I figured it out, I was locked up in the cell with the others. The trolls were everywhere. They sacrificed the others one by one upon this very altar. I can still hear their screams."

"Why would he do that?" Ziegler asked.

Deltys pointed to the crystal still hovering in the air. "He used the life force of others to fuel this crystal."

"Why?" Ziegler pressed.

Deltys shrugged. "I don't know. All I know is, when the door was left open, I watched one time when the troll killed one of the others. His life force was drained out and absorbed into this crystal."

"Then we should destroy it," Ziegler said.

"Wait!" Ruben cautioned. "It isn't wise to try and simply attack something like this. If what he says is true, it could strike back with a magical ward, or it could explode and bring the whole crypt down on top of us."

"Jason, go in the office and see what you can dig up."

Jason nodded and rushed back into the office.

Jonathan watched Deltys as Ziegler continued to pull information out of him.

"Where is Larkyn now?" Ziegler asked.

"Said he had what he needed from us. Said he was going to Sierryn," Deltys replied.

"What is in Sierryn?"

Ruben interjected. "That is the ancestral home of the Sierri'Tai. They lived in a vast system of underground caves."

Deltys shivered and rubbed his arms. "It's said if you go far enough into Sierryn, you can find the underdark and harness its energy. It is where necromancy was born in Terramyr, and the reason for the schism between the drow and the rest of us."

Ziegler pulled his sword back and placed it into his sheath. "You said you are a mercenary?"

Deltys nodded.

"But you are not Pes'Tai. You are Svetli'Tai."

Deltys nodded again. "Most of my kin are endowed with magic. I am not. I was given the gift of the sword, and I used it to my advantage. I hired out with a group of mixed elves." He pointed to the room with the iron cells. "Go and see for yourself, there are not only Pes'Tai piled in heaps in that chamber."

Ziegler nodded and folded his arms. "How long ago did Larkyn leave here?"

Deltys shrugged. "I'm not sure, maybe a day or two, maybe more. I can't be sure how long I have been down here."

"We should go back to Gwyndoltai. If Larkyn is in Sierryn, then the council can arrest him and put him on trial," Ruben said.

"You can't arrest Larkyn," Deltys said with a vigorous shake of his head.

Ziegler shook his head as well. "Deltys is right. You cannot arrest a person like Larkyn. He will fight his way out."

"Then let the council take their warriors," Ruben said.

"You can't have forgotten that some of the council's warriors tried to murder us, can you?" Ziegler shot back.

Deltys shook his head. "I heard Larkyn talk about the council. He has allies there. I don't know who, but he has a friend there who would help him for sure."

"Maybe this letter will shed light on who that friend is," Jason said as he came out of the office with a piece of paper in hand.

Ruben frowned and moved to take the letter from Jason. He mumbled as he read through the words and then his mouth dropped open and he shook his head. "This letter is written to Larkyn by none other than Isylian." Ruben turned to look at Jonathan.

Jonathan knew the name well. It was the fiery red-eyed Svetli'Tai councilman. "He sat in the council meeting with me," he said.

"Isylian speaks for the Svetli'Tai people," Deltys said. "His is the oldest family to sit on the council. If he is partnered with Larkyn, then Gwyndoltai will be a death trap if we go there."

Ruben nodded his agreement. "This letter lays out terms for Isylian's fees in exchange for helping Larkyn acquire certain artifacts."

"Is Nebenuk's amulet listed?" Jonathan asked.

Ruben shook his head. "No, but other items of necromancy are listed. According to this letter, Isylian acknowledges Larkyn's ambition to control a seat on the council and reestablish the legitimacy of the drow nations in Tanglewood Forest."

"For that, Larkyn would need an army. Even with Isylian, the council will not sit idly by and let Larkyn overtake a council seat."

"And that is why he is going to Sierryn," Ruben said as he dropped the letter onto the altar. "Sierryn has a sacred crypt where all of their past warriors were buried."

"No, that doesn't make sense," Jonathan blurted out. "Nebenuk's amulet controlled the weather. It didn't help control armies brought back from the dead." He then snapped his fingers and his eyes grew wide. "Larkyn gave the amulet to the troll king to control the weather in the Murkle Quags. That's how the monsoons spread northward."

"We know that already," Ziegler said.

Jonathan smiled. "Larkyn wasn't trying to raise an army of undead elves, he was trying to bring a nation of trolls north to help him reclaim his family's seat at the council table. It must have been a simple deal. Offer the trolls power to conquer the peninsula, and then in return they offer the warriors needed to take back the council seat. We've already seen many trolls out here. It's the only thing that makes sense."

"Then why would Larkyn need sacrifices, and why would he run to Sierryn?" Miranda asked.

Ruben moved close and inspected the red crystal hovering in the air. He hummed and stroked his chin for several moments.

"What are you doing?" Ziegler asked.

Ruben waved him off and kept staring at the crystal. Finally, he turned to Deltys and asked, "Have you ever seen power leave this crystal?"

Deltys shook his head. "No, but most of the time the door was closed."

"Nebenuk's amulet was altered to feed upon life force to enhance its power. Maybe Larkyn has figured out how to store life force indefinitely."

"That doesn't explain why he needs it." Ziegler quipped, his patience obviously shortening.

Ruben snapped his fingers. "If Larkyn's first plan to bring the trolls northward failed, then he would have to look for something to replace them. Sure, a few trolls remained loyal and relocated up here somehow, but most of the survivors scattered after the war was won. So, in the same way that he could use Nebenuk's amulet to control the weather, maybe he can use this crystal, and the life forces inside, to control something much more dangerous." Ruben pointed to the list of items on the letter and nodded. "Of course. He isn't after an army of undead elves. He is trying to reach the underdark. If he can unleash just a handful of the demons found in the bowels of Terramyr, even the council would be hard pressed to defend Gwyndoltai from such an attack. This must be his plan."

"If that is true, then why leave this crystal here?" Jonathan asked.

Ruben shrugged. "There are several crystals listed in the letter. This is only one of them. Perhaps he has them strategically placed to help control the demons once he releases them, or maybe this one is being kept here for safe keeping until he needs it. All I know, is if he has a few days' head start on us, we will need to hurry to catch up to him."

"Then we have no time to lose," Ziegler said. "We must go to Sierryn and stop him before he can attain his goal. With any luck, we'll find Raven there as well."

"I might know a way," Deltys said. "I don't know if he still operates out here, but I used to know of an elf who captained a river boat. If we find him, then he can take you to Sierryn much faster than you can travel by land."

Ziegler huffed and looked to Deltys. "Not just *us*," he said. "You're coming too."

Deltys balked. “No, Larkyn has more trolls with him, I’m sure of it.”

Ziegler smiled wide. “If there is one thing we are good at exterminating, it’s trolls.”

# CHAPTER 13

The group was back on the raft and heading downriver just as quickly as they could forage for equipment and food. Deltys spent his time cutting small sticks into poles and gathering thin, long vines. Ziegler found him a sword and the mercenary grudgingly put it on and followed them out to the raft, though he didn't look all that pleased about being part of the group.

They navigated the river as best they could with their raft, doing their best to steer clear of large rocks jutting out from the waters. Deltys made use of himself by fishing. He cut the poles he had brought along so that the front was a tri-pronged spear, complete with barbs carved out of the wood. On the back end of each pole, he cut through the wood just enough to slip the vine in and tie it around the pole.

Jonathan watched as Deltys walked to the back of the raft, one spear in his right hand and the rest he dropped by his feet. The mercenary tied the loose end of the vine to his right wrist, and then he lifted the spear and peered into the water for some time. Suddenly, he launched the spear into the water. The raft drifted downriver so fast that the slack in the vine was pulled tight in a couple of seconds. A fish came up to the surface, splashing and thrashing about.

"There's one," Deltys commented as he began to pull the vine in. He dragged the fish and spear out of the water and then turned to Jonathan. "Get me one of the backpacks," he said.

"Not mine," Jason commented wryly. "I am not about to carry fish around in my bag."

"Here," Ruben said as he emptied a leather bag of fruit. "We can redistribute the fruit to other bags and we can store the fish in here."

"It's only for a little while," Deltys promised. "Just until we stop for the day. Then we can cook the fish and clean out the bag."

Jonathan smirked, doubting very much that washing the bag in the river would rid it of the fishy smell that was sure to develop throughout the day. He took the bag once Ruben emptied it, and then went to work pulling the wriggling fish from the spear. He placed it into the bag and watched it gasp for breath while it twitched twice more.

There was another splash, and Deltys reeled in a second fish. This one was slightly larger than the first, nearly two feet long. It had a brown stripe along its otherwise silvery side with black spots over the spine and fins. Jonathan stayed near the bag, retrieving the fish from the spear and putting them into the bag. He and Deltys spent the entire first half of the day filling the bag with fish. It helped the time pass a lot faster than just sitting upon the raft, watching the forest pass by.

Around the middle of the afternoon, Ziegler steered the raft in to shore and they made camp for lunch.

"I'm hungry," Ziegler had said just before locating a gentle eddy to pull into. "I could use more than bread and fruit, too."

Ruben and Miranda set about gathering wood and building a proper fire. Jason went around cutting saplings to make roasting spits with so they wouldn't have to use the spears Deltys had made. Jonathan drew the thankless job of cleaning the fish.

He didn't mind it so much. It was just that afterward his hands would feel so slimy, and it would take a lot of effort to clean them off. He always hated that part about fishing. Catching and eating them was just fine, but he sometimes wished the fish could come up from the water already clean and ready to fry. He tossed the guts back into the river and then slipped a roasting stick through the mouth and into the tail of each clean fish. Jason would take each fish as soon as it was ready and carry it toward the already crackling fire, and soon the smell of cooking fish filled the little camp.

Once Jonathan had finished his task, he rubbed his hands vigorously in the river, and then turned to a large fern to scrape of the remaining grime and blood. It didn't work as well as he had hoped. The fern leaves were fragile, and ended up breaking and sticking to his hands, along with their little brown seeds. Jonathan went back to the water and dunked his hands and forearms in again. He used his nails to scrape and pull the muck off of him. Trails of slimy fern leaves wriggled out into the current and were pulled away from him down the river as he continued to scrub and scrape.

Finally satisfied that he was clean, he pulled his hands out of the water and turned toward camp. However, as he walked and the air moved around his hands, he could feel that he had missed some spots. He looked down and saw a mess of slime and fish scales clinging to the underside of his right wrist. He sighed and went back to the river a third time.

This was exactly why he hated cleaning fish. The very phrase itself was an oxymoron.

After the third wash, he wiped his hands on his trousers, no longer caring to keep his clothes clean. After all, he would be wading out into the river again after lunch. Better to let the fish goop cling to the pant legs than his hands.

He walked back to the fire and Jason held out a slightly charred trout for him.

"Thanks," Jonathan said with a nod.

"Better catch up," Jason warned. "Most of us have already had two or three."

Jonathan took the fish and ignored his brother's baiting. He bit into the crisp skin and flaky meat and his stomach awoke with a hunger Jonathan had not even realized was there. He devoured the fish, barely tasting the thing before all that was left was a rather intact skeleton on a stick. Jonathan tossed that to the side and took a second fish. This time he slowed down enough to enjoy the food, smiling at it as he ate. The meat was thick and good. Had he been at home, Memaw would have prepared it with her spices and a hint of lemon rind, but it tasted just fine as it was.

After the meal, Jonathan and Jason laid back on the ground and stretched out. Had they not been in such a hurry, the two would have likely taken a nap, as they often did after lunches in the fields back home, but Ziegler was up and ready to break down camp the moment he finished his last bite.

"Douse the fire, gather the equipment," he said.

Jonathan and Jason slowly rose up from their spots and started to gather their things when they heard a voice from the river.

It was an elf, and he was speaking in Taish.

The group went for their weapons, but Deltys was quick to put them at ease. "This is Ryrden, he is the river captain I was telling you about," the mercenary said.

Jonathan turned to see a rather large barge coming up the river against the current. There were a few barrels on the deck, but otherwise the boat was empty. As the aft portion came into view, Jonathan saw a strange, very short, elf. Tufts of white hair stood straight out from the elf's head around the ears and over the scalp, but it wasn't long like all the other elves Jonathan had seen. Apparently, this elf had also traded in the slender facial features of most elves for a big, bulbous nose. He wore simple clothing of brown and green fabric, and was furiously working some sort of contraption with his feet while he steered the barge with a large wheel.

Deltys walked to the bank and waved at him.

Ryrden turned the barge around and brought the bow toward the shore. Jonathan watched Ziegler, waiting to see what he would decide about Ryrden before offering to help pull the barge in to shore. Deltys, on the other hand, jumped into the shallow water and used his hands to guide the barge up and onto the sandy bank.

Ryrden said something in Taish, and Deltys nodded and then pointed to the group.

"These are my friends," Deltys said in Common Tongue.

Ryrden walked to the front of the barge and hopped off, landing upon dry ground and then moved up alongside Deltys. "Deltys, the last time we met, you were with a band of young Svetli'Tai." The diminutive elf looked up at Deltys. "Where are they now? Did you all find the fortune you sought?"

Deltys' eyes lost their sparkle and he frowned and shook his head.

"Where was it you all were going?" Ryrden asked. "You went to Sohn, right? Did you fare well out there hiring on with the sea captains?"

"Jeryn died that winter fighting against the merfolk," Deltys said. "Huryn died the following spring when the ship was overtaken by a terrible storm."

"Oh, Deltys, I am sorry to hear that." Ryrden reached up and patted Deltys' arm.

Deltys nodded. "We quit the seafaring life then," Deltys said.

Ryrden nodded thoughtfully. "Decided better to go home, did you?" Ryrden asked.

Deltys shook his head. "We went north. We hired on with a nobleman in Telward for some time. Then we moved on out toward Inghali, in search of greater fortune and fame."

"No!" Ryrden gasped. "You hired out to those, those, degenerate Pes'Tai!" Ryrden wagged an accusing finger at Deltys.

Deltys smirked and nodded. "We spent many years fighting against the Kratii. We made good coin. Diryk retired and settled down back in Telward. Geori also retired and went to Tirnog."

"And what about your cousin, Dorliit?"

Deltys frowned. "Killed just recently by a troll."

"A troll?" Ryrden asked skeptically. "Where in Scale Valley did you come upon trolls?"

Deltys shook his head and recounted how they had been hired on with a larger group of mercenaries to help Larkyn. From the expression on Ryrden's face, Jonathan could see that the river captain had heard of Larkyn, but had obviously never heard of his crimes. Ryrden's eyes filled with tears by the time Deltys was done, and then the river captain bent down to kneel upon one knee to Ziegler.

"Kind sir, I am in your everlasting debt," Ryrden said.

Ziegler glanced around and then bent down to lift Ryrden up.

Ryrden smiled and looked to Ziegler with big, blue eyes and smiled. "Deltys is like a nephew to me," he said. "When he was younger, he used to work the river with me. I taught him how to spear fish, and he helped me fill my barrels with all the fish you could ever eat."

Ziegler smiled back and looked to Deltys. "We are just happy we got to him in time, and sorry we couldn't save the others from their terrible fate."

"Deltys was only thirteen the first time I saw him on the banks of this river. He was orphaned, his mother having died in childbirth and his father abandoned him in the woods. He spent ten years with me on this river. I took him in as one of my own," Ryrden said with tears in his eyes. "As he grew, he spent less and less time with me in Neez, and began making his own way in the larger cities."

"But I would come back and visit every few summers," Deltys said.

Ryrden nodded. "Until that summer more than five decades ago," the river captain said. "Come, we shall feast in Neez tonight. The others will be excited to see you have returned."

"I'm afraid that will have to wait until later," Ziegler said. "We need to make our way to Sierryn as quickly as possible." He gestured to the barge then and asked, "How fast can that go?"

Ryrden smiled wide. "That there is the finest ship to move upon these waters. I can have you to Trivilk in less than a day."

"That's several hundred miles from here," Ruben said.

Ryrden nodded. "Come, I will help you hunt down the blackguard, and then we shall east in Neez together."

Deltys put a hand on Ryrden's shoulder. "This venture will be very dangerous, my old friend. Permit us to take the ship ourselves. I can drop you in Neez, and then come back for you once we are finished."

"Nonsense," Ryrden said with a shake of his head. "It's about time I join you on an adventure. Besides, no one has the stamina I do to keep her going." Ryrden winked at the group then and turned, waving them on after him. "Let's all get on board. Sit down in a line in the middle of the deck, and I will take care of the rest."

Jonathan and the others moved onto the barge. The wood creaked slightly underfoot as they all moved into position. Jonathan sat in the rear of the line, trying to get a better look at the strange contraption by the wheel.

"Give her a shove," Ryrden instructed Deltys, who was standing ankle deep in the water and waiting for the signal.

Ryrden clambered up onto a leather seat and put his feet onto pedals attached to a wheel of sorts. Ryrden began pedaling backward and the wheel turned a gear which in turn caused a chain to loop around it. Jonathan followed the chain with his eyes, but it disappeared below deck.

"I'll bet you have never seen one of these before," Ryrden called out to Jonathan.

Jonathan shook his head and smiled as the barge lurched out into the river.

Deltys hopped up over the side and walked back to stand near Ryrden. "Please, reconsider coming with us. I can pilot your vessel safely enough. You taught me how, remember?"

Ryrden shook his head. "I'm going with you. Now take your seat so I can get up to speed and keep her balanced."

Deltys shrugged and moved to sit behind Jonathan. Jonathan watched as Ryrden worked the wheel to point the vessel down river. The current started taking them along, but then the small elf smiled and bent forward.

"You might want to hold on to something," he said. He then pulled a strange pair of goggles up and placed them over his eyes.

Jonathan saw Deltys take a breath and steady himself, bracing with his palms against the deck. Then, Ryrden began pedaling forward and the vessel lurched in the water. It was a short jerk followed by a slow, gradual acceleration at first, but the more the elf pumped his legs, the faster the barge began to move. Soon everyone on board was hunkering down and trying to hold on to each other as they careened down the waters while Ryrden laughed at the top of his lungs.

"I once raced an eagle down this river," Ryrden called out. "I beat him so badly that he had to leave Tanglewood Forest! Ha ha ha!"

Jonathan could barely keep his eyes open for the wind was now rushing into his face so furiously it made his eyes water if he looked forward. The pace never let up. The little elf continued to pump his legs to maintain the speed while he worked the wheel to avoid the rocks and debris in the river. The party all hollered as they went down a steep grade and water splashed up around them, but Ryrden only continued to laugh and scream with delight as he pushed the barge faster and faster through the waters. Within two hours, they were coming upon Neez and Ryrden was forced to slow for a time.

"Have to make sure no one else is in the waterway around here," he called out as he stopped pedaling and let the boat slow to match the river's current.

Ruben took the opportunity to crawl to the side and vomit.

"Oh, don't do that!" Ryrden chided. "It scares the fish away for hours."

Ruben glanced up with a pale face and then turned back to retch again.

"Eesh," Ryrden commented. Ziegler and the others got up to stretch their legs a bit.

Jonathan moved toward Ryrden and then tried to mentally trace the chains under the boat as he walked to the back of the barge and looked down into the water.

"Deltys, take the wheel for a moment," Ryrden said. The little elf hopped off the seat and walked up to Jonathan. "You like it, eh?" he said with a proud grin.

Jonathan nodded. "Very much."

"The pedals turn a set of pulleys that make the dual propellers move," Ryrden said.

"The what?" Jonathan asked.

"Propellers boy, propellers! At least, that's what I call them. Here, kneel down and have a look."

Jonathan knelt down and leaned over to look where Ryrden was pointing. Several inches below the water he saw a strange contraption with three blades. It was just sitting in the water, doing nothing.

"It's motionless now because I am not moving the pedals, see? But, when I move them, the propellers churn the water and either push the barge forward, or pull it backward. It helps me move against the current, or if I use the current to go downriver…"

"Then you can move faster than an eagle," Jonathan said with a nod.

Ryrden smiled and then looked up and frowned. "Deltys, what are you doing? You're steering her into the docks." Ryrden jumped up and pushed Deltys away from the wheel. Jonathan watched as Deltys tried to convince Ryrden to go ashore, but the river captain would have none of it. Finally, Deltys shook his head and his face grew red as he walked away and turned his back on Ryrden.

Within a couple of minutes, the river captain was calling for everyone to move back into their line sitting upon the deck.

"And get that one a bucket," Ryrden shouted as he pointed to Ruben.

They had barely passed by Neez, of which Jonathan had only seen the docks with a handful of smaller canoes and a couple of short elves, when Ryrden picked up the pace once more.

"If I work hard, we can make Trivilk in about four hours," Ryrden said.

Jonathan heard Ruben shake his head just before he whined and pulled a bucket up to his face.

True to his word, they came up on Trivilk four blisteringly fast and wet hours later.

"Deltys, come hold the wheel," Ryrden called out.

Jonathan turned to see Ryrden now slowing down so he could pedal backward. The young man stood up and looked around. The river was about a mile wide at this point, and off in the distance was a foamy, brown rapid that dropped off into what appeared to be the edge of the world. The forest on both banks stopped where the rapids began, seemingly disappearing as if into nothing.

Ruben pointed over to it in the few seconds he had his face out of the bucket and called out. "Trivilk is a giant waterfall that drops nearly three hundred feet into a great pool below, then the river splits into three smaller rivers."

"Aye, and we need to make landfall before the current carries us too close to the edge!" Ryrden said. "Hold tight, Deltys will work the wheel and I'll work the pedals. We've done this plenty of times." Ryrden looked up and saw that Deltys was steering for a spot on the southern bank and shook his head. "Deltys, you dolt, Sierryn is that way," Ryrden said, pointing to the north bank. "We need to land over there. We can't cross the river by swimming it, and you can't reach Sierryn from the southern side."

Deltys nodded. "Ryrden, I will drop you off over here, then I will take the others to the north shore."

Jonathan wondered why Deltys was so set on getting Ryrden off the vessel. He agreed that the elf was small, and he was doubtless as ancient as many of the larger trees in the forest, but he seemed fit enough considering he had powered the barge for most of the day without stopping to rest other than the time they drifted past Neez.

"Deltys, stop trying to get me off the boat. I'll take you all across, and then I am going to Sierryn with you."

Deltys turned away from the wheel and grabbed Ryrden's shoulders. Jonathan noticed the intense focus in the elf's eyes. "My friend, please, go ashore here. You cannot come with us to the other side, it is too dangerous."

There was something in the mercenary's voice that unnerved Jonathan.

"Enough, Deltys," Ryrden said as he pushed him away. "I can work the wheel and the pedals from here."

Deltys sighed and backed away from the wheel. Jonathan watched the mercenary move to the other side of the barge as Ryrden set them toward a landing spot on the north shore. The process was slow going, for Ryrden had to angle the barge slightly upriver to keep from going with the current. It took nearly ten minutes to come within fifty yards of the north shore, and it would likely take another ten to reach the bank.

That was when Jonathan noticed Deltys grumbling to himself. He wasn't making any noise, but his mouth was moving and he was shaking his head. Finally, he reached down to fumble with his sword belt. A silver chain with charms on it fell out from Deltys' sleeve and caught on the sword's hand guard, popping one of the charms off from the chain. Deltys didn't seem to notice as he fiddled with his sword and situated it around his hip. The small charm hit the deck and bounced toward the middle of the barge, near Ryrden's pedals.

Something compelled Jonathan to stand up and walk toward the charm. He bent down to pick it up and saw upon it a round sigil. Stamped into the metal was the same very symbol he had seen twice before. The first time was in the mushroom hut in the mystical preserve. The second time was in Gadrien's house, where all the scorch marks had been found. Jonathan looked up to Deltys and saw that the elf was now looking at him with cold, deadly eyes.

"It was you," Jonathan shouted.

Deltys nodded.

"Him what?" Ryrden said as he continued to work the wheel.

Deltys lit a fire in his palm and let loose on the steering wheel of the barge. The fire exploded into the wood, splintering it apart and sending embers up into the air as Ryrden yelped and fell backward to land upon the deck.

The barge lurched forward then, submitting to the current.

"What is the meaning of this?" Ziegler shouted as he drew his sword.

"I told you to go ashore!" Deltys shouted at Ryrden. "Why didn't you listen?"

Jonathan seized the moment to hold up the charm for the others to see. "Deltys is the assassin who attacked us in Tirnog, and the same one who killed Gadrien."

"Gadrien was a fool!" Deltys shouted. "He never understood our cause. His loyalty to Nebenuk was misguided!"

Ruben stood up, but his sea sickness had left him drained and weary. He fell to his knees.

Jason rushed in to cut Deltys down, but the assassin threw a fire bolt at Jason. Luckily, the Telarian steel of Jason's blade was able to deflect the fire.

Deltys laughed and pointed to the north shore.

Jonathan looked up to see a line of elven archers taking position.

"They are here for you," Deltys squealed with delight. "You were hard to kill, I will give you that, but it ends now."

"You have been after us the whole time, haven't you?" Jonathan said as he stepped closer.

Deltys pulled another ball of fire into his palm and poised himself to strike. "The master will be pleased with my work."

"Deltys! What is the meaning of this?" Ryrden asked as he pushed himself up and rubbed his head. "This isn't the boy I knew."

Deltys then looked to the old elf and his confidence waned.

"Stop this," Ryrden pleaded.

Deltys shook his head. "Too late; the master has already sentenced these humans to death. They must be killed."

Ryrden shook his head and stepped closer to Deltys. "Put this away," Ryrden said. "Look, you can use magic now. Isn't that what you always wished for? You don't have to be anyone's mercenary any longer. Come on, end this foolishness."

Deltys turned his eyes to Ryrden and shook his head. "You don't understand. The master is the one who gave me my magic. He made me what I am."

"Why serve a drow?" Ruben asked as he tried to straighten up again.

Deltys laughed at them. "Larkyn is not the master. Larkyn is a ghost, a campfire story we tell in the night and whisper of in the shadows. The master is not a drow."

Ryrden placed a hand on Deltys' forearm. "We can still fix this. Let me rescue you again, as I did once before."

Jonathan then noticed the cloud of arrows rising up from the bank. "Take cover!" he shouted.

Ruben turned his hands to the sky, but Deltys threw one of his fireballs at him, catching him in the side. Miranda fired upon Deltys, but the assassin created a shield of fire that absorbed her spell and then he turned to attack Jonathan.

From behind, Jonathan couldn't see exactly what happened next. Ryrden's right hand moved so quickly, and then Deltys' eyes shot wide and the magic faded away into the air. The assassin stumbled back two steps, and only then did Jonathan see the small fish knife protruding from Deltys' abdomen.

Deltys looked to Ryrden with pained eyes, but the small elf took no pity upon him. He pointed one hand toward Deltys and shouted a single word. A blast of air shot out from Ryrden's hand and Deltys flew out from the barge and splashed into the water.

"You are not the boy I found those many years ago," the short elf said with a hint of sorrow in his voice. Ryrden then turned his left hand to the air and shouted again. A great gust of wind swept away the incoming arrows, saving all in the barge.

"We need to make for the other shore," Ziegler called out.

"We'll never make it now," Ryrden said. "The current has us, and even if I had my wheel back, I wouldn't be able to pedal fast enough to go against the current here."

Miranda stepped to the side of the boat and her amulet glowed bright as she sent focused spells toward the archers. She was able to take down a few, but there were scores of them still lining up along the shore and taking aim.

"I can't take them all," Miranda said.

Jonathan went for his bow, but even he knew it was a lost cause. There were far too many enemies.

"Do you have a plan?" Ziegler called out.

Ryrden nodded. "Come and stand here," he said as he hopped up onto his seat and placed his feet on the pedals. "I need something to hold onto. You two boys try and keep us pointed forward. There are a pair of long oars in the compartment there."

Jonathan looked to where the elf was pointing and saw a metal ring sticking out from one of the boards in the deck. He pulled on it to find a pair of oars. He handed one to Jason and took the other.

Ryrden shouted again and a thunderous gust swept away another volley of arrows. Ruben sat up then, crying out from the pain in his side.

"I can help with the arrows," he said.

Ryrden nodded and grabbed onto Ziegler's belt as he put his head down and began pedaling.

Jonathan and Jason did their best to point the bow of the barge downstream while Miranda and Ruben fired off spells to attack the enemy and try to intercept the arrows.

"What is the plan?" Ziegler asked. It was the first time Jonathan had ever heard fear in the man's voice.

"We're going with the current," Ryrden announced.

Everyone stopped and looked at the crazy elf.

"Don't look at me, focus on your jobs!" Ryrden shouted. "You two steer the barge, you two keep those arrows off of us!"

The current picked up and the thunderous roar of the waterfall came ever nearer as Ryrden pedaled with all of his strength. Soon they were zipping along faster than they had ever been going before. The water rolled and churned under them, sending the barge up and down to crash in the rough waters.

"They stopped!" Miranda said about the archers on the shore.

"Because they know we're about to die!" Ruben shouted.

The only sound loud enough to be heard over the din of the roaring water was that of Ryrden's laughter as the barge shot out over the edge and flew through the air for several yards.

"Where are the eagles to race now? Ha ha!" Ryrden yelled as they sailed out into the open air with nothing but the mist and spray of the waterfall around them.

Jonathan sucked in a breath and his heart stopped as he looked out over the expanse of lush, green forest below. Then his stomach rose up within him and he felt a tingling sensation just before his feet lifted from the barge and he floated into the air. He looked around, terrified as the air rushed in around them and the others also floated up from the barge.

The vessel angled to point downward and then dropped faster than the rest of the party, who were all now flailing about and screaming wildly. The barge continued to flip end over end as it fell below them.

The white and brown water behind Jonathan seemed to be suspended in the air with him. Bits of liquid morphed and split into droplets before rejoining again and twisting in front of him. It was almost peaceful, if not for the sound of rushing air around him and the pool below racing up to meet him. He looked down into the dark pool and thought of his home. He said a silent prayer for his grandparents, and then he closed his eyes and gave in to his fate.

Jonathan passed out moments before impact, causing his body to relax as his feet broke through the surface and he drifted into the depths below. The waterfall churned the pool into a muddy brown where it crashed down. The heavy force of the water was enough to pull Jonathan's limp body toward it, forcing him down toward the bottom of the pool and refusing to let him float upward. Then, a great turtle swam to him and grabbed his belt in its mouth as it effortlessly swam away from the churning waters.

The turtle took the boy to the surface, and then turned his face upward toward the air as it continued to push him through the pool.

Jonathan woke just as his body was pushed onto a beach of pebbles and sand. When he opened his eyes, he saw the massive beak of the turtle and screamed, scrambling to get away.

He heard Jason laughing and looked around to see many large turtles along the beach and in the water. Jason and the others were already ashore and watching Jonathan.

"It's a turtle," Ryrden said. "It won't hurt you, boy."

Jonathan turned back to the turtle that had been looming over him and he waved at it.

The turtle mad a clicking noise and then shuffled its way back to the water.

"Well then, now that we are all accounted for, let's take a ride with my friends here," Ryrden said as he patted a green and brown turtle that was affectionately nuzzling his leg with its head.

"Your friends?" Ziegler asked.

Ryrden balked, as though shocked anyone should ask such a question. "Well they certainly aren't *your* friends," he fired back. "I told you I had a plan."

"And when were you going to tell us that you would have giant turtles waiting for us at the bottom of the waterfall?" Ziegler pressed.

Ryrden laughed and shook his head. "No, no, if I had told you something like that, you would have thought I was crazy!"

Ziegler shook his head and bent down to retrieve his sword from the ground where another turtle had dropped it.

"Come on, quickly now, we need to get back into the water before the elves from above spot us cavorting on the beach."

Ziegler scoffed, but he didn't say anything to the contrary. The group made their way back into the water and Jonathan watched as the others each held onto one of the turtles and let the creature pull them through the waters. They all did their best to remain low to the surface as the turtles carried them into the northernmost of the three rivers branching out from the pool.

Jonathan occasionally glanced up the cliff wall to the top of the waterfall, but he never saw any sign of the enemy. Soon they were back inside dense tree cover where the branches extended out over the river and obscured the view from above. From that point on, the party was able to sit atop the turtles and ride them down through the river without soaking their entire bodies.

The turtles swam for about two hours before coming to a gently sloping beach and letting the party off to make camp.

Ruben and Miranda were quick to set about gathering wood, but Ziegler forbade a fire, saying the light of a fire would be seen from far off, and they were too close to take such chances now. Ryrden disappeared into the forest and came back with an arm load of fruit and dirty roots to use for food. Then he went to Ruben and inspected the wizard's wound.

"Did you cast a ward?" Ryrden asked. "The wound is not deep."

"No, I wasn't even looking at Deltys," Ruben admitted.

"I tried to negate the fire spell," Miranda said. "But I wasn't fast enough."

Ryrden whistled through his teeth. "Well, you managed to save his life. That spell should have burned a hole right through him, so you can take pride in the fact that you did, in fact, stop it. Just some superficial burns here, and only a few spots where it burned through the top layer of skin. I can create a poultice that should prevent infection."

"Shouldn't you have done that before our long swim with the turtles?" Jason asked.

Ryrden shook his head. "The water here is clean. Part of it is connected with Heart Spring, which has healing properties. Besides that, it likely did good to soak him in the cool water. Burns can continue to damage tissue long after the flame has been removed because the heat can remain within the skin and continue to cook a person's body."

Ryrden then turned to Ruben. "Does it hurt?"

Ruben nodded.

"A lot, or a little?"

Ruben glanced to Miranda and then answered, "I can manage."

Ryrden turned to Miranda and winked at her. "Be a dear and turn the other way, would you?" Miranda nodded and complied, then Ryrden turned back to Ruben. "Now, you don't have to try to impress the young lady. Just nod yes or shake your head for no. Does it hurt a lot?"

Ruben nodded his head.

Ryrden smiled. "Good, then that means it isn't so deep. If it didn't hurt a lot, then I would be worried that it had managed to burn away your nerves." Ryrden pointed to the food he had set down. "Everyone eat. The fruit is sweet and good for a quick burst of energy. The roots are good to help you feel full, and they can alleviate sore muscles and joints as well. The turtles will carry us into Sierryn tomorrow."

# CHAPTER 14

If not for the roots Ryrden brought them, which also acted as powerful sleeping aids, Jonathan would likely not have caught a single minute of rest that night. Thanks to the short elf's scheming however, Jonathan and the rest of the party was fully rested and ready to move again once the sun rose.

Riding upon the turtles once more, they traversed the final hundred miles of river in a little more than four hours, reaching the giant mountain just before midday. The great, jagged spire of black rock stabbed at the clouds in the sky as if attempting to conquer the heavens themselves. A series of caves permeated the lower level of the mountain, and the trees had been cleared away all around the base.

As Jonathan looked at the ominous growth of rock, he realized that the river flowed into the mountain as well. He followed Ryrden's lead in slipping off the turtle's back and hanging on with only one arm as they neared the mountain.

Then, just before reaching the rocks, the turtles dove under the surface, dragging the party along with them. Jonathan strained his eyes to see in the darkness. He could just make out the sharp rocks jutting out from above and the ridges and spikes below. Had it not been for the turtles, it would have been nearly impossible to navigate the treacherous waterway. Fortunately, the turtles were adept at maneuvering around them and the entire party was taken through the underground waterway safely, arriving in a cave pool just a minute later.

Ryrden and Ziegler swam to the side of the pool slowly, trying not to make much noise. Jonathan and the others followed. Once they were all out of the water, the turtles dove back under and disappeared once more.

Jonathan looked around and saw buildings made of stone near the walls. Torches, sconces, and braziers were lit throughout the large chamber they were in, illuminating the cave.

Ziegler motioned for everyone to follow him. They each kept a low profile as they made their way around a large boulder the size of a house and then crept into a tunnel nearby.

They followed it downward into the bowels of the mountain. The air grew warm and moist, with a musky odor hanging upon it. The torches grew fewer and farther between the deeper they went, but they didn't stop. They continued down, winding their way until the tunnel opened into a large chamber that dwarfed the caves in the Murkle Quags that the trolls had called home.

A vast city of three and four-story buildings rose from the floor of the chamber. There were towers and wells too. Yet, unlike the troll caves, this cavern was illuminated with an ethereal glow. Bioluminescent plants as well as rocks that gave off light all mixed together to create something that was very similar to the daylight experienced above ground. This allowed Jonathan to survey his surroundings easily.

That's how he spotted a pocket of trolls that came around the corner of one building and entered into another some hundred yards to the right. Jonathan crept up to Ziegler.

"I saw them too," the captain said. "You and Jason go and put them down. I'll take the others along the other side of the city. We have to find whoever is leading them."

Jonathan nodded.

He and Jason stalked down to the nearest building, and the skulked around the back. Jason led, while Jonathan kept scanning the area for any sign of danger. Their feet fell silently upon the rocky floor of the chamber as they padded along to the two-story building the four trolls had entered. They snuck up to the door and pressed it open.

A single troll was sitting with his back to them and hunched over a table. Jonathan could hear the monster chewing and crunching on something. Jason drew his sword quietly and moved up to the troll with absolute silence. His sword went up, and then it came down in an arc that removed the head from the troll's neck.

Jonathan moved in then and took the dead troll's sword.

"Where's your bow?" Jason asked.

Jonathan shrugged. "Didn't survive the waterfall."

"You really are bad with bows aren't you?" Jason prodded. "I don't think there has been a bow you haven't either broken or lost."

"Shut it," Jonathan urged. He pointed to the stairs nearby. Jason nodded. They moved up the marble steps slowly, careful not to let their footsteps announce their presence. Fortunately, they found the other three trolls sleeping in beds in an upper room. Jason and Jonathan positioned themselves near two of the trolls and raised their swords over the trolls' hearts. They watched each other, and then mouthed, "One…two…three!"

On three, they both came down, piercing the heart of the troll they were over.

The two trolls grunted, but not loudly enough to do more than cause the third to snort loudly and roll over in his bed. Jonathan moved to the other troll and took its head from its body, jumping back as the severed head bounced down to the floor near his feet.

"Good, now let's go and find Ziegler and the others," Jason said.

Jonathan nodded. They exited the building carefully, not wanting to be spotted by any other trolls. They worked their way through the streets, cautiously examining each one before sprinting across to remain close to buildings for cover.

When they came upon a pair of trolls playing with an old skull, they decided it best to skirt around two building to the left in a wide arc rather than risk an open confrontation that could alert others to their presence. The choice proved wise, for as they crossed the street a couple hundred yards down from where they had nearly run into the two trolls, they spotted a larger group of troll warriors just another twenty yards away.

"There are a lot of them here," Jason commented.

"Maybe they came here after the war was over," Jonathan replied.

Jason shrugged.

They continued onward until they reached the tunnel that Ziegler had intended to go to. This one was much darker than the rest of the mountain. A blueish-gray light pulsed from somewhere within the tunnel, stretching and shrinking the shadows along the wall as Jonathan and Jason watched.

"Let's hurry," Jonathan said.

The two brothers moved through the tunnel, swords at the ready as it wound down and around to the left. The air turned colder, and the scent became sweeter the deeper they went. A couple of smaller chambers branched off from the main tunnel, but upon inspecting them, Jonathan and Jason didn't find anything inside other than rubble and the occasional pile of bones.

They continued on for nearly an hour before they heard voices.

"What is that?" Jason asked.

"Sounds like chanting," Jonathan replied.

They moved through the winding tunnel and then hunkered low as it spilled out onto a stone precipice overlooking a strange structure. It was as if someone had carved a chapel out of the very mountain rather than build with stones or bricks. A great mural of carved stone depicted a large, winged demon over a set of metal gates that appeared to be shut. Massive columns held up the ceiling above. There were pews carved from the stone in the floor, and an altar of stone in the front.

Around the altar were several elves. They were kneeling upon the stone and chanting as they waved their arms up into the air and then bent their faces low to the ground again. Jonathan didn't know what to make of any of it.

"Look," Jason said.

Jonathan peered over the edge and looked straight down to where Jason was pointing. He raised a hand to his mouth when he saw the terrible sight at the bottom, some hundred feet down from the precipice they were on. Ryrden was lying broken upon the ground. One of his arms had been cut off and two spears protruded from his chest. All around him bodies were strewn about. There were trolls and elves. Blood stained the floor, and weapon littered the area.

"What happened?" Jason asked. "Where are the others?"

Jonathan pointed further off to a small, square building in the center of the grotesque chapel. The side they could see showed a depiction of a demon wearing a crown and elves bowing to it. "I bet they went in there," Jonathan said.

"I don't hear anything," Jason replied. "Think they're okay?"

Just then a door swung open on the building. Four tall elves walked out from the doorway. Behind them, Ziegler, Ruben, and Miranda were hauled along in chains. There were a dozen trolls around the prisoners, shouting and pulling on the chains. Ziegler tried to fight and pull against the chains, but a group of four trolls dragged him forward against his best efforts.

"We have to get down there," Jonathan said.

Jason nodded. "We need a plan," Jason replied.

Jonathan shook his head. "We don't have time for that." He stood up and looked around, then he found a narrow walkway leading from the left side of the precipice down to an area where there was a large rock outcropping they could hide behind for cover. "There, we can wait there until they bring them closer to the altar."

Jason shook his head. "You don't think?"

"What else is an altar for?" Jonathan shot back as he ran down the walkway. Jason huffed angrily and was two feet behind Jonathan the whole way down.

They leapt from the walkway to hide behind the outcropping of rock while the other elves and trolls brought the three prisoners in front of the grand metal gates.

"I am so very glad you could join me," a tall elf said.

"I know that voice," Jonathan told Jason. The two brothers pressed into the rock and strained to listen as they peered around the edge to see what was happening.

"I would love to have witnesses to my moment of glory."

"It's Isylian, yeah?" Jason asked. "He is the councilman that was helping Larkyn."

Jonathan shook his head. "No, Deltys said there is no Larkyn, remember?"

"But Nebenuk told us about Larkyn too."

Jonathan nodded and waved at his brother to shut him up.

Just then, the tall elf turned and drew back his hood to reveal his face. Long, shining white hair flowed down around his face and Jonathan's mouth dropped open. It was not just any council member, it was the one who had led the council while Jonathan was there."

"I must admit," the elf said as he paused and turned back to the prisoners. "You have proven my greatest challenge. Not only did you slay the troll king and break the curse of the monsoons, but you survived my assassin in Tirnog. Not to mention you were able to escape with the disciplinary record and escape my agents there as well."

"Why worry about the record at all?" Ruben shouted in a courageous outburst. "If Larkyn is dead, what difference would it make?"

"Because, you fool, I needed others to believe he was still alive!" the elf roared. "But then you came and took the maps from Eustinian as well. You figured out that elves had been in the Murkle Quags before the war. You poked your noses where they didn't belong!"

"You started a war in our homeland," Ziegler shouted.

"War!?" The elf threw his hands up and yelled in frustration. "You humans know nothing of war. You are so very consumed with your empty, short lives, that you fail to grasp the power that is available, waiting to be taken!" He made a fist as if grabbing something from the air and then whirled around. "You should have been finished in Inghali, after my servants gave you the false lead about mercenaries, but you not only escaped, you survived my ambush in the forest as well."

"Don't forget Deltys," Ziegler spat. "We killed him too."

The elf took in a deep breath, walked up to Ziegler, and backhanded him. Ziegler tried to fight back, but the trolls held his chains steady.

"Now you will die," the elf said. He turned, and the trolls brought the prisoners up close to the altar. They secured their chains to iron loops in the floor, and then the trolls took their seats upon the stone pews.

"We have to do something," Jason urged.

Jonathan looked back to him and nodded. "We have to wait for the right moment."

"If you knew anything about our history, you would know that this is about much more than a council seat," the elf laughed. "It makes for a good story, but a seat upon the council is not nearly worth such sacrifice as I have put in over the last several hundred years. However, now that your souls shall fuel my goals, I shall let you in on a little secret.

"There is a crystal, a crystal with such power that you cannot even imagine. It would allow the holder to walk into the astral plane and subjugate it to his will. Can you imagine? It grants the wielder power over life and death."

"Yes, it's a powerful artifact used in necromancy, we understand," Ziegler spat out sarcastically.

"NO!" the elf shouted. "It doesn't raise the dead, but it can make someone immortal! It would grant powers like those of a demigod. That is what we are after. It was lost, and now I have been searching for it these many hundreds of years. I was so very close before you came along. The trolls had almost completed their tasks for me and victory was within my grasp, but then you took it out of my hands and I have had to start anew. Not to worry!" The elf pointed to Ruben. "You undoubtedly saw the crystal in Tomyn, yes? It hovered above an altar not unlike this one. It absorbed life force in an effort to help me locate the Astral Shard. I have nearly located it now." He paused and closed his eyes as a satisfied smile crossed his lips as he considered it. "Mmm. The key to Astral Plane! Now, all I need is an army willing to go and fetch it for me. That is where you all come into play."

The elf turned and walked back to the altar. "While I do not have my heart set upon necromancy, it does have its uses. You see, a long time ago, the Sierri'Tai used the powers of necromancy to seal away a very powerful demon." The elf pointed to the gates at the other end of the hall. "Now, with your sacrifices, I shall unlock that gate. You shall give your lives and your very souls to me so that I may free the demon, and set him loose upon the world. In the confusion that ensues, I will take my faithful servants and collect the Astral Shard. Then, I shall claim Gwyndoltai not only as the king of all elves, but as god of this world. I shall build a kingdom such has never before existed, where the Vishi'Tai will be immortal and have ultimate control over all life on Terramyr, as is our calling."

"Bah!" Ziegler shouted. "I thought the commander at Battlegrym had a superiority complex, but you, my friend, you are far and away the most insane person I have ever met."

The elf's face grew cold and he placed his hands upon the altar. "Isylian," he said.

One of the elves that had been kneeling in front of the altar rose up and approached. "Yes, my king?"

"Explain to this fool why we seek the Astral Shard."

"Yes, Master Brykith." Isylian turned to Ziegler and smiled. "Because, after the great wars, when the gods where chased back across Bifrost and hid themselves, the world has fallen into chaos. The only way we can ensure peace is to forge peace for ourselves."

"Now tell them why you would put me as high king over all others," Brykith commanded.

"The Vishi'Tai are the oldest of all races, and the wisest. They will rule fairly, with justice."

Brykith stepped next to Isylian and draped an arm over his shoulders. "You see? I am destined to rule in this manner. The elves will cleanse the world of its chaos. We will cut out humanity like the disease it is, and then we will purge the world of orcs, goblins, giants, dwarves, and all other manner of filth!" Brykith motioned for Isylian to step back into place, which he did immediately. "Bring the girl, we'll start with her." Brykith then took a golden dagger from the top of the altar and waited.

"Now?" Jason asked.

Jonathan shook his head. "Almost."

He watched as a pair of trolls moved to unhook Miranda's chains from the floor. They walked her up toward the altar and her eyes flicked up to lock with his. He nodded to her, and she nodded back and the purple amulet began to glow softly.

"Now," Jonathan said suddenly. He ran around the rock. Miranda head butted one of the trolls and then turned to unleash a blast of fire on the other. Brykith moved to intercept her, but Jason was already out from around the other side of the rock and he hurled his sword out at the leader. The weapon flew end over end, flying directly for Brykith, but at the last moment, Isylian leapt up and pushed the leader out of the way, taking the sword in his own chest and slumping over the altar.

The other three elves around the altar stood to fight, but Jonathan overtook them from behind. He stabbed the first through the upper back, then pulled his sword and chopped down on the second elf's neck. A spray of blood shot out as the elf twitched and fell. The third turned to defend himself, but Jonathan lunged with a forward thrust that put his sword through the elf's heart.

Brykith cursed and fired a ball of lightning toward Jonathan. Jonathan dropped to the ground and the ball of magic sailed past to explode one of the columns holding the ceiling. A great tremor rocked the chamber and a thunderous rumble roared through the mountain as a crack appeared in the wall that stretched up to the ceiling.

Miranda turned and blasted Ziegler's chains. He yelled angrily, grabbing a length of chain and whirling it overhead like a heavy whip. He came down on one of the elves behind him, crushing bone and sinew with his assault. Then he ran forward and kicked a second elf in the groin, grabbed a fistful of hair, and brought the elf's head down to meet his knee as he drove it up into the elf's nose. Ziegler then ripped the scimitar from the elf's belt, slashed across the dazed warrior's neck, and pierced the third elf's chest as well.

Miranda blasted Ruben's chains then and he jumped up to unleash a furious bolt of lightning at a group of trolls rushing toward them. The silvery-blue energy burned through the trolls' chests, obliterating their hearts and dropping them like sacks of wet clay.

"NOOO!" Brykith cried as the battle turned against him. He leapt down and ran toward the gate with the carving of the demon above it.

Jonathan gave chase while the others battled the trolls.

The elf turned to him and snarled. "Why won't you die?" He raised his hands and lightning jumped from one palm to the other in a network of sizzling energy. Then, Brykith shot out at all of the remaining pillars, laughing maniacally as he stepped through a portal and vanished.

Jonathan never reached him before the portal slammed shut and Brykith was gone. The remaining pillars sizzled and groaned as the magical energy ate away at them. Hunks of stone fell away and Jonathan knew this would end exactly the same as the arena in Inghali.

He rushed back toward the others, shouting the warning, but none of them could hear him. Miranda and Ruben were firing spells at trolls while Jason and Ziegler were locked in vicious melee combat. Only the terrible quake that threw everyone to their knees broke the ferocity of the battle. The one single crack in the wall and ceiling instantly became three, and a great chunk of granite fell from the ceiling.

"Retreat!" Ziegler shouted. The group ran for the walkway, as did the trolls. Ziegler cut one down that came too close to the group, but otherwise the battle had been suspended while everyone attempted to flee out of the chamber.

A massive hunk of stone crashed into the floor and crushed the pews and corpses there, driving them into the ground and turning everything to dust and rubble. The quaking then resumed, throwing everyone down to the ground once more as they were about half way up the walkway.

Another chunk of rock fell out of the ceiling and smashed into the walkway before them, wiping out a thirty-foot section and making the escape impossible. Jonathan caught up to them then, and stabbed a confused troll through the heart. Miranda, nodded her head and blasted the final two with a fireball that sent them careening over the edge and back down to the chamber floor, where they were soon buried in tons of igneous rock.

"Hold on!" Ruben shouted as he ran to the edge of the walkway. He pointed his left hand down at a long strip of stone and chanted a spell. His ring began to glow and the stone answered to his call, flying up and moving into place where the gap was. To steady it, a flurry of lightning swirled out from Ruben's hand and bolstered the rock up.

The group started running across, but then a great rumble sounded and a section of the wall behind them broke and collapsed out toward them.

Ruben shot his right hand up and a storm of lightning created a shield, pushing against the rocks and holding them in place just a few feet above them.

"GO!" Ruben grunted. "I can't hold this much longer."

"If we go, you'll die!" Miranda shouted.

Ruben looked to Jonathan and smiled. "Get her out of here, my friend."

Jonathan dropped his sword and ran toward Miranda. He and Jason lifted her up and carried her across the suspended strip of stone and up out of the chamber. She screamed angrily through eyes full of tears when the sound of the lightning stopped and was replaced with crumbling stone slamming into place.

It was all Jonathan and Jason could do to hold onto her and carry her up the tunnel.

A pair of trolls were running down into the tunnel from above, but Ziegler slew them quickly and pushed them out of the way so the group could continue their escape. The tunnel groaned and shook, but only smaller bits of rock fell inside along with pockets of dust. Miranda screamed and cried, fighting against Jonathan and Jason nearly half the way back up, and then she went silent and limp. Jonathan tried to talk to her, but she didn't respond to anything he said. She was inconsolable.

Then, the rumbling stopped and the group reached the top only to discover a horde of seventy trolls standing in a semi-circle around the opening, waiting for them.

"Didn't they all run away last time?" Jason asked.

"Looks like they aren't running this time," Ziegler said.

"What are we going to do?" Jonathan asked.

Miranda then gently pulled away from the two brothers and took in a deep breath. She turned to the angry, snarling horde of trolls and stood there, staring at them.

"Miranda," Jonathan called. "Come back, get behind me." Jonathan moved to step in front of her, but she shot him a warning glare and shook her head. The amulet around her neck was glowing so brightly that a ball of purple light engulfed her as she turned back to the trolls and screamed with all of her rage and hate. Fire swirled out from her hands and formed a protective ring around the group while a stream of white flames shot out of her mouth and engulfed the enemy horde. Shrieks and howls went up around them, and then all was turned to silver ash as the trolls were destroyed. Miranda's black hair flowed out behind her as the power continued to surge through and around her. Then, her hair turned as white as snow and the fire faded away. Her knees went week and she collapsed to the side. Jonathan rushed in to catch her just before she hit the ground.

"Miranda?" he cried.

Ziegler was there in an instant, with a finger on her neck. "Her heart still beats," she is just exhausted. "Come, let's go and take shelter."

"Think there are any more trolls?" Jason asked.

Ziegler glanced to the piles of ash and then shook his head. "I don't think so. We'll be safe enough now. Come on."

"What are we going to do?" Jason asked.

Ziegler sighed and took Miranda in his arms to carry her. "When we were captured, Ruben overheard the elves talking about the missing crystal in Shuldern. We should try to go there."

"You mean the Astral Shard?" Jason pressed.

Ziegler shook his head. "No, there is some other crystal Brykith was looking for. The elves didn't realize that Ruben could understand them, so they spoke fairly freely. It's something like the one we found in Tomyn. Ruben described them as pieces to some sort of large, magical scrying device that can be used to find the location of the Astral Shard."

"If Brykith can teleport, we may not reach Shuldern before he does," Jonathan put in.

Ziegler nodded. "We can't carry Miranda that far over our shoulders. Besides, Ruben said they only thought the crystal was there. It didn't sound like they were going to march in and take it from the dwarves. Ruben said that it sounded as though it was something they were planning to do at some point in the future, after they released the demon. But, seeing that now they failed to release the demon, I will bet that the elves involved will have to act much more covertly from this point on."

The group moved into the nearest structure and located a bedroom to lay Miranda down in. Then, Jonathan and Jason went out to surrounding buildings to find food and other supplies.

As soon as Miranda was ready, they would begin the journey to Shuldern.

# Epilogue

Nagé sat upon a cloud as it drifted over Tanglewood Forest. She always loved riding the clouds at night. It made Terramyr appear so much more peaceful than it really was. Up here, she could almost forget about the troubles and strife she had witnessed since the dawn of time. Her deep brown eyes watched the quiet trees so very far below as she gently floated eastward upon the cloud. The moon rose high in the sky, bathing everything in its silvery light below. It was her favorite time of day; the few moments in the quiet of the night, just before she started her rounds retrieving the souls of the dead that had died during the day, and were worthy enough to be brought to her husband Tangui, Icadion's younger brother. Of course, the gates to Bifrost had been closed for millennia, and only few souls ever justified opening the bridge to Volganor, but Nagé and Tangui did their best to provide a peaceful rest in Zintara, where Bifrost connected with Terramyr.

She stood on the cloud and unfurled her great, white wings, preparing to take flight and search for the just souls waiting for guidance below, but just then something caught her eye. Even from her position high up within the night sky, she could see a great building collapse upon itself down below, just east of Tanglewood Forest and west of the Nahktun Mountain Range.

Nagé knew the place well, for Inghali was a city of ill repute among the gods, known for the bloodthirsty souls that thrived there. A great sound of weeping rose up through the air and filled her ears. Her heart grew heavy for the suffering they experienced. Her head dropped low and a tear formed in her left eye. She closed her eyes and looked away as the sounds of crying and screaming grew louder, for it was not only the mourning survivors she heard, but also the souls of the dead, who were only now becoming aware that they had been ripped from their mortal bodies.

The goddess flew down toward the ruin as the dust settled.

Flashes of light twinkled through the ruins and the rubble even before she reached it.

As she had expected, there were far more scarlet hued lights than there were blue.

The souls began pouring out from the ruin, wandering around, confused and in shock. When she stepped down in the midst of four Pes'Tai nobles, they cowered away from her. They could not see their own lights, Nagé knew; that was only a gift she and a couple other gods possessed. However, those who had been unjust in their mortal life were brought to feel their guilt and shame before her as she walked among them.

A young Pes'Tai girl, who was perhaps only four years old in terms of time upon Terramyr, stood up from the rubble and grew into a full woman before Nagé. The soul twinkled blue, and Nagé pressed her thumb to the elf's forehead. The elf smiled and drifted away toward Zintara.

Nagé looked upon all of the others with pity, for none of them had the blue light that signified they were worthy to go to Zintara.

A great streak of black lightning broke from the ground and grew into a rift before her. Nagé waited patiently as Khefir, the son of Khullan, stepped through the rift. He was a god, like Nagé, but he no longer had a body of flesh like she did. Icadion had punished him many years before, and stripped him down to a skeleton as retribution for an injury Khefir had inflicted.

His loose, black robes hung around the skeletal hand that reached out to point at the nearest soul that twinkled scarlet. Like Nagé, Khefir could see the lights. His job was to collect the souls of the unjust, and lead them away to Hammenfein, where his older brother Hatmul would pronounce judgments in accordance with their wicked deeds, and assign them an appropriate level of hell.

Many in the mortal realm cursed Khefir, as did many of the souls revile against him now as he appeared, but Nagé understood his role for what it was. She bowed her head to him, and then continued walking as he began to collect souls and send them to his brother.

Nagé saw only two more blue souls in the rubble. They were not elves, but human. One of them was extremely tall and muscular, the other shorter, but by no means short. In them she saw something that she rarely saw, even among the souls found worthy enough to send to her husband. In the center of their blue lights there was a bright orb of white.

She smiled at them and reached out her hands. They stepped forward and each placed a hand up to hers. As they did so, she saw their lives from the moment they were born, until their tragic, self-sacrificing deaths.

Nagé wept for them and then pulled her hands back. "Moose and Bull," she said in a soft voice. "Your sacrifice here has done more than you could have possibly known. You have brought down the largest clans of the Pes'Tai, which will put an end to their unjust, vicious wars against the Kratii for many years to come. You have saved countless lives. More than that, you made it possible for your comrades to escape."

"Will they find Raven?" Moose asked.

Nagé smiled and looked to the tall man and shook her head. "I do not see the future, for I do not have such gifts. However, I can tell you that I have not seen Raven's soul. He is still alive." She stepped forward then, moving closer to them and flared out her wings. Neither of the men flinched in her presence. They stood tall, and proud. She smiled at this, and made her final decision. "If you will accept it, I have a special role for the two of you to play. Reach out your hands, and I will make you instruments of my will."

Moose and Bull reached out without hesitation. A shining light, like a bright star, formed in their hands as she placed her palm over theirs. A loud, high-pitched ring expanded out over the air around them, and then all three vanished into the night.

# About the Author

Sam Ferguson is a fairly average guy.
That's it.
No, really, that's it.
Oh- you are actually reading this?

Well… the truth is that Sam is a very *lucky* guy. He juggles work in such a way that he makes sure to spend enough time with his loving wife and six sons. His goal is to make writing his fulltime career so he can have even more time with them (assuming they can handle having him around that much every day…). If he can carve out an extra hour for himself during the day, he'll hit the gym to try and regain the body he used to have in his youth (but he eats too much junk food to ever accomplish that goal).
He spent nearly five years serving as a U.S. Diplomat and absolutely loved the experience, but decided to move back home. Outside of the U.S. he has lived in Latvia, Hungary, and Armenia. He speaks Russian, Hungarian, and Armenian. (He used to speak some Latvian too, but he has no one to practice with anymore…)
He also has two dogs.
He plays the Elder Scrolls series.
His favorite superhero is Wolverine, but Batman is a close second.
If the kids go to bed at a reasonable hour, he will cuddle up with his wife to watch Scrubs reruns, the Big Bang Theory, Castle, and Burn Notice.
See, really just an average guy after all.

If you enjoyed this book, then join Sam Ferguson's Facebook page, sign up for alerts on his Amazon page, and by all means leave a kind review!

Thanks for reading Brothers Haymaker!

Tell your friends about it, and please consider leaving a review on Amazon or Goodreads.

Be sure to check out other great stories brought to you by Dragon Scale Publishing

The Sorceress of Aspenwood Series

The Dragon's Champion Series

The Dragons of Kendualdern Series

Haymaker Adventures Series

The Netherworld Gate Series

The Dwarves of Roegudok Hall comic books and novels

The Fur Trader

Tales from the NoWhere & NeverWhen

The Annals of Esparia Series

Go to: www.dragonscalebooks.com

You can enter monthly giveaways for books and other prizes by signing up for Dragon Scale Publishing's newsletter and keeping up with the authors and publishing company via Twitter, Facebook, and Goodreads.